D1521795

**Books by Victoria Malvey**

Portrait of Dreams
Enchanted
Temptress

# VICTORIA MALVEY

## Temptress

SONNET BOOKS

New York London Toronto Sydney Singapore

An *Original* Publication of POCKET BOOKS

 A Sonnet Book published by
POCKET BOOKS, a division of Simon & Schuster Inc.
1230 Avenue of the Americas, New York, NY 10020

ISBN: 0-671-02072-2

First Sonnet Books printing December 1999

10  9  8  7  6  5  4  3  2  1

SONNET BOOKS and colophon are
trademarks of Simon & Schuster Inc.

Cover art by Ben Perini

Printed in the U.S.A.

To all my nieces and nephews that bring such sunshine to my life.

Nathan David Brindley
Travis Lane Brindley
John Livingston Conover IV
Amy Elizabeth Frey
Emily Anne Frey
Melissa Ellen Frey
Patricia Eileen Frey
Abigail Ann Lindamood
Elizabeth Owen Lindamood
Leah Day Lindamood
Rebecca Burke Lindamood
Dayna Marie Malvey
Jonah William Malvey
Luke Sebastian Malvey
Margaret Hayley Reagan
Samantha Lee Reagan
Theodore John Verstraete IV

Whew! That's what happens when you come from a large Catholic family.

I love you, guys!

Aunt Vicky

# Acknowledgments

Thanks to Barb Shaeffer for introducing me to her pals, Strunk Jr. & White.

Thanks to Pam Hopkins for her encouragement, support, and time. You're a wonderful agent, Pam, and I am so thankful I met you in NYC at my first RWA conference. We make a great team!

And, as always, a special thanks to Amy Pierpont for believing in me and not allowing me to say "It's okay; let's just leave it." I truly appreciate that you always ask for more, Amy, and, by doing so, you make me a better writer.

# Prologue

## Harpsden, England
### February 1784

*The* coldness from the hard stone floor of the chapel seeped through his knees and up his legs, stiffening his muscles into painful knots. Edward welcomed the pain, accepting it as penance for his guilt over breaking one of God's sacred laws. All his life he'd honored the rules of the Church . . .

But now he had faltered.

His love for his wife, his beautiful Katherine, overshadowed all else. He would do anything for her—even damn his soul to Hell. Edward bent his head, resting it against his clasped hands as he begged the Lord for forgiveness.

Feeling the pew shift as someone sat down next to him, Edward didn't look up; he knew who it was. "It is done," Edward rasped, his voice raw with pain.

"I know. I've been to see Lady Katherine."

Slowly, Edward raised his head to look at Basil

Whitmore—his pastor, his confessor, his friend. "Has she let go of the babe yet?"

Basil shook his head. "No, but can you blame her? After having three children born lifeless, she's unable to believe that this miracle has occurred."

"I know. God forgive me, I know." Edward felt his heart lurch. "And if she found out that the sweet boy she holds in her arms isn't her natural child, it would destroy her."

Basil placed a comforting hand upon Edward's shoulder, but remained silent.

"Why do you not agree?" Edward asked. "I love Katherine with all that I am, so I have created this . . . lie. And by doing so, I have destroyed myself. Do you not think I know that I have betrayed all I am, all I believe, to arrange to have the babies switched at birth?" He buried his face in his hands. "Today I fouled myself by taking another child and claiming it as my own, deceiving my beloved wife into believing she'd finally given birth to a healthy child, then burying our own sweet babe without her knowing."

Basil's sigh filled the church. "Don't destroy yourself over your choice, Edward. It was a hard decision you made. I saw how agonized you were when the doctor told you your unborn child lay unmoving within your wife. You *knew* she would be unable to face birthing another . . . still baby." He shifted on the pew. "Did you sin against God with your lie? Yes, but as the Bible says in the book of Proverbs, 'Honest scales and balances are from the Lord; all the weights in the bag are of

his making.' Only He can judge you, Edward—
not I."

Edward ground his fingers against his temples.
"I know you don't judge me, Basil; I know my time
for retribution will be when I stand before the
Almighty. Still, I cannot help but judge myself.
How can I live knowing that I bought my child
from a stranger? How can I carry around the
knowledge that the mother of the babe suffers too
because of my actions?"

"No, Edward, she suffers not. You've saved her
as well," Basil protested. "That wastrel, Griffin
Kingston, took her innocence, leaving her life in
ruins, her hopes gone. You merely offered her an
escape from her plight."

Edward raised his head, looking at his friend,
almost afraid to hope that he might speak the
truth. "Do you believe that to be so?"

His nod was emphatic. "Sarah Thane told me
herself that she was relieved to give her child into
a good home, to give him a title, to offer him a
chance at a privileged life. And with the compen-
sation you bestowed upon her, she is able to move
up to the north country and purchase a small
house for herself."

Relief rushed through Edward. At least he could
dismiss that guilt. A new thought took hold.
"What of Katherine? The child she now holds is a
few weeks old. Do you think she noticed that the
babe is not a newborn?"

"Absolutely not," Basil reassured him. "Lady
Katherine delights far too much in counting the
baby's toes, pressing her face into his neck, and

listening to him breathe to question your son's size or health."

"My son," whispered Edward, sitting back on the pew. For the first time since he'd arranged for his doctor to switch the children, he allowed himself to look far into his future—a future now holding a son, an heir. True, he had sinned against the teachings of God, but in doing so, he'd saved the lives of many—himself included. "My son," he said again.

Basil smiled at him. "Indeed. Teach him well; help him to overcome his less than perfect lineage."

Inside, Edward bristled over the comment, already feeling protective toward the child he'd claimed as his own. Looking toward the front of the church, he gazed up at the crucifix where the Lord's only son rested. "I will raise him in the eyes of God and with the honor befitting his rank."

"As it should be." Basil clasped his hands together. "I have faith in you, Edward."

"My thanks." He turned toward Basil once more. "I cannot express how grateful I am to you for all your help and support."

Basil shrugged lightly. "We are all searching for the path to Heaven. As I said before, who am I to judge another man for the choices he makes?"

"You are my pastor," Edward replied, knowing that Basil's ascension into Heaven was a certainty. "That alone gives you the right."

Basil sat back in the pew. "I am a man, Edward, just like you. I'm uncertain if I would have chosen differently than you if faced with a similar circumstance. I pray I never have to discover that truth within myself."

"As do I." Edward stood, his muscles tight and stiff. "I need to see to my wife now—and my son."

Basil made the sign of the cross and gave Edward a parting blessing. "Go with God," he said.

"I pray I do," Edward responded as he left the chapel and walked toward his future, carrying with him the sins of his past.

# 1

*Northampton, England*
*September 1810*

*F*reedom!

Even the air tasted sweeter to Rosaleen as she wandered near the pond. She'd tethered her horse nearby, and was walking along the water's edge, trying to forget the dreadful weight of spying eyes and wagging tongues she'd left behind at Lady Foley's country house.

Tossing a pebble into the water, Rose listened to the satisfying splash break the silence. For two days now she'd suffered through this country affair, only bearing it because Lord Foley was a close friend of her father's and her parents had insisted she attend with them.

She'd accompanied them reluctantly, but had held out a glimmer of hope that at least here, where her father was welcomed, there would be no talk of her family's scandalous beginnings. Yet, it had been foolish to imagine that members of the ton would pass an opportunity to gossip about her mother, a former courtesan, and her father, the man who had been her mother's protector. The fact that Rose was born well after their marriage did little to overcome this heritage of shadows.

A flare of anger burst to life within Rose. Who were these paragons of society to believe they could judge her mother and find her lacking? Her mother—and her father—were two of the most wonderful, loving, joyous people Rose knew. However, few people made the effort to look beyond her mother's reputation to see her warmth and, in truth, her family was rarely issued invitations to social events.

Yet another reason why Rose could not have turned down her father's request that she attend the Foleys' weekend party, and why she was on her best behavior, trying though it was. All day she'd avoided the dandies as they'd whispered innuendos in her ear or stroked a hand down her arm. Feeling as if all of the men she knew simply assumed she'd be willing to become their mistress, Rose had been forced to set them down with scathing remarks.

But now, for the moment, she was free! Wearing a smile, Rose tilted her head up toward the warm afternoon sun, feeling the tension inside of her melt away. Her eyes closed against the brightness, Rose began to sing a bawdy tune she'd overheard her father and Lord Foley croon one night when they'd been deep in their cups.

"A gentle old lady I knew
was dozing one day in her pew.
When the pastor yelled 'Sin!'
She said, 'Count me in! —
As soon as the service is through!' "

The last word of her song was drowned out by the sound of clapping. Stunned, Rosaleen whirled about, her cheeks aflame.

A gloriously handsome man stood before her—laughing.

"I don't believe I've ever heard that song performed by such a lovely lady," he managed to say once he'd regained his composure.

Well accustomed to being in embarrassing situations, Rosaleen lifted her chin, determined to brazen it out. "Thank you," she murmured, trying to act unaffected. "It is a particular favorite of mine."

"I gathered as much from the . . . *hearty* manner in which it was sung." The man took a step closer, his lithe body encased in stylish riding clothes, his highly polished Hessian boots crunching on the stones. "Allow me to introduce myself. Lucien St. Cyr, at your service," he said, bowing before her.

Rose could hardly believe her eyes. Was this man actually *bowing*? If his manner had been in the least familiar, she would have been quick to respond in a tart fashion. But, to be offered an introduction in such a gentlemanly way, well, she didn't quite know how to react. Instinctively, she sank slowly into a curtsey. "Rosaleen Fleming, my lord. It is a pleasure to finally meet you."

"Finally?" His eyes flared. "You know me then?"

Know him? Rose couldn't keep a small smile from playing upon her lips. Who in all of society didn't know the handsome, reputedly charming Lucien St. Cyr, Earl of Berwyn? With thick black hair, brilliant blue eyes, and perfect features that were surely created by angels themselves, there wasn't a lady who hadn't sighed over him in longing.

Still, it would hardly do for her to admit these facts to him. Instead, she merely nodded. "My father pointed you out to me when we were last in town."

Her heart leapt as he grinned down at her. "Then you have the advantage." He took two more steps, moving to her side. "I hope you don't mind the intrusion. I saw your horse and wanted to ensure your well-being."

Rose struggled to remain collected beneath his welcoming gaze. "I am perfectly fine, thank you."

"So I see, but now that I've met you, I fear I am reluctant to leave your company so soon." He offered her his arm. "May I accompany you on your stroll?"

She nodded silently, unsure of her voice, before accepting his arm. His friendly acceptance of her was a novel experience. Most of the men of Rose's acquaintance treated her as an object of desire, rather than a true lady. Perhaps they all thought that if her mother had followed a path into the world of a Cyprian, then she would as well. While Rose knew this wasn't true, none of the men she'd met seemed to accept that fact.

It only made the comfort she felt around Lucien St. Cyr more rare.

It amazed Rose that Luc apparently hadn't heard any of the gossip surrounding her and her family. Still, she wasn't going to question her good fortune. Allowing herself to fantasize that they were of like status couldn't harm anyone. Just for this afternoon, she'd pretend that she was a proper young lady with an unblemished background being courted by the glorious Lucien St. Cyr.

As they began to stroll along the water's edge, Luc said, "Though I shouldn't question my good fortune, I can't understand why a gracious lady such as yourself would be out here all alone."

She couldn't tell him the truth—that she'd needed a moment away from the glaring eyes. Instead, she responded with a quick retort. "Perhaps I prefer my own company than to suffer the dull wit of others."

He erupted with a laugh. "Then I must work very hard indeed to ensure that I entertain sufficiently."

"It would be appreciated, my lord," she returned, glancing up at him. Her heart skipped at the expression of warmth molding Lucien's features.

"Shall I tell you of my latest adventure then?"

"Please do," Rose said, enjoying Luc's sense of humor.

Lucien wrapped his hand atop hers. "I was off at Lord Atherby's fox hunting party last weekend. My dogs had finally managed to trap a fox in his burrow, and since I arrived first, I dismounted and fired into the hole."

"The poor fox," Rosaleen murmured.

"Don't feel too sorry for the devil yet," Lucien assured her. "Trust me. That 'poor fox' managed to make me look the fool."

"And pray tell me how he did that?"

"Quite easily. For, you see, I had knelt down and reached deep into the hole to pull the fox free, when I spotted him standing on the rise before me—whole, healthy, and, I tease you not, grinning down at me."

Rose broke into laughter as she imagined the picture he must have made.

"There I was, my knees in the mud with the crafty fellow laughing at me. Worse still, when I tried to pull free, I found my sleeve had caught on something in the burrow." With a grin, Luc shrugged. "I was stuck."

"Oh, how the fox must have enjoyed that."

"I'm sure he did. I tried to slip out of my jacket, but my arm was too deep in the hole to maneuver. Then, when I didn't believe things could get any worse, my dogs spotted that bloody fox and lunged for him." Lucien slanted her a wry look. "Unfortunately, I was kneeling between them. So, as the dogs took off after the creature, they bounded over me, nearly trampling me in the process."

"Whatever did you do?" Rose finally asked after she managed to contain her laughter.

"What else could I do but remain there until the rest of the hunting party stumbled upon me?" Lucien grinned broadly. "In order to fully appreciate this adventure, you must use your imagination and envision me, kneeling in the dirt, my arm stuck into the ground up to my shoulder, my posterior facing the riders as they approached, and muddy dog prints covering my jacket."

It was all too easy to see it in her mind. Another gale of laughter broke from Rose. Finally, she wiped the tears from her eyes. "Ah, my lord, you are indeed a very entertaining gentleman."

"Thank you, Miss Fleming," he responded, bowing slightly to her. "I am happy to make a fool of myself in order to amuse you."

"It is appreciated." If Luc kept her company, perhaps the Foleys' affair wouldn't be so dreadful after all, Rose thought. "And I do hope you will share any future adventures with me."

"On my honor," he promised, before bringing them to a halt. "We've wandered around the entire pond. May I escort you back to the estate?"

The spark inside of her dimmed as Rose realized the reality of Luc being a houseguest of the Foleys. This pleasant little interlude would come to an end and Lucien would undoubtedly learn of the gossip plaguing her family. It would be only natural for him to mention meeting her and Rose was positive that someone would eagerly impart the titillating gossip surrounding her family.

Rose squeezed Lucien's arm, smiling up at him. "I cannot adequately express how much I have enjoyed this time with you, my lord."

"It has been my pleasure." Luc bent over her hand, kissing the back of it.

Rose folded the memory into her heart, appreciating the brief fantasy of Lucien paying court to her.

She held back a sigh as he escorted her to their horses, leaving the sun-kissed afternoon behind.

Lucien returned Rosaleen's wave of farewell, then watched as she made her way into the manor house. It was impossible to tear himself away from the sight of her incredible beauty, from the way her hair captured the sun and created a shimmering veil of gold. Knowing that his parents arrived today, Luc had gone riding to calm his thoughts, to still his yearning to be back in town, because he had no desire to reveal this restless side of himself to them. Their respect mattered dearly to him and he never wanted his parents to realize how difficult it was for him to abide these tiresome social gatherings.

So, with the restlessness swirling inside of him, he'd raced off to find peace, but he'd found Rosaleen instead. Luc felt his lips curving upward at the memory of her bawdy tune. She'd been utterly refreshing and when she'd gazed up at him with her blue eyes sparkling with delight, he'd been entranced by her.

Ah, yes, Rosaleen's beauty was renowned through society . . . as was her lineage. He'd known at a glimpse who she was, but never had he imagined that it would be her wit that captured his interest. She'd responded to him with an openness rare within this jaded world. Perhaps the stories he'd heard of her wild behavior were merely tales bantered about with no base in reality.

"You're a sly one, St. Cyr."

Luc turned to face his friend, Lord Peter Ridgely. "And how is that?"

"Going for a ride with the luscious Rosaleen," Peter drawled.

Luc's fingers tightened around the reins in his hands. "I insist that you refer to Miss Fleming in a proper fashion, Ridgely."

The young lord lifted his blond brows. "Calm down, Luc. I meant no offense." A lopsided grin spread across his face. "Sometimes I forget that you're such a stickler for proprieties— never one to indulge your curiosity in a good bout of gossip."

"I can only imagine what I'm missing," Luc said, the knot in his stomach loosening. "How can I live without knowing such valuable information as who was caught with their maid in the pantry?"

"So you *did* hear last week's news!"

Lucien shook his head in defeat. "Why don't you make yourself useful, Ridgely, and help me bring these horses back to the stables?"

Peter took the horse Rosaleen had been riding by the reins. "I'd be happy to help you, Luc. That will give me a chance to tell you the latest bit of goods. The Earl of Ross arrived today."

"Griffin Kingston?"

"Do you know him?"

Luc shook his head. "No. I know him only by reputation. And if even half of the stories about him are true, why on earth would he come to an affair like this? It's a bit tame for a man like him, isn't it?"

"That is precisely what makes this news so delicious," Peter said with a grin. "The man is quite beyond the pale. Kingston is a veritable living scandal!"

"I shall make a point to avoid him," Luc said, giving his horse a pat.

"Ah, yes, wouldn't want to sully that fine reputation of yours."

"Scoff at me if you want, but a man's honor should not be taken lightly." Hearing himself, Luc winced. "Lord, now I'm starting to sound like a prig."

Ridgely slapped Luc on the back. "A stiff one at that."

In his efforts to control his baser desires, was he slowly turning himself into a pompous bore? A shiver ran through Luc. "Promise me something, Peter."

"Anything . . . as long as it doesn't require too much effort," Peter quipped.

"If I ever become too much of a prig, take me into a pasture and shoot me."

Rosaleen's fine mood darkened the moment she stepped into the parlor to find Lady Foley and Lady Howard enjoying their tea. Nothing could destroy the wonderful glow of her afternoon as swiftly as the sharp tongues of these formidable ladies.

"Rosaleen, dear," Lady Foley called out, her false welcome grating on Rose's ears. "How lovely of you to join us."

Rose forced a smile. While Lord Foley and her

father were great friends, Lady Foley left something to be desired. "I didn't mean to interrupt your repast," Rose murmured politely. "I was looking for my mother."

"Then I suggest you look in the study," Lady Howard suggested snidely. "That's where the men usually are."

Anger flared within Rose. She knew only too well why Lady Howard was so venomous toward her mother. Still, Rose struggled to hold her temper, not because of Lady Howard, but because of her mother's request. "While I appreciate your suggestion, Lady Howard, I believe I'd be better off checking her rooms. She might be resting."

Lady Howard sniffed, before turning toward Lady Foley to murmur, "Resting? Oh, I don't doubt she's abed, but alone? Hardly."

It was all Rose could bear. She lifted her chin, glaring at the two ladies who didn't even try to hide their snickers of vicious amusement. "I'm quite sure that my mother is alone, Lady Howard, as my father is off hunting today with Lord Foley." Rose turned to leave, but paused mid-stride, looking over her shoulder at Lady Howard. "However, I do believe I saw Lord Howard heading out toward the gazebo with Lady Stanton." She frowned slightly. "Now why does that remind me of something . . . oh yes, I've heard in town that Lord Howard and Lady Stanton are *quite* the close companions."

Lady Howard's outraged gasp made Rosaleen smile as she left the room, her head held high. If there was one thing Rose understood, it was the power of gossip. It didn't matter one whit that she'd not even glimpsed Lord Howard today. Everyone knew Lord Howard chased the ladies, and caught them, more often than not.

After all, hadn't he been her mother's first lover?

Rose thrust that distasteful thought aside as she headed up the stairs to her parents' bedchamber.

# 2

"*W*ith the way you've made yourself scarce these past few months, Lucien, it makes me think you're trying to avoid your mother and me," Edward St. Cyr remarked casually, keeping his eyes fixed upon the dancers twirling past.

"Of course not," Luc returned quickly, praying his voice held a ring of truth despite the lie. He had no wish to hurt his father's feelings. "I've simply been extremely busy taking care of my affairs."

"Hmmmm."

Fighting the urge to squirm beneath his father's gaze, Lucien pointed toward the dance floor. "I see Mother is enjoying herself this evening."

Though he tilted an eyebrow at him, Luc's father didn't comment on the change of topic. "She certainly appears to be," Edward agreed. "But I believe a dance with her son would make her happier."

"And relieve you of dancing with her?"

"That too." Grinning, Edward shrugged. "All I can say is that you didn't inherit your ability to dance from me."

A shadow flickered quickly across his father's face, making Luc guess at its source. "There's nothing to be embarrassed about, Father," Luc said, placing a hand on his father's shoulder. "Your good works toward others far outshine my skill at dancing."

It was obvious that Edward felt uncomfortable with the topic. "All I do is arrange for food and clothing to be distributed to the needy." An expression of chagrin twisted his features. "And I do that with the help of Pastor Whitmore."

"Oh, well then, that's another matter altogether." Luc rocked back on his heels, his hands clasped behind his back. "If you can't do your miracles for the poor by yourself, then I do believe you're quite right; my ability to dance *is* of greater value than all of your puny efforts."

While Edward smiled over Luc's dry wit, his tone was quite serious as he replied, "Don't underestimate the value of making one person supremely happy." He nudged his shoulder against Luc's arm. "Now if we combined our talents, then we'd have the perfect—" Edward broke off with a gasp. "Dear Lord in Heaven!" he whispered, his voice choked.

"Father? Are you all right?" Luc asked, placing a hand upon his father's shoulder.

Edward didn't answer; he merely shook his head. Lucien grew alarmed as he took in the paleness of his father's skin and the wild glaze filling his widened eyes.

"Father?" Lucien asked again, stepping closer.

"Not now," Edward whispered, his gaze fixed across the room. "Not after all this time."

Lucien glanced around sharply, following Edward's gaze. A tall gentleman stood across the dance floor staring back at them. Luc frowned slightly, trying to match a name with the startlingly familiar face.

"I don't recognize that man, Father." Luc returned his attention to Edward. "Do you know him?"

"N-n-n-o," Edward stammered. "I don't know him."

Stunned, Lucien didn't know how to reply to his father's blatant lie. Finally, Luc said, "It is rather obvious that you know him, Father."

"I don't, I tell you." Edward shook his head. "I've never spoken to the man."

Lucien frowned again. "If you say so, but something about him seems extremely familiar."

Though he'd have thought it impossible, Luc watched as his father paled even further, looking like a ghostly version of his normally robust self.

"Please excuse me, son." Edward's voice cracked on the last word, before he turned and strode away.

His eyes narrowing, Lucien looked back at the man who had disturbed his unflappable father. Luc squared his shoulders and stood firm as the man crossed the ballroom, coming to a stop a few feet from him.

"Do I know you, sir?"

Lucien's demand was met with a grin. "Griffin Kingston, Earl of Ross."

Something about Kingston's intense stare disturbed Lucien. It was almost as if the man were waiting for something, some type of reaction. Perhaps Kingston understood that his reputation preceded him everywhere he went. Wary, Lucien returned the greeting. "I am Lucien St. Cyr, Earl of Berwyn."

The man's brow arched upward. "You are, are you?"

What the devil did he mean by that? Luc met Kingston's gaze with a cool glare. "Excuse me?" Lucien asked, his tone tight and formal.

Instead of answering, Kingston looked toward the door through which Edward had just exited. "My pardon—" Kingston shot him a mocking glance, "—my lord St. Cyr, but I have matters to attend that are long past due."

As Kingston went to move around him, Luc side-stepped into the man's path. "Would these matters have anything to do with my father?"

"Your father?" Kingston's bold laugh attracted the attention of nearby revelers. "Yes, indeed it does."

There was no way Luc was going to allow this madman to confront his father, especially not after Edward's odd reaction to Kingston's presence. Lucien nodded tersely. "If you are determined to speak with my father, then I shall accompany you, sir."

Kingston's mouth twisted before he answered,

"Perhaps it would be best if you did join us." His expression grew solemn. "After all, you're a part of this as well."

"A part of what?" Lucien demanded, though he was uncertain if he wanted to hear Kingston's response. It was as if some part of Luc, deep inside, already knew the answer . . . and dreaded it.

"In good time, my impetuous young lord. All in good time."

Lucien pressed his lips together, heartily sick of Kingston's cryptic statements. "Then let us go find my father and be done with it."

Kingston agreed readily. "Yes, Lucien, it is time you found your father."

They came upon Edward in the study. Sitting with his head in his hands and his shoulders slumped forward, he appeared the very image of a man utterly defeated. Stunned, Lucien paused at the open door.

Kingston didn't hesitate for an instant.

He nudged Luc inside. "I suggest, my lord, that you stand to meet your destiny."

The bleak expression on his father's face as he lifted his head shocked Lucien into speechlessness for a moment. "Please spare him this," Edward pleaded in a low voice.

Spare him? Spare who? Confused, Luc stepped forward. "What is going on here, Father?"

As Edward made to rise, Luc moved to assist him to his feet. "You are the best son any man could hope for," Edward rasped fervently, squeezing his son's hand tightly between his own.

A chill raced through Lucien as he stepped back, sensing that his life was about to change. "What is the matter?" he asked again, not sure if he wanted the answer.

"I'm positive that your *father* is merely disturbed to find that his past has returned to haunt him." Kingston lifted an eyebrow. "Isn't that right, St. Cyr?"

Edward spread his hands out, imploring. "Why are you doing this now? After all these years, why can't you simply let it be?"

"Let it be? Hell, man, I just found out you'd robbed me of my legacy, and you expect me to blithely ignore it?"

"I have not robbed you of anything, sir. I merely cleaned up after your—" Edward broke off, glancing at Luc with an apology in his gaze.

"My mistake? Isn't that what you were going to say, St. Cyr?" Kingston laughed aloud. "Is that any way for a father to talk?"

"I wasn't referring to the result, merely the process," Edward retorted quickly. "You have no right to do this."

"Right? You dare to speak to me of right?" Kingston's eyes narrowed. "Why, you sanctimonious, lying bastard."

"Enough!" Lucien stepped in front of his father. "You will leave at once."

"Damn, boy, you do my aging heart good," Kingston said with a grin. "You'd face the Devil himself to save this old man, wouldn't you?"

"How can I be certain that I'm not doing that right now?"

Kingston's bark of laughter did not ease the tension in the room.

"Lucien, please." Edward placed his hand on Luc's shoulder. "This is something I need to address."

"But, Father—"

Edward cut him off sharply. "I need to speak with him. Alone."

Luc started to protest, but amazingly enough, Kingston did it for him. "Absolutely not, St. Cyr. It is time he knew the truth."

"The truth?" The muscles in Luc's stomach tightened.

"Come now. You seem an intelligent fellow; surely you can figure it out." Kingston rocked back on his heels. "Haven't you ever wondered why you're a good foot taller than your father? Or why your coloring is so different?"

Lucien listened in stunned silence as Kingston asked him questions that he'd asked himself. Still, Luc shied away from the answer that hovered at the edge of his consciousness.

"Stop this; I beg of you," Edward pleaded. "Don't destroy him this way."

"Him?" Kingston sneered. "You're just afraid to lose your precious heir."

"No, this was never about me." Edward seemed to shrink before Luc's eyes. "Never."

"Father?" Lucien whispered hoarsely. "What is he talking about?"

Before Edward could answer, Kingston interrupted again. "Use your eyes, Lucien," he reprimanded sharply. "Look at me and tell me that you don't see a younger version in the mirror every day."

The screaming awareness in his head drowned out all his thoughts but one.

This man was his natural father.

There could be no other explanation, Luc realized, even as he tried to deny the evidence. "No," he groaned desperately. "It can't be. You're lying."

Kingston crossed his arms over his chest. "If you don't believe me, ask him," he said, nodding toward Edward. "If he'll finally tell you the truth, that is."

Luc turned to face the man he'd always called Father. "It can't be true."

Edward sank into a chair, looking ancient. Slowly, he lifted his head, and Luc could see the fear and desperation in his eyes.

"No!" Lucien shouted. "I will not believe that this wastrel is my flesh and blood."

"Oh, I assure you I am," Kingston stated softly, the quiet pronouncement so at odds with Luc's fierce denials.

"You cannot be my sire." Rage poured through Lucien, its strength stunning. "I've heard all about you, Griffin Kingston. London is awash with sordid tales about your activities in the seediest whorehouses to the rankest gaming Hells." Luc fisted his hands. "I will never claim you for my father!"

"Then you'd rather claim him? The man who has lied to you all these years, telling you that he was your father when in fact you're nothing more than my bastard?"

The question slammed into Lucien's gut. For even as he denied it, the truth was apparent . . . even to his disbelieving eyes.

"I will not believe that my mother took you into her bed when—"

"Never!" Edward said, thrusting to his feet. "Your mother never knew about any of this. She is innocent . . . just as you are."

"Innocent?" Lucien staggered backward, grasping on to a chair to hold him upright. "Are you saying that she isn't my mother?"

Edward couldn't meet Luc's desperate gaze.

"I never touched the lady," Kingston pronounced with a cocky smirk.

"Dear God," Lucien whispered. "Then who am I?"

Edward's shoulders slumped forward. "You are this man's son, in truth."

"*Truth?*" The word scraped out, tainting Luc's voice with raw bitterness. "You've just told me my entire life is a lie, Father. Why would I look to you for the truth?"

Edward flinched at the question, but Lucien didn't care. A wave of fury swept over him, but he fought it, needing to know the entire truth now.

Lucien raised his eyes to Kingston. "Who is my mother?" he asked, his voice taut with suppressed anger. All the loving touches, the gentle reprimands, had come from a woman he couldn't claim as his true mother. "Tell me."

"Her name was Sarah Thane."

"Was?"

Kingston nodded. "It was upon her death that I received a note from her explaining all of her sins. Her letter was quite thorough, listing not only the exact amount St. Cyr paid her for her son, but also their arrangement that she never contact you."

"Paid for me?" Lucien gasped. Horrified, he turned his gaze onto his father. *"You bought me like a piece of meat?"*

"It wasn't like that, Lucien," Edward protested, pounding his hand against the arm of the chair. "Sarah Thane had been abandoned by this scoundrel, left to face the scorn of a child born out of wedlock. After learning of her situation through Pastor Whitmore, I offered her a solution to—"

"You offered to purchase yourself an heir, is what you did, St. Cyr," Kingston interrupted.

"And what if I did?" Edward asked, his voice reverberating with anger. "In the process, I not only helped Sarah Thane, but Luc and my wife as well." He shook as he stood. "I don't know what you hope to accomplish with this revelation, Kingston, for if you make Lucien's parentage known to the world, then you destroy him."

"Do you think I'd label my son a bastard when he is in line to become the Marquess of Ansley?" Kingston snorted in derision. "I'd no sooner cut off my own hand."

The walls began to close in upon Lucien as he listened to these two men—one his natural father, one the father he loved—argue over his future, as if it even mattered anymore.

Lucien stared at Kingston, searching for some sense of kinship, but finding none. The years of debauchery had not been kind to Kingston, and yet Lucien couldn't take his eyes off of the man because he knew exactly what he was looking at . . .

His future.

Throughout his entire life he'd striven to please his father. He'd tried so hard to be honorable, to follow the teachings of his parents, to do God's bidding, wondering all the while why it was so hard to conform. But now it all made sense and the struggle in and of itself seemed so futile, such wasted energy, because he finally knew the truth—his destiny lay elsewhere.

A bastard son of one of the greatest wastrels of all time was certainly pre-ordained to damnation in the eyes of society and God.

"Lucien," Edward began, reaching out a hand to him.

Luc stepped back swiftly, not wanting to be touched by the hand that had betrayed him.

Smirking, Kingston taunted Edward. "You can no longer hide your sins behind the cloak of pious acts, St. Cyr. You've finally been exposed as the liar and fraud you are."

"You are evil incarnate," Edward charged. "You care nothing for Lucien's fate. What comes next? Blackmail? I wonder just how much it will cost to keep you silent." He took a step forward. "But understand this, Kingston, Lucien is a fine man because of me, my teachings. I raised him, loved him, taught him and—"

"Lied to him his entire life," Luc finished for Edward, bitterness dripping from every word.

"That's my boy," Kingston said with a laugh.

Lucien pulled back his shoulders, gathering in the tattered remains of his self-control. "I am not, nor will I ever be, *your* boy," Luc said to Kingston, before turning his gaze to Edward. "While it is true that you have raised me as your natural son, in doing so, you've deceived me, giving me false hope that my future could be different than my destiny decrees."

"What are you talking about?" Edward asked, spreading his hands wide. "You are a good man."

"No, Fath—" Lucien cut off the word, agony searing him. Still, he forced himself to continue. "No, I am not. I have only pretended to be in order to make you happy." He flicked a glance at Kingston. "Now at least I know why my struggle has been so difficult."

"He has nothing to do with who you are," Edward protested.

His anger exploded. *"Don't you understand? He has everything to do with who I am. His blood runs through my veins."*

"Lucien—" Edward's protest was cut off by Kingston's booming laughter.

"So right, my boy, so right." Kingston waved a hand at Luc. "Blood will tell, so return with me to town and I'll show you all of my favorite vices. I'm certain we'll enjoy the same sort of . . . entertainments."

The foul thought disgusted Lucien. He had to

escape this room, these men, while he still held
onto his sanity. His hand on the doorknob, Lucien
turned to face his natural sire, the Earl of Ross,
making no attempt to hide his contempt. "Perhaps I am damned because of you, sir, but I prefer to find my own path to Hell."

# 3

"$\mathcal{I}$ have always admired that shade on a
woman, Rosaleen. It's so . . . appealing to the
senses."

Rose turned to face the two gentlemen leaning
against the fence of the cantering ring. *Drat!* she
thought; she'd been so caught up in thoughts of
Lucien St. Cyr that she hadn't been aware of her
surroundings.

And now she'd been caught off guard.

Immediately, Rose smoothed her features into
the cool, slightly mocking mask she preferred to
don when facing such "gentlemen." "I apologize
for not thanking you more quickly for your lovely
compliment, Lord Hughes," she murmured
sweetly. "I was merely surprised at the notion that
you had senses at all, not to mention that you actually apply them."

While Lord Hughes scowled at her, his compan-

ion, Lord Atherby, chortled, sending an elbow deep
into Lord Hughes's side. "I warned you not to toy
with this one. No one escapes unscathed from her
tongue."

The dull flush coloring Lord Hughes's flesh did
little to aid his already ruddy complexion. "Foolish me," he ground out. "What else did I expect
from a courtesan's daughter?"

Gasping at the harsh retort, Rose struggled to
maintain her composure, having learned long ago
that the torment only worsened if she allowed the
taunts to hurt her . . . or, rather, if she allowed the
gentlemen to *see* that their insults hurt her. "Yes, I
imagine a keen sense of wit would be beyond your
expectations, my lord. After all, it is common
knowledge that the Hughes line is filled with
bores and lackwits."

Lord Hughes took a step toward her, a growl
rumbling from his throat. Though intimidated,
Rose stood her ground, refusing to show her fear.

"Far better to have bores than whores in one's
background," Lord Hughes returned, sliding his
gaze over her, the look itself a deliberate insult.
"Though I must say your background is well
suited to my . . . needs at the moment."

Rose let loose a gusty sigh. "Really, Lord
Hughes, while I understand your failings, you
should try to be more original in your insults. I'm
sorry to say but your snide remark fell quite short.
In fact, I do believe it's the insult I hear most often,
other than 'like mother, like daughter,' of course."
She tipped her head to the side. "But then again, I
don't consider that much of an insult, since I hold

my mother in such high regard. Still, someone as . . . intellectually challenged as you might consider it an absolutely fabulous taunt."

"Why, you . . . you . . ." Lord Hughes sputtered as Lord Atherby clutched his stomach in laughter.

Rose nodded encouragingly. "Come now, my lord. I know that if you try hard enough you might be able to think up a smart reply."

"You're wrong, Miss Fleming. Waiting for a witty response from Hughes would be a complete waste of your time."

Lucien! Rose spun around to face him, dread filling her as she wondered how much he'd heard. She'd rather face an hour of teasing from Lord Hughes than one moment of disapproval from Lucien. Not after yesterday, not after she'd finally found a friend in him.

Luc glared at Lord Hughes over her head. "You could give Hughes two days to come up with a suitable retort and you'd still find it lacking."

"I say, St. Cyr—"

"I already heard what you have to say, Hughes, and I find it extremely offensive." His features hardened. "You owe Miss Fleming a most sincere apology. You as well, Atherby."

"Me?" Lord Atherby squeaked, raising his hands in the air. "But I didn't say anything."

"My point exactly," Luc said swiftly. "You should have defended the lady's honor."

Lord Atherby's mouth flapped open and closed like a fish gasping for air.

Rose stared at Lucien, unable to believe that he was coming to her aid.

"I'm still waiting . . . gentlemen." Lucien's voice darkened, almost as if he welcomed a disagreement.

Apologies stumbled out from both lords before they hurried off, leaving her alone with Luc. Once again, she didn't know what to say. Rose glanced down at her clasped hands.

Slowly, Lucien tipped her face upward until her gaze met his. "You face the insults of those two fools without faltering and now you're shy with *me?*"

Warmth curled around her heart, so she gave Luc the truth. "I've often faced situations like the one you just witnessed, but with you . . ." She shook her head, not certain if she could adequately explain how wonderful, how special, he made her feel. Rose took a deep breath and tried again. ". . . with you I don't know how to act, what to say." She allowed her emotions—relief, admiration, gratitude—to show in her expression. "Thank you, Lucien."

"There's no need to thank me," Luc said softly. "I did nothing less than what any true gentleman would—" A shadow darkened his features, erasing the warmth from his gaze, his hand dropping back to his side. Pain flashed in his expression before he smoothed his features into a smile once more—"would do," he finished.

Rose studied Luc; there was something different about him today, something that wasn't there yesterday. Taking a step forward, she placed a hand upon his sleeve. "Are you all right, Lucien?"

The shadow flickered in his gaze once more, but

it was gone so quickly, Rose wondered if she'd just imagined it. "I am perfectly fine, Rose," he murmured politely. "Thank you for asking. You're looking in fine spirits as well, despite your trying confrontation."

"Thank you," she said automatically, waving a hand dismissively, "but there is something—"

"Ahhh," Luc murmured, glancing over her shoulder. "Excuse me for interrupting, Rose, but I see my mount is ready." Before she even had a chance to ask if she could accompany him on his ride, Luc said with a bow, "It was a pleasure as always and I look forward to seeing you this evening at the ball."

Rose shut her mouth with a snap as she watched him mount swiftly and kick his horse into a trot, looking like any hero should—tall, confident, and handsome.

The dancing had already begun when Rosaleen entered the ballroom with her mother that evening. Automatically, Rose searched amongst the gentlemen, seeking out Lucien.

"Is he here yet?"

A blush warming her cheeks, Rose turned to face her mother. "Is who here yet?"

Elinor laughed brightly, patting her auburn hair. "Don't play coy, Rosaleen. You're far too intelligent for anyone to ever believe you to be naive."

"True," Rose said, "and you know that better than anyone else as you made sure I received an education to equal most men's."

"No, my darling, you're far brighter than *most* men." Her lips twitched as Elinor quipped, "And that is before one considers how much schooling you've received."

Shaking her head, Rose smiled at her mother. "You'd better not let Father hear you speak so disparagingly about men."

"Why not? He knows perfectly well *he's* not most men."

"Indeed not," Rose agreed readily as she watched the dance floor fill with couples, seeing all too clearly how often the other ladies were partnered—while she stood off to the side. "Sometimes I wonder if it is not easier to be coy."

Elinor's brows drew together in a slight frown. "Of course not, my darling. What would make you think such a thing? While coyness might attract a husband, intelligence is what will keep him at your side." She nodded firmly. "Besides, who would want to marry a dullard?"

"Certainly not me," answered Rose's father as he moved to join them. "But then, neither would you."

Elinor simply laughed at his assertion.

Leaning down to press a kiss upon his wife's cheek, Reggie murmured, "I believe I'll accept that as a yes."

"You do that, my love," Elinor said, patting Reggie's arm.

Rose smiled as she watched her parents; they had always been open with their affection.

"We must be serious now, Reggie," Elinor said briskly. "Our daughter needs our help to find a certain gentleman."

Rose groaned. "No, I don't, Mama."

"Shhh," Elinor said, raising up onto her tiptoes to peer around the ballroom. "Perhaps he stepped out into the garden for a few moments."

"Who are we searching for?" asked Reggie.

"No one."

Elinor waved away Rose's statement. "He's certainly not no one, dear. We're looking for the Earl of Berwyn."

"Lucien St. Cyr?" Reggie looked at Rose. "Did the young earl catch your eye?"

Rose felt herself grow warm again beneath her father's quizzical gaze. "No," she stuttered, lying poorly. "Mama simply makes too much of my chance meeting with Lord St. Cyr yesterday." She had not spoken of this morning's incident with Lord Hughes and Lord Atherby. There was no point in doing so because it would only upset her mother.

A bemused expression shifted onto her father's face. "So, someone has finally captured my little girl's interest."

"Are either one of you listening to me?"

"Of course we are, darling," her mother assured her. "We're simply hearing what's in your heart instead of the denials coming from your mouth."

Chagrined, Rose didn't know how to respond. It would seem that her parents knew her far too well.

"St. Cyr seems like a decent fellow." Her father paused for a moment, gazing out over Rose's head. "And I do believe he's headed this way."

A gasp escaped Rose as she turned, trying to

keep her heart from racing as Lucien approached. In his smart evening clothes, he outshone every other gentleman in the room.

Coming to a stop before her, Lucien bowed low. "Miss Fleming."

"Good evening, my lord," Rose murmured softly, as she dipped into a curtsey.

Luc smiled at her, then turned his attention to her parents. "Forgive the intrusion, but since I've already boldly introduced myself to your daughter, I felt it only proper that I do the same with her parents." Once more, he bowed. "Lucien St. Cyr, Earl of Berwyn."

Approval glimmered in Reggie's gaze as he returned the gesture. "Reginald Fleming, Viscount of Howland." He drew Elinor forward. "And may I present my viscountess, Lady Elinor."

Lucien accepted the hand Rose's mother proffered, bending to press a light kiss upon the glove-encased fingers. "I am honored."

Reggie eyed Lucien. "I am acquainted with your father, the Marquess of Ansley. He's a good man."

The tremor that shook Lucien bewildered Rose. After a moment's hesitation, he murmured, "Indeed."

Shadows crept into Lucien's blue eyes again, just as they had this morning. Still, she had not a moment to dwell upon it as Lucien turned to her.

"May I have the honor of this dance?"

Joy spread through Rose at the thought of dancing in his arms. Just moments ago, she'd longed to be one of the couples on the dance floor and now, with Luc's escort, she would join them. Finally.

At her pause, he added, "I promise not to be dreadfully dull."

"Well, in that case . . ." she began with a smile as she accepted his arm. But when Lucien led her onto the dance floor, her pleasure faded as she noticed the scandalized looks she was receiving from the gaggle of matrons in the corner. Lady Howard sat in the midst of them, undoubtedly urging on the gossips.

A pang of guilt struck Rose as she glanced up at Lucien. By escorting her, he became the target for their slurs as well. She couldn't allow him to be hurt simply because he was kind enough to befriend her.

"Is the thought of dancing with me so unappealing?"

Startled, Rose shook her head. "Of course not! What would make you think something like that?"

"I don't know . . . perhaps it's because you've been frowning since we stepped onto the dance floor," Lucien murmured, positioning himself across from Rose. "Do you wish to return to your parents?"

"Oh, no," she whispered, desperately aware of the people watching them. "Though I would like a private moment with you afterward."

"It would be my pleasure," Lucien agreed. An instant later, the ensemble began to play.

Her skirts spun outward as Luc swung her around, exchanging places with her. Smiling into her eyes, Luc moved around her, before clasping her hand to send her twirling out, then reeling her back toward him, until she rested against his arm.

Pleasure rippled through Rose as Luc held onto her, pressing her close to his side, as he led the promenade through the other couples.

Almost giddy, Rose pushed aside her worries, concentrating only on the swell of emotion inside of her. Every time she swung about and faced Lucien, her heart felt light. For this moment, she would pretend that she was accepted, that she belonged.

The music ended far too soon for Rosaleen, though she tried to mask her disappointment as Luc guided her off the floor, leading her into a private alcove.

"Thank you for the wonderful dance," Rose said, smiling, unable to hold in her happiness. "I will always treasure the memory."

Puzzlement drew Lucien's brows together. "You tell me you enjoyed partnering me, yet you make it sound as if it will be the last time we dance together."

"I believe it would be best," Rose whispered, looking up into Lucien's handsome face. "There are things you don't know about me."

His lopsided grin made her heart ache. "Isn't learning about one another part of building a relationship?"

Excitement feathered inside of her for an instant, but died the moment she realized his enthusiasm would fade once he knew the truth about her background. "Yes, that's true, Luc, but there are things about me that you don't know, things that—" Rose's explanation faltered. How could she explain it without sounding defensive?

"Are you referring to the gossip about your family?"

"Gossip?" she squeaked. "You've heard it?"

A dull flush stained Lucien's cheeks. "While I don't normally listen to gossip, I have overheard a few bits and pieces here and there. I only mention it because I thought it would make it easier to discuss it openly," he hastened to reassure her.

Rose tilted her chin upward. "Please understand, Lucien, not all of the stories are rumors. My mother truly was my father's mistress before they wed."

"And what bearing does that have on us?"

"How can you ask that?" Stepping forward, she placed her hands upon his arm. "If you are seen in my company, the gossips will start involving you in their sordid tales."

Lucien's gaze gentled. "I care not what others say."

"That's only because you haven't felt the sting of disapproval," Rose whispered, her throat tight.

Lucien shook his head. "That's not true, Miss Fleming. I enjoy your company far too much to deny myself simply because someone might remark upon it." A wry smile tilted up his mouth. "Besides, I pride myself on being a gentleman, and a true gentleman always ignores the rumormongers."

Hope swelled within her. "So, even though you've heard the stories, you wish to spend time with me?"

"Have I failed to make myself clear?" Lucien laughed, his eyes crinkling in the corners. "Which time did you misunderstand me? Was it the first time I expressed my intentions or the fifth one?"

Rose's confidence soared at the teasing note in his voice. "Don't be droll," she finally said, happiness brightening her smile. "I only wanted you to know what you'd be facing if we remained friends."

"Now, I never said that I knew what I'd be facing with you." Lucien leaned in a bit closer. "In fact, Miss Fleming, it is the excitement of discovery that intrigues me the most. For I'll wager you are a woman of depth and it will take me years before I understand exactly what I'm facing with you."

Years. He'd said it would take years. Shaken, she managed to murmur smoothly, "Perhaps the same could be said of you, my lord."

Lucien's smile faltered. "I believe it could."

"What do you mean?"

Abruptly, Luc stepped back, a stiff smile upon his lips. "All I meant, Rose, was that everyone has a few skeletons rattling around in their family closet." He offered her his arm. "The trick is to keep them there."

Rose allowed Lucien to escort her from the alcove. It would appear that she wasn't the only one who had secrets.

Lucien escaped by way of the garden, hurrying out into the night air to take his first deep breath since entering the ballroom. All day long he'd done nothing but evaluate his life and his future. He'd ridden deep into the woods, alone with his thoughts, trying to decide how to go on, now that his entire world had been tossed upside down.

Finally, anger had come to his rescue. While his blood might run true, he'd controlled his inner yearnings for years. Surely he could continue onward, ignoring the wildness that called to him. His fate if he failed was too bleak to consider. He need look no further than Kingston to see it.

Despite his intentions, Luc felt like a fraud. The entire time he'd been at the ball, he'd imagined that someone would turn and point to him, exposing him for the bastard he was. How had he not suspected the truth just from comparing his looks to those of his parents? Everything about him was so different, so foreign to Edward and Katherine's natures. As a child he'd been so loud and rambunctious, his mother used to look at him as if he were something incomprehensible. Even as a young man at Oxford, Luc would sow his wildness with his friends, praying that his father wouldn't find out and be disappointed. More often than not, though, his friends would plan a wild night of women and drink, but Luc would cry off, afraid to unleash the pulsing desires within him, terrified that once released, he'd never regain control over his emotions.

Anger bubbled up inside of Luc once more, but he tamped it down. If he were going to continue forward, he needed to keep a close rein on his temper.

He was still a gentleman.

Something in Luc's gut twisted at the thought, but he ignored it and continued to repeat it over and over in his head, praying that if he told himself he was truly a gentleman, he might actually come to believe it.

Please, God.

"Lucien, my angel."

At the hail, Lucien lowered his bow and arrow, dread filling him as he turned to face the woman approaching him. "Mother," he said, hoping the pain within him wasn't showing on his face. He placed the bow on the nearby table and went to greet her. "It is wonderful to see you," he murmured.

"I'm sorry I missed you last night," Katherine replied, hugging him and pressing a kiss onto his cheek. "Your father told me he'd seen you at the ball. Playing favorites, my Lucien?"

"Of course not," he replied, his voice cracking on the last word.

"I was just teasing you, dear. After all, we both know I would be your favorite."

He tried to smile, but feared he'd failed miserably. He'd struggled over whether or not to continue his father's charade, then realized he'd no choice in the matter. To tell her would be to break her heart . . . and that was not something he would ever be able to do.

So, like his father before him, he would look into this sweet woman's face and lie.

Luc eased out of her arms, forcing himself to act naturally. "Would you like to take a stroll around the garden with me, Mother?"

"How delightful," Katherine replied, accepting

his arm. "We can catch up with each other. I want to hear everything that has happened to you lately."

"Certainly," Luc agreed, knowing he would never be able to tell her the truth.

Patting his arm, Katherine said, "The last time I saw you I believe you mentioned you were going to be investing in . . ."

As they began to stroll toward the gardens, Lucien tried to keep his expression light, a difficult task, to be sure, with the burden of a heavy heart.

# 4

⹋

$\mathscr{T}$he minute she realized she was staring at Lucien through the bushes, Rosaleen caught herself with a start. A flush warmed her face as she turned toward her mother and the other ladies once again. Despite the fact that she was utterly fascinated with the play of Lucien's muscles beneath his white shirt as he drew back his bow, it wouldn't do to be caught peering at him.

Rose began to fan herself slowly, trying to cool not only her face, but her thoughts as well. Who would ever have guessed that archery could be such an appealing sport? Luc unnerved her, disarming her with his charm and polite attention. Never again would she wonder why females fluttered and preened to catch a man's attention. If she'd known that this magical emotion, this wonderful floating sensation, was the reward, then she too might have . . .

"Rose? Are you all right?"

Her mother's question snapped Rosaleen from her reverie. "Certainly," she murmured, stuttering slightly before calming her voice. "What could possibly be wrong?"

Elinor leaned in closer. "An odd look crossed your face a moment ago," she began, "and I wondered if—"

"It would appear that we are boring the Viscountess of Howland and her daughter."

Rosaleen bristled at Lady Howard's tone, but before she could utter a word, her mother replied smoothly, "Of course not, your grace. I was merely inquiring after my daughter's well-being. I did not mean to interrupt."

Lady Howard sniffed, her lips pursed tight.

Rose wanted to rail at the old crone, but again her mother stayed a rebuff by lifting her hand. Rose's stomach tightened in rebellion against the silence her mother had requested. Frustration roiled inside of her, partly toward Lady Howard and the other nasty gossips, and . . . partly toward her mother.

Rose felt ill at that realization, but there was no denying it as the truth. Her mother's repeated requests for unending patience and unchallenging silence were driving her mad. Trying to push her frustration away, Rose focused upon the exchange between her mother and Lady Howard.

"I assumed, Lady Fleming, that you didn't add to the conversation because you were uncomfortable with the topic," interjected Lady Foley.

Another woman snickered behind her fan.

Elinor shook her head. "Not at all. The news from the town is always welcome."

"Even when it concerns the death of one of your own?"

"I'm not certain what you mean," said Rose's mother, a wary note creeping into her voice.

Lady Foley widened her eyes, false innocence brightening her gaze. "Why, I assumed that you'd heard about the brutal murder of that infamous Cyprian, Lucienda Perth."

"Oh, dear God." Elinor's hand fluttered to her chest as she swayed against Rose.

Unwilling to expose her mother's pain to this gaggle of gossips, Rosaleen wrapped her arm about Elinor's waist and guided her away from the women.

"Elinor's distress proves my theory about her. You can take the woman out of the bed, but you can never erase the stain on her soul," Lady Howard pronounced in a loud voice.

"Mother, are you all right?" Rose asked as she brushed away the tears streaming out from behind her mother's closed eyes.

"Lucienda was a dear friend." Elinor clasped Rose's hand against her chest. "She helped me survive in the beginning. She took me under her protection and showed me how to build a life for myself."

Her mother's tearful admission surprised Rose, for Elinor never spoke openly of her past. Uncertain of what to say, Rose simply stroked her mother's back.

"When I met Lucienda, my life had become a nightmare, nothing at all like the one your father and I have given you, Rosaleen. It would be impossible for you to understand."

"I can try," Rose offered.

"I had no choice as to my fate." Bitterness crept into her mother's voice. "My father saw to that. He was a miserable man, a drunkard who treated me like his servant, making me wait on him and his friends until I dropped from exhaustion." Elinor pressed her eyes together tightly. "I'd thought my life couldn't get worse, but when my father finally lost our home, I'd discovered how wrong I'd been. We moved to London, and my father told me he planned on finding a husband for me, someone with money who could keep my father in drink."

In her heart, Rose wept for her mother. "What happened then?"

"I was terrified of who my father would bring home, of who I'd now belong to, so I ran off one night. There I was, in a strange city with no money, no friends, no way to survive." Her lips quivered into a soft smile. "That's when I met Lucienda. She taught me how to become a Cyprian, a courtesan."

Rose didn't know how to respond. The truth of her mother's past was more horrific than she'd ever realized.

"I know you must think that becoming a mistress was just as terrible a fate as being bartered by my father, but, Rose, you must understand that I didn't feel I had a choice. If I'd stayed with my father or the man he would have found for me, they would have destroyed me, first in spirit, then in body. So I ran far away, but I needed to live, to survive, and in order to do that, I had to support myself. Becoming a courtesan was the only way I could accomplish this."

Rose asked the one question that had haunted her. "But what about becoming a maid? Or a servant? Surely there were other ways to support yourself."

Elinor's smile darkened into a sad shadow. "I didn't have any references nor any idea as to how to fashion myself into a proper ladies' maid. All I had was a friend named Lucienda who lived in a glamorous world of balls, exotic parties, and, as she told me, endless pleasure." Elinor's gaze pleaded with Rose to understand. "Perhaps you would not have made the same choice I made, but please don't judge me too harshly, Rosaleen. I took the only path I saw. And, unlike the fate that awaited me with my father's edict, I would be able to control my own destiny."

Instinctively, Rose wanted to shy away from thoughts of her mother as a mistress, but the strength of her love kept her in place, stroking her mother's back. "I understand," Rose murmured softly.

Relief eased the lines furrowing her mother's forehead. "Thank God," Elinor said, closing her eyes for a moment, before opening them again to capture Rose's gaze. "I was afraid to tell you sooner. I have always been careful to shield you from the rest of my past."

"Why? You must have known that I would sympathize with your plight."

Elinor turned her head to the side. "It is hard for me to even speak of it."

"Then why now? Why tell me after all these years?"

"Because I wanted you to know why I am so devastated by Lucienda's death . . . and because I believe it is past time you learned the truth." Her mother squeezed Rose's hands. "I want you to know, Rose, that there were only two men in my life. I've already told you that Jonathan Howard was my first lover."

Rose flinched, remembering clearly when her mother had explained the reason behind Lady Howard's anger toward them. "Please," she asked, unwilling to hear more.

"I want you to know, Rosaleen; I want you to understand how much your father means to me." Elinor's tears began to dry as she pushed into a sitting position. "Lucienda helped me choose Lord Howard because he was rich and influential. He purchased a house for me, provided servants, and only visited occasionally. It was an ideal situation. I felt nothing for him other than mild affection."

"Mother." Rose tried to shift away, but her mother held her firm.

"No, Rose, please listen. It is time I was completely honest with you."

Though it bothered her, Rose remained on the bed, silent, allowing her mother to share her past.

"I first saw your father while under Lord

Howard's protection." A faraway look brightened Elinor's eyes. "I was visiting Lucienda's salon, where men would mingle with courtesans, when your father walked into the room. He was so self-assured, so confident. He took my breath away. I know the attraction was mutual because the instant he saw me, this wonderful, beautiful smile spread on his face and he made his way over to me."

Rose listened to the tale, caught up in the magic she heard in her mother's words.

"But it was the warmth, the kindness, I saw in his beautiful blue eyes that captured my heart." Elinor looked back at Rose. "Knowing that my interest lay in another, I ended my arrangement with Lord Howard that very evening. He was most generous, giving me the house in gratitude for my months of affection. The next night, I returned to Lucienda's and found your father waiting for me. I took him into my arms and into my heart and he did the same with me." Her mother smoothed back Rose's hair. "And when we discovered we were to be blessed with a baby, your father married me, despite the protests from his family and friends. Neither one of us have ever regretted forsaking the rules . . . except for the price you've been forced to pay."

Rose shook her head. "Please, don't."

"How can I not regret that you too must feel the sting of rejection and condemnation because of our past? It's not fair to you, Rose. You are innocent of any wrongdoing, but there is no swaying the small minds of some people."

Compassion spread through Rose. "No, Mother, please don't regret anything. If your past were indeed different, then I would never have been born, never experienced what it felt like to be cherished and loved by my parents."

"Your father and I were truly blessed when we had you," Elinor murmured, reaching for Rose.

Rose hugged her mother, accepting the love given so readily and returning it in full measure.

Lucien glanced at Rose's note in his hand once more as he made his way to the gazebo that stood in a remote corner of the elaborate hedge maze. Having received the missive less than an hour ago, he'd immediately come at her request for a private meeting, though he had no inkling as to why Rose wanted to see him. A rush of anticipation filled him at the thought of spending a private moment with Rose, but he tamped it down. From the tone of her note, Rose was in need of a friend, not an admirer.

One last twist in the path revealed the gazebo with Rosaleen pacing in the middle of the ornate building, her hands clasped in front of her. He'd thought her beautiful two days ago by the pond, but something about how she looked now, so anxious, so vulnerable, he found breathtaking.

The moment she saw him, Rose stopped pacing and rushed toward him, her hands outstretched. "Lucien," she said, relief coloring her voice. "I appreciate your coming to meet me."

"Never let it be said that I turned away from a

friend in need," Luc returned, clasping her hands. "What has upset you so, Rose?"

Rose dropped her gaze away from him. "It is hard for me to speak of my family's past with anyone, including my parents," she whispered.

"I thought we'd agreed that your family had nothing to do with our friendship."

Her smile warmed him. "We have, Luc. My concern is not our growing friendship. I needed to know if you could shed more light on a bit of news from London that greatly distressed my mother."

Lucien frowned slightly. What had happened recently that would have upset . . . Understanding smoothed his forehead as he nodded slowly. "Are you speaking of Lucienda Perth's murder?"

"Yes." Rosaleen lifted her chin. "She was a friend of my mother's."

"I'd guessed as much from your distress," Luc said without hesitation, watching as her challenging expression slipped away. "What would you like to know?"

"Anything you can tell me."

Seeing her so unguarded for the first time affected Luc far more than he thought possible. Though the details were gruesome, Rose wanted, no, she *needed* the truth.

He could see it in her eyes.

"When Lord Hampton arrived last night, he brought the terrible news with him. Apparently Lucienda was murdered in her bedchamber two nights ago. Her maid found her early yesterday morning." Luc paused, then continued as he realized there was no gentle way of telling the truth. "Someone had stabbed her through the heart."

Rose gasped, pressing her hands against her mouth. "Dear God," she whispered.

Grimly, Lucien nodded, holding back the rest of the information. There was no need for Rose to know that the murderer had taken the time to arrange Lucienda's body, even brushing her hair. No, it would do her no good to learn all the macabre details.

Rose's hands trembled as she dropped them back to her sides. "Do the authorities know who killed her?"

"No."

"Do they have any clues?"

"I don't know," Lucien said, wishing he had another answer when he heard the slightly desperate tone in Rose's voice. "All I know is that a note was found with the body."

"A note?"

"Yes," Luc verified. "Lord Hampton had no specifics as to what it said, but supposedly it's from the killer to his victim and is of a nature that led the magistrate to believe that a lover, current or former, is behind the crime."

Rosaleen rubbed at her temples. "It's so horrible to imagine anyone capable of murder."

The horror mingled with fear in her voice stirred Lucien's compassion for the beautiful woman before him and he wrapped his arms around her, silently offering her comfort.

Eagerly, she accepted it, winding her arms around his waist, burrowing her face into the breast of his jacket. Gently, Luc slid his hands along her spine, pressing her close, feeling a wave of protectiveness crash over him.

Yet, even as he comforted her, the sweet scent of lavender drifting up from her hair tempted Lucien to bend his head closer. Soft, golden tendrils brushed against his cheek as he inhaled deeply, overcome by the delicious sensations Rose created within him, knowing it would be so easy to tilt her chin up and kiss her as he longed to do.

The rare combination of emotions soaring through him made Luc almost light-headed. How could this one woman arouse so many conflicting feelings within him in the space of mere minutes?

When Rose stepped back, Lucien wanted to pull her close once more, but he forced himself to end their embrace.

"Thank you, Lucien," Rose whispered before leaning in to press a kiss upon his cheek. "You are a true gentleman and I consider myself blessed to be able to call you a friend."

Rosaleen smiled softly at him, her gaze sparkling with gratitude and warmth. "Thank you," she said again before hurrying from the gazebo.

Lucien watched Rose leave, feeling like an absolute fraud. Little did she know that the "true gentleman" she'd trusted to hold her in comfort had been imagining the sweetness of her kiss.

His bastard blood ran strong.

# 5

A calm settled over Rosaleen as she slowly walked back to the Foleys' manor house. She'd been right to turn to Lucien, to trust in his kindness. Sighing softly, Rose remembered how it had felt to be in Luc's arms, how aware she'd been of him as a man. Part of her had yearned for him to lift her face, to gift her with her first kiss, but she'd been glad that nothing had come of the easy embrace.

It only proved once more that he truly respected her as a lady of breeding.

The unique experience was a heady one indeed, Rose thought, as she slowed her steps. Lucien's treatment of her gave life to dreams of true acceptance among the ton. Wonderful, comforting images of meeting a man like Luc, falling in love, being welcomed into everyone's home with a smile instead of a sneer . . .

The sound of a woman's laughter broke through Rose's thoughts.

". . . her reaction did not shock me in the least."

Rose's stomach clenched as she recognized all too well Lady Howard's voice coming from the other side of the hedgerow.

"I will admit, though, that I've never before seen Elinor lose her composure like that."

Lady Howard's dear friend, Lady Foley, once again discussing her mother, Rose thought. Instinctively, her steps slowed because she had little desire to see those two harpies.

"Well, what did you expect?" asked Lady Howard. "I'm quite sure that despite her title, that . . . that *woman* has kept in close contact with her kind."

"I fear it as well."

"If you are in doubt, you need look no further than the Fleming whelp. Why, her disgraceful boldness leaves little doubt of her heritage."

Lady Foley quickly agreed. "It's true; breeding will always tell."

"And, I might add, that the gentlemen seem to notice as well," Lady Howard stated firmly. "It is blatantly apparent that the Fleming chit has captured the eye of the Earl of Berwyn. I've no doubt that he will soon offer for her . . . to be his mistress, that is."

Lady Foley twittered with laughter.

Raw fury blazed through Rose as the nasty gossip shattered her new-born illusions of acceptance. She'd been deceiving herself; the ton would never accept her.

*Then damn all the gossips,* Rose decided, her hands fisting at her side. She could no longer respect her mother's wishes to remain silent regardless of the insult.

It was far past time that Lady Howard and Lady Foley be taught a lesson. One they'd never forget.

Rose was prepared for battle.

Her hair flowed in bright, blond curls over her shoulders as she fastened a glittering sapphire necklace to emphasize her scandalously low bodice. Her skin had been scrubbed until it looked silky smooth, her hair brushed until it gleamed, and her eyes enhanced with a touch of kohl.

She was ready to seek her vengeance.

Tonight she would make those old witches, Lady Howard and Lady Foley, regret their vicious attacks upon her family.

Rosaleen skimmed her hands downward, smoothing out her skirts, as she rose from her settee. Taking a deep breath, she squared her shoulders and headed down to the ballroom.

Dancers occupied the center of the room with groups of people chatting along the outer edges. A quick scan located her victims sitting next to each other, huddled behind their fans. Though Rose couldn't see their mouths, she had little doubt that their lips were moving furiously with all sorts of nasty tidbits.

Anticipation filled Rosaleen as she set her plan into motion. She'd arranged for her parents to enjoy a private dinner in their sitting room, so she would be able to enact her revenge without their notice. Continuing to look around the room, Rose finally saw Lord Howard standing amidst a group of older gentlemen, all with reputations for enjoying the ladies.

Perfect.

Rosaleen glided toward Lady Howard with the thrill of the hunt racing through her veins. Her skirts swayed as she came to a stop before the gaggle of gossips. Lady Howard's eyes widened when she saw Rose standing before her.

"What is the meaning of this?" Lady Howard gasped, pressing her fan against her bosom. A moment later, her mouth dropped open as her gaze beheld Rose's ample cleavage, the sight obviously rendering her speechless.

The same wasn't true of Lady Foley. "Miss Fleming!" she exclaimed as she began to fan herself furiously. "That gown is utterly disgraceful!"

Allowing a mocking smile to curve upon her lips, Rose dipped down into a low curtsey, giving them an even more shocking glimpse of the gown. "I thought my attire would provide you with this evening's entertainment," Rose murmured, rising slowly, satisfied at their scandalized looks, confident that she was providing fresh fodder for their wagging tongues.

"I say!" Lady Foley drew herself upright, her lips pressing together in blatant disapproval.

"Indeed you do," Rose agreed. "You say quite a lot, but nothing is ever of a pleasant nature. No, you and Lady Howard merely voice your narrow-minded opinions to anyone who will listen." Rose glanced at the other ladies who had moved closer to catch the latest *on-dit* occurring before their very eyes. Their astonished expressions let Rose know she'd accomplished her goal to shock everyone.

"Who do you think you are to insult me?" Lady Howard asked, drawing back her shoulders. "You're nothing but the daughter of a whore."

Even Lady Foley gasped at the unveiled insult. "Really, Marianne," she murmured, shifting on her seat. "While Miss Fleming is behaving in a most vulgar manner, there is no need for you to join her."

Rose merely smiled, allowing Lady Howard's vileness to wash over her. Now, finally, she faced the true spirit of this woman, unmasked for all to see. "No, Lady Foley, please allow Lady Howard to speak. After all, what she said is true," Rose replied, her voice clear. "I am my mother's daughter and am proud to call myself such."

"We can all see that!" Lady Howard exclaimed, her expression twisting into harsh lines. "You're nothing but a harlot yourself."

"Marianne," Lady Foley murmured, placing a restraining hand on Lady Howard's arm. "Please remember yourself."

"How can I when I am confronted with such atrocities?" Lady Howard demanded.

"Do I distress you so much?" Rose asked softly, her heart pounding from her success at undermining Lady Howard's composure. "I suppose I could apologize for upsetting you . . . but I don't believe I will." Rosaleen twirled a curl around one finger. "In fact, I'm beginning to feel even more outrageous. What would you think if I were to stroll over to your husband and boldly ask him for a dance? What would he say?"

Lady Howard's gurgled exclamation answered the question.

"Hmmmm," Rose murmured, running her hand along the edge of her bodice. "Do you suppose that he might be easily swayed to seek my . . . companionship? From all accounts, your dear husband is always eager to make new friends. Isn't that right, Lady Howard?"

Lady Foley restrained her friend. "Everyone is watching us," she whispered furiously to Lady Howard.

"So true." Rose leaned closer. "And while such scandalous behavior is only expected of me, you have a reputation to maintain. I know it must be difficult to sustain your calm when you hear all the whispers about your husband's varied dalliances. It must be completely mortifying to watch him try to sneak off with one of the parlor maids or even one of your so-called friends."

Rose looked pointedly at the other women circling around their drama, noting quite a few blushes caused by her last words.

She returned her attention to Lady Howard. "Then again, perhaps you prefer that your husband turns his attention to others. That way, you're not forced to suffer his brutish embrace. Is that it?"

Lady Howard thrust to her feet, coming face to face with Rosaleen. "You are a vile creature," she hissed, her face reddened.

Rosaleen smiled in response. "And what do you consider yourself, my lady? With your harsh judgment on others, unforgiving nature, and vindictive gossiping, you put to shame even my most outrageous behavior."

Rose looked at Lady Foley and the women surrounding them, including the entire group in her censure. "All of you consider yourselves true ladies, yet you condemn my mother without hesitation. She has never been anything but kind and charitable to all of you, yet you sneer at her to her face."

Rose shifted her gaze back to Lady Howard. "But you, Lady Howard, are the worst. Your nastiness is directed at women whose reputations were often created by your very own husband." Her throat tightened, emotion choking her, as she whispered, "Just like my mother."

A strangled gasp gurgled from Lady Howard. "Why, you—"

Sharp pain lanced through Rosaleen as Lady Howard's hand slapped across her cheek. Something inside of Rose hardened even further. She refused to acknowledge the pain burning on the left side of her face as she glared at Lady Howard.

"You have just sealed your fate," Rose vowed, lifting her chin. "Now I will show you how easily I could tempt your husband into humiliating you once again."

"You wouldn't dare."

Despite the throbbing in her cheek, Rose forced a smile onto her face. "Watch me."

# 6

$\mathcal{F}$ueled by rage, Rose began the seduction of Lord Jonathan Howard. Forcing her gait into a smooth roll and swaying her hips gently beneath the length of her gown, Rose moved toward Lord Howard, who stared at her with a lecherous gaze. The sound in the room dimmed to a murmur as everyone froze, all of them watching the fascinating scandal unfolding before them.

Instead of wavering beneath the weight of their stares, Rosaleen forced her lips to tilt upward, a sensual curve she'd seen thousands of times on her mother's face. Whenever her mother gave this look to her father, he'd always stop whatever he was doing to kiss her. Surely, her sultry expression would have the same effect upon Lord Howard.

She couldn't have been more right.

Stepping forward to clasp her hand, Lord

Howard's gaze lowered to her décolletage as he bent to press a kiss to the back of her hand. "Miss Fleming, how delightful to see you again."

"Thank you, my lord," Rose murmured, dipping into a shallow curtsey.

She slanted a glance at him in time to see his eyes glazing over with a haze of lust. Rose looked away, her stomach roiling in protest. Still, she forced herself to continue with the game; Lady Howard needed to be taught a lesson.

"Might I say you are looking particularly fetching this evening, Miss Fleming."

Rose tilted her head to the side, hoping that it looked coquettish. "Miss Fleming? Surely we can disperse with the formalities—what with us being old, shall we say, family friends."

Lord Howard's chuckle crawled along her flesh. "Indeed we are." He leaned closer. "However, I would prefer to become *better* acquainted with you, my dear Rosaleen."

His breath feathered over her, making her feel unclean. Tapping his arm, Rose tried to act playful. "So bold, sir, when all eyes are upon us."

"Shall we seek privacy then?"

The dark promise in his voice caused Rose to stumble back as doubt assailed her.

"Rose?" Lord Howard asked, grasping her elbow in his hand. "Are you all right, my dear?"

"I . . . I'm fine," she stuttered, trying subtly to pull away.

"I'm so glad to hear it." Lord Howard leered at her.

Unable to look at him one moment longer, Rose

glanced away over Lord Howard's shoulder . . . only to meet the burning gaze of Lucien St. Cyr.

Dear Lord! Luc had witnessed her disgraceful behavior. All at once the realization of how she'd acted, how she'd demeaned herself, hit her full force.

Unfortunately, it was too late.

Rose watched, helpless to react, as Lucien's gaze traveled down her neck, pausing on her deep bodice, across her clinging skirts, and back up to her face. He stared at her, his expression intense, for a long moment before turning away.

No doubt in disgust, Rose thought a bit frantically, her heart aching.

Bile rose in her throat as Rosaleen jerked free of Lord Howard. She choked back her tears while she raced from the room, unable to face herself, Luc, or anyone else.

But even as she fled, Rosaleen knew she could never outrun her demons.

Lucien turned away from the sight of Rosaleen, his breath caught in his throat, his gut gripped with desire. Praying for his self-control to return, Luc fought off the urge to go to Rose, to capture her lips beneath his and see if their taste was as sweet as they promised. He closed his eyes against the hunger burning within him.

Even then, the seductive image of Rose remained, branded into his very soul. When she'd smiled, that sensual little tilt to her mouth, he'd felt the tug of desire clear down to his loins. Her very gown tempted him to . . .

Luc brought his thoughts to a fierce halt, guilt assailing him at the realization that he hadn't even given a moment to wonder *why* Rose had been acting so wantonly. Why would an innocent miss flaunt her beauty to a lecher like Howard? It didn't make any sense.

And how had he reacted to her odd behavior? No differently than Howard, Luc berated himself, disgusted at his own actions. Despite his best attempts to act the gentleman, it was obvious that he couldn't control his baser desires in her presence. She deserved someone to love her, to care for her, to treat her with respect—

Someone other than a bastard by birth and by nature.

Was he even capable of love? As Luc stood there, his manhood stiff and aching from just a glimpse of Rose, it seemed safe to conclude that he wasn't . . . just like his father before him.

Looking around the ballroom, Luc mentally bid farewell to the trappings of his life. He no longer belonged here within the boundaries of polite society.

He was, it would seem, his father's son after all.

Rose's heaving sobs had calmed into gentle tears, leaving behind deadened emotions. Curled into a ball upon her coverlet, Rose tried to hide from the painful thoughts swirling madly about in her head.

"Rose?"

Rose flinched at her mother's soft voice and she buried her face in her pillows, not wanting to expose her shame to her mother.

The bed shifted as Elinor sat down. "Oh, my poor darling Rose."

Fresh tears started as her mother gently stroked her hair. Anger, disappointment, those were emotions Rose could have dealt with, but compassion? It destroyed her fragile walls of defense, exposing her pain-laden heart once more. "Please, don't. Please let me be," she whispered, the last word ending on a choked sob.

Ignoring her plea, Elinor shifted to lie next to Rose. "I can't leave you alone," she answered, wrapping an arm about Rose's waist. "You're my daughter and you're hurting."

To her mother, it was that simple, Rose knew, but the thought of admitting her embarrassing actions made Rose cringe even more. "I need to be alone," she pleaded.

"No, Rosaleen, we can face this together."

Her mother's calm statement created a horrible suspicion within Rose. She twisted onto her back to look at her mother. "You already know about the scene I created?"

Compassion gentled her mother's gaze. "Lord Foley came to tell us." Elinor smoothed her hand down Rose's cheek. "Apparently, Lady Foley was concerned that you might have been hurt from the slap, so she retrieved her husband from the salon."

"Did you say Lady Foley?" Rose couldn't believe it. "You must have been mistaken."

Elinor shook her head. "No, Lord Foley was quite specific."

Rose swallowed. Hard. "Specific? About everything?"

"Very," Elinor said, her brows drawing downward. "What possessed you to confront Lady Howard like that in the first place?"

"I caught her speaking ill of us again this afternoon."

Elinor blinked. "Yes, but why would this cause you to confront her? It's a common occurrence."

Rose thrust up into a sitting position. "That's the very problem! Every time we're insulted, we turn away and ignore it. I couldn't *bear* to simply turn the other cheek . . . yet again."

"I see." Elinor sighed deeply, sitting up as well. "So you sought your revenge."

Remnants of anger began to simmer within Rose once more. "Yes, I did." She stood, facing her mother. "Why should we allow them to malign us time after time?"

"Because we have no choice. There are only two ways to handle the gossips—ignore their taunts or challenge them like you did this evening." Elinor's expression remained cool as she asked, "Tell me, Rose, did you find your solution preferable?"

A wave of disgust rolled over Rose as memories of events just past consumed her. "No," she admitted quietly.

Rising from the bed, Elinor paced with her arms wide. "Do you see how difficult it is to find a suitable way to handle their constant slurs? I know my solution may not seem the best to you, but it *is* the best for me."

Rose looked at her mother. "How can it be the best if you are constantly insulted?"

"Because their opinions matter less than nothing to me." Elinor leaned toward Rose, her expression intense. "Try to understand, Rose. I knew what my life would be if I accepted your father's marriage proposal all those years ago. I knew that I would never be welcomed in society, nor would my child." Her gaze took on a faraway cast. "Still, I would not change a thing, for if I did, my life might not be as wonderful as it turned out to be."

"But it's not fair that you treat those so-called ladies politely, yet receive no respect in return."

"No, it is not, but that is my life." Elinor shrugged lightly. "Nothing I do or say will ever change the fact that I was once a Cyprian."

"But doesn't it anger you to listen to those gossips tear you apart?" Rose couldn't understand how her mother accepted such treatment.

"At times," Elinor admitted. "However, I have found that anger is a useless emotion. Nothing positive ever comes from negative emotions, Rosaleen. So, I choose to ignore it and concentrate instead upon my family."

"It is so difficult to do that, Mother. So hard to pretend you didn't hear the snide remark." Dropping her head down, Rose murmured, "But after tonight, I know that I was wrong to confront Lady Howard."

A bittersweet smile touched Elinor's face. " 'Tis a hard lesson to learn, but as my mother always used to tell me, you can never grow without pain."

"I'm sorry, Mother, but I don't find that of much comfort," Rose replied with a half-smile.

"Hard truths never are."

Rose sighed deeply. "There are times I wish my life were different, that I found a man who cherished me and made me feel special."

"And what of your Lucien?"

"I've only just met him, Mother," Rose responded, shaking her head. "Besides, he witnessed my behavior tonight and from the look on his face, I've thoroughly disgusted him."

"I rather doubt that is true, Rose. Your young lord struck me as a gentleman who wouldn't be so quick to judge someone."

She could still see Luc's expression all too clearly in her mind. "No, Mother. I'm not mistaken."

"Well, then he doesn't deserve you," Elinor pronounced firmly.

Her mother's unwavering support warmed Rose.

"So now there's only one thing to be done," Elinor said brightly. "We need to introduce you to someone just *like* Lucien."

"Gentlemen, true gentlemen, are a scarce commodity," Rose pointed out dryly.

"Here in England, yes, but perhaps on the Continent?" Elinor's eyes widened. "That's it! We can send you on an extended tour of Europe."

Rose couldn't even speak a word before her mother continued.

"Think on it, Rose. Wouldn't it be marvelous to leave all of the rumors, the gossip, behind? You could start fresh where no one knows your family history."

"I'm certain that other people from England tour the Continent as well."

"Of course, darling," her mother replied, waving her hand in dismissal. "But not everyone will know your background when they learn your name as they do here in England. It will allow a new acquaintance to form an opinion of you based on your wit, charm, and kindness, rather than on your heritage."

"And what happens if someone is so kind as to inform this new acquaintance of our past?"

"Hopefully it will not matter by then." Elinor grasped Rose by the shoulders, gazing into her eyes. "Oh, Rose, I know it's not the perfect solution, but there is hope that your life will be easier in Europe. Why don't you just try? You deserve happiness."

Yes, she did. A weight lifted off of Rose's heart at the thought, no, the hope that she might find a life in Europe free of innuendos and shadowed glances. Smiling at her mother, she nodded slowly. "It is well worth the try."

"Oh!" Elinor cried happily, pulling Rose into a swift embrace. "We can make our excuses to the Foleys and leave first thing tomorrow. Then we can begin to plan your grand excursion without delay."

Rose held up a hand. "Before we leave, I need to find Luc, to explain why I behaved the way I did this evening."

"You don't owe him an—"

"He's been a friend to me," Rose interrupted gently. "He's earned the right to an explanation."

Elinor pressed her hands onto her hips. "Very well, but as soon as you've seen him, we'll start home."

With her heart feeling lighter than it had in years, Rose smiled at her mother. "And then on to Europe . . . and, with any luck, the future of my dreams."

# 7

## Three Years Later
## London, England

"Are you feeling up to a bit o' sport?"

Fighting to clear his thoughts, Lucien looked up at the two wenches, one blond, the other brunette, pressing against his side. His mouth felt dry and wool-laden from the amount of drink he'd poured into it, yet he longed for another pint. He still had the ability to remember who he was . . . and what he was.

Turning away from the bountiful breasts, Lucien raised his mug and called out for another drink.

Not rebuffed, the two women separated, one on each side of him, before running their hands through his hair and across his neck. "Cor, he's a beaut."

"I told ya, Bev," murmured the dark-haired girl. "I've 'ad the pleasure of 'is company before." She leaned down to lick at Luc's ear. "And 'e's delicious."

The blonde on his right giggled, the sound piercing through the lovely haze beginning to cloud Luc's brain. He shrugged the women aside as the waitress brought him another round, taking a deep draw from the goblet. The liquor burned down to his gut, the familiar fire comforting because he knew that complete oblivion wasn't far behind.

"Wot's a gent like 'im doing in Charlie's place?"

Luc slanted a look at the blonde. "Because this is where I belong," he replied, his words slurred.

The brunette cradled Luc's head against her breasts. "That's right, Bev. 'E's one of us now, a regular."

"Indeed I am," Luc agreed, allowing the feel of the woman's flesh to mellow the harsh edges of his mood. "I fear I'm no longer welcome at White's or any other respectable place." He motioned the blonde closer. "It's because I'm a drunken bastard."

"Pissah," the brunette scoffed with a laugh. "If that's all it took to keep a gent from fine places, then I'd wager the proper establishments wod all be empty, woddn't you, Bev?"

Again the blonde giggled, but this time, with a lovely haze covering his senses, Luc didn't mind the sound.

"What do you say about comin' upstairs with Bev and me for a while?" the brunette whispered, rubbing her body against his.

Through his blurry vision, Luc saw the two women smiling down at him, their expressions encouraging him to accept their offer. "Both of you at once?"

"You seem man enough to 'andle us," the blonde said, leaning closer to slide her hand along the length of his thigh.

"Indeed I am," Luc agreed. In fact, the man he'd become had often taken on more than two at a time. His descent into darkness had been laden with ladies such as these, gallons of alcohol, crooked games of chance, and even a few wagers of a most sordid nature. Glancing up at the two women, he nodded slowly. "I'm just the man for the job."

Lucien swayed slightly as he levered himself out of his chair, but the women steadied him. Reaching for his drink, Luc took another long swallow before following the women upstairs.

"Have you heard the latest news?"

Katherine St. Cyr hid her grimace at the way Lady Foley seemed to savor the words. Her teacup clicked gently against the china saucer as Katherine set it down. "You know I'm not one to listen to gossip," she said, loudly enough so that the other women in the room could hear her.

"Oh, but this is news of the best sort," Lady Foley protested, pressing a hand to her chest. "I certainly wouldn't call it gossip because it is completely true, of course. Everyone here knows that I would never repeat a tale if it were a vicious lie."

It would be rude, Katherine thought, to disagree with that terrible falsehood in public. Instead, she remained silent, allowing her lack of response to speak for her.

Apparently, the subtlety escaped Lady Foley,

and she continued on as if Katherine had eagerly asked for the news. "The Fleming girl is returning to England."

All of the ladies in the room exclaimed at once, each one demanding more details.

Lady Foley sat back in her chair, wearing a cat-in-the-cream smile. Katherine looked away, wishing she'd never agreed to attend this tea party.

"It's quite true, I assure you." Lady Foley took a sip of her tea. "What is even more shocking is that the girl has become the toast of Europe."

Now this caught Katherine's interest. Wasn't it Rosaleen Fleming who had captured her son's eye all those years ago? She focused her attention back to the conversation.

"Isn't that the girl who aroused Lady Howard's ire at your country affair?" asked Lady Evans.

Lady Foley's lips pursed. "Yes, though I'd rather forget the entire event."

"Forget?" Katherine arched an eyebrow at Lady Foley. "But wasn't Marianne Howard your dearest friend?"

"*Was* being the proper word in that statement, Katherine." Lady Foley shook her head. "Marianne's actions were shocking. While it's true the Fleming girl was overly bold, I must say I expected far more of Marianne. And to make matters worse, when I called Marianne to task, she had the audacity to challenge me."

"Whatever do you mean?" asked Lady Evans, latching on to the gossip like a dog with a bone.

"I'm certain I told you this before," Lady Foley began, "because I was most distressed over Mari-

anne's actions. That . . . that *woman* had the gall
to ask me how I would react if faced with someone making improper advances toward my husband." Lady Foley paused dramatically, playing
her enraptured audience like a master. "Then *she*
pursued him! Isn't that utterly disgraceful? Mind
you, my husband would never even consider such
a thing, but that doesn't make Marianne's actions
any less shocking."

Looking pointedly at her guests, Lady Foley
said, "Naturally, after that horrid event, I could no
longer suffer her presence."

"Quite shocking," Lady Evans murmured.

"Indeed, but then I *knew* Marianne was less
than a lady when she slapped the Fleming chit."
Lady Foley helped herself to a crumpet. "I must
say, though, Rose Fleming stood firm beneath
Marianne's venomous attack, but that really
shouldn't have surprised me. After all, it is a well-
known fact that I've always admired Miss Fleming's strength of character."

Katherine almost spilled her tea. "You have?"
she choked out.

"Well, of course, Katherine. Why, I've often spoken about it."

"When was that?" Lady Evans asked, a frown
darkening her brow.

With a huff, Lady Foley crossed her arms, dismissing the questions. "Oh, come now, I'm sure
you must remember how dreadful I felt when the
poor girl was slapped." When Lady Evans shook
her head, Lady Foley sniffed loudly. "Well, I did
defend the chit at my country affair. You should

remember it, because it was there that we learned of the first murder."

Katherine shifted on her chair. "Yes, I remember now. Since then, six more have been murdered."

"Three in the past year," Lady Evans interjected.

"Perhaps it is God's wrath finally coming down upon those wicked women." Lady Foley glanced at the ladies in the room. "No decent woman has been harmed."

Offended by Lady Foley's opinion, Katherine quickly replied, "It was not God's hand that killed those poor, misguided souls, my lady. Our Lord is our Savior . . . not a murderer."

"The hand of God wipes out plagues."

"Mistresses are hardly a plague, Lady Foley, and the hand of God is merciful. He would forgive those ladies their sins if they repented."

Lady Foley waved her hand. "I have no desire to get embroiled in a theological debate with you, Katherine. I was only trying to refresh everyone's memory as to what transpired before Marianne's fall from grace."

"She was your friend," Katherine pointed out softly. "Could you not forgive her the one slip in judgment?" Though she didn't care for Lady Howard, Katherine disliked Lady Foley's harsh rejection of her friend even more.

Lady Foley puffed up her chest, indignation tightening her expression. "I simply could not, in good conscience, condone Marianne's behavior. From the Fleming girl I expected no less, but from Marianne Howard . . . well, I found it reprehensible."

Katherine didn't bother to respond, knowing

Lady Foley wouldn't hear what she had to say anyway.

"In fact, I feel so awful about the way Marianne treated poor Miss Fleming while at my house that I'm going to be holding a ball in her honor."

"You are?" Lady Evans gasped.

"Absolutely."

Katherine blinked at Lady Foley's pronouncement. "It comes as somewhat of a surprise to me as well."

"What could be more fitting, I ask you, than to make retribution to the girl?" A satisfied glint reflected in Lady Foley's gaze. "Of course we'll have to be careful to leave Marianne Howard off of the guest list, though I will send an invitation around to Lord Howard since he's still a dear friend of my husband's."

Lady Evans's eyes widened. "Oh, my, I fear that will greatly distress Marianne."

"Ah, well, that can't be helped," Lady Foley said, far too cheery for anyone to think she felt even the slightest remorse.

Suddenly, Katherine knew why Lady Foley was so determined to embrace Rosaleen Fleming—spite, pure and simple. Still, Katherine rejoiced at Rose's change of fate, not only for Rose's sake, but for Luc's as well.

Remembering clearly how Luc responded to Rose, Katherine couldn't help but wonder if he would delight in seeing her again. For the past three years, Luc had been slipping further and further away from her and he'd virtually withdrawn from polite society.

Oh, she knew it was pitiful to hope that Rose would spark something inside of Luc that would make him want to mend his ways and return to his life within the ton, but all she had left now was hope.

Feeling a glimmer of excitement, Katherine turned her attention to Lady Foley. "I'd be more than happy to assist you in arranging the reception for Miss Fleming."

Surprise widened Lady Foley's eyes. "Why, Katherine," she sputtered. "How generous of you."

Allowing Lady Foley to think her offer purely altruistic, Katherine bowed her head once. "I'm glad to be of help."

"Our baby is coming home!"

Elinor moved into her husband's arms, laughing in delight as he twirled her about the room. She smiled up at him as he finally brought them to a halt.

"Why, my dear viscountess, I don't believe I've seen you so happy in years."

"It's true, Reggie," Elinor admitted, pressing a kiss onto her husband's cheek. "I hope I haven't been too melancholy for you. It's just that I've missed our Rose dreadfully these past few years."

"As have I, but our sacrifice has been well worth it."

Elinor moved out of her husband's arms. "That's true. Your Aunt Jane's letters were full of stories about how Rose has taken Europe by storm."

"Just as we knew she would," Reggie replied

proudly, before chuckling softly. "And I suppose we should be overjoyed that none of Rose's many suitors managed to sweep her off her feet and into a hasty marriage on the Continent."

Surprise sent Elinor whirling toward her husband. "Why on earth would you be happy about that?"

"Because I don't wish to be cheated out of attending my only child's wedding," Reggie said without hesitation.

Sighing deeply, Elinor dropped into a chair. "As much as I'd love to be there when Rose gets married, I was praying that she would fall desperately in love and marry while in Europe."

"But this will be even better, for now she can find an Englishman to marry and we'll be able to see her often even after she's wed," Reggie replied.

Distressed, Elinor gazed up at her husband. "Have you forgotten what life was like for our Rose in England? Don't you remember how the men treated her?"

"Not all of them," Reggie protested. "Take Lucien St. Cyr, for example. He showed the utmost respect for our daughter."

"Yes, but he was the only one." Elinor stood again, agitation making it hard to remain still. "And look at him now."

Disappointment flickered in Reggie's gaze. "Ah, Elinor, I thought you of all people would know better than to base your opinion of someone on gossip."

Shame filled Elinor. "You're right, but there's no denying the fact that he's no longer welcomed by polite—" She broke off, hearing her own words and realizing just how ironic they were. As if she'd ever known acceptance from the ton. "I'm sorry, Reggie. I *do* know better," she admitted softly. "I'm simply afraid that Rose hasn't let go of her dreams of Luc."

"Dreams of Luc? Lucien St. Cyr?"

"Of course," Elinor replied. "She's mentioned him in quite a few of her letters and I'm worried that she still has lingering feelings for him."

Grasping Elinor's shoulders, Reggie stopped her pacing. "I don't understand why you're concerned, even if she does carry fondness for him."

"Because when our daughter returns, she needs to focus on building a life for herself here in England, a daunting task, to be sure." Elinor gazed up at her husband. "And Luc, in his present state, would be a burden Rose doesn't need."

"Oh, Edward! There you are!" Katherine strode into the library. "I have some hopeful news."

Glancing up from his accounting ledgers, Edward was pleased to see the sparkle in his wife's eyes, a sparkle that had been absent for far too long. "Please share it with me."

"Do you remember the Viscount of Howland's daughter, Rosaleen?"

Edward didn't have a chance to respond before his wife continued.

"The one that Lucien seemed so attracted to before . . . before . . ." Katherine stuttered to a halt. "Before he changed," she finished lamely.

A change caused by his son's learning the truth of his heritage.

Edward knew all too well what had caused his son to change so drastically, to embrace a life of debauchery, but his wife had no idea. Luc had never told Katherine the truth, and though he knew she deserved to know, he couldn't bear to hurt her. Still, it cut Edward deeply to see the pain Lucien's unexplained withdrawal had caused Katherine.

Would it be better to simply tell his wife the truth? Or would it be less painful for her to be left wondering why their son had changed overnight? It was a dilemma that haunted him.

"Yes, I remember the girl," he admitted softly, trying to hide his torn heart.

Katherine's faltering smile regained its strength. "Splendid. She returns from Europe in a few days."

Though Edward couldn't even guess why this news would be so hopeful, he smiled at his wife's enthusiasm. "That is wonderful news indeed."

"I thought so as well." Katherine began to pace. "Lady Foley is hosting a ball for her return. Now, all I need to do is make sure that Luc attends."

"Lucien?" Unease shifted inside of Edward. "Why?"

"Because of Rosaleen, silly."

Edward wasn't able to piece the two bits of information together. "He needs to attend because of Rosaleen?"

"Exactly."

Edward lifted his shoulders. "Why?" he asked again.

Katherine's laugh trilled out. "Because I'm hoping that she will remind Luc of the life he once led." Her smiled dimmed. "Perhaps seeing her again will make him cease wasting his days in worthless pursuits."

"I'm still unclear as to what Miss Fleming has to do with anything," Edward said gently.

Katherine sank onto a chair. "Oh, I'm well aware that I'm being silly and praying for a miracle, but I can't let go of the thought that maybe, just maybe, Rosaleen will make Luc feel an urge to rejoin society."

Edward reached out and captured her fingers within his grasp. "Don't get your hopes up only to have them dashed, my dear."

Shadows gathered in her eyes once again, making Edward sorry he'd brought them back. "We've tried everything else to reach him, Edward, but yet he still avoids us. Stories of his excesses reach me every day. Whatever happened to our sweet Lucien?" Bowing her head, Katherine drew in a deep breath. "I just want my son back."

His wife's voice broke on the last statement, adding to the weight of his guilt. Squeezing his wife's hand encouragingly, Edward murmured, "Would you like me to ask Luc if he will attend the ball in Miss Fleming's honor?"

Katherine's eyes widened. "Would you? I didn't think you set much stock in my idea."

While he didn't believe her idea would work, Edward said, "You might be right after all, Katherine. This girl, this Rosaleen, might just be the one to bring him around."

The frail light of hope once again shone from

his wife's beautiful brown eyes, making Edward glad of his lie. After all, what did one more matter?

With every one, he merely added another footfall on his descent into Hades.

"To what do I owe the honor of this visit?" Luc drawled, propping a foot on his library table. "Come to tell me yet another lie?"

Shaking his head, Edward refused to rise to the taunt. "I've come on behalf of your mother."

"Ahhhh." Luc raised his glass toward his father. "Forgive me; I'd forgotten for a moment that everything you do is for her."

Annoyance flickered in Edward's gaze. "Haven't you had enough of this yet, Lucien?" he demanded. "Perhaps you haven't realized, but while you're so busy punishing me for my sins, you're also hurting your mother—deeply. And she, like you, is an innocent in this whole bloody mess."

Luc felt the weight of his father's words settle into his gut. "I know."

As suddenly as Edward's anger had come on, it faded away. "Ah, Lucien, I can only apologize for the thousandth time and beg your forgiveness."

Luc waited for the rush of fury that overtook him whenever he spoke to his father, but this time he felt nothing. Absolutely nothing. It was as if he were already dead inside.

Taking another sip of his brandy, Luc murmured, "You needn't keep apologizing. It changes nothing."

An expression of defeat etched its way onto Edward's face. "No, it doesn't," he admitted softly. Squaring his shoulders, he took a step closer to Luc. "Then I won't speak of it further. The reason for my call is to ask you for a favor on your mother's behalf."

A spark of guilt flared within Luc, but he tamped it down, remaining silent.

Edward's jaw tightened. "I can see you are determined to make this as hard on me as possible. Very well, Lucien; you've earned that right." He swallowed once. "Your mother would like you to attend the Foleys' ball in three days."

Surprise rippled through Luc. He'd imagined his mother asking him to call upon her, to escort her to an opera, or to simply spend time with her, but not to attend a ball. Immediately suspicious, Luc narrowed his eyes. "Why?"

"Does it really matter, Lucien?" Edward asked, setting his hands on his son's desk. "Say you'll grant your mother her wish or you won't, but let's cease this game of cat and mouse."

"Very well."

Vexation brought Edward's breath rasping out. "What precisely does that mean, Lucien? Are you saying we will stop the baiting or were you promising to attend the ball?"

Luc curved his lips into a mocking smile. "I meant, 'Very well, I will attend the ball,'" he murmured softly.

Edward nodded once. "Thank you, Lucien," he said quietly.

Taking a long sip from the snifter, Lucien simply stared at the man before him.

At the continued silence, Edward finally cleared his throat. "Well, then, I shall be off."

Moving toward the door, Edward paused with his hand on the knob, before glancing back at Luc. "Damn, but I miss you, son."

Without displaying a hint of emotion, Lucien watched his father walk from the room. When Edward was gone, Luc drained his brandy, muttered an oath, and flung the glass headlong into the fire grate.

Having paused only to give his wife the news that Luc had promised to attend the Foleys' affair, Edward had headed straight to his study. He'd watched the sun drop below the horizon, but hadn't moved to light even a single candle. In his current frame of mind, he found comfort in the darkness.

A soft knock on the door roused Edward from his morose thoughts. "Enter," he bade.

Basil Whitmore peered around the edge of the door. "Edward? Are you in here?"

"Yes," he responded, not moving from his chair.

Basil stepped into the study, reaching to light the nearest candle. "Why is it so dark in here? Are you resting?"

Resting? Edward doubted he'd ever be at rest again. "No. Please come in, Basil, though I warn you I'm not fit company at the moment."

Basil sat in the chair across from Edward. "Ah, then it appears I've come at the right time. Now why don't you tell me what's bothering you."

Edward closed his eyes, unable to meet Basil's gaze. "I went to see Lucien today."

"I can only take it that the meeting didn't go well."

"No," Edward replied, a harsh laugh scraping from his throat. "No, it didn't go well at all." He opened his eyes to look at Basil. "He despises me, but no more than I do myself. As I stood in the middle of Lucien's library watching him drain his glass of brandy, I searched for a sign, the smallest sign, that the son I'd raised and loved was still alive within him." Edward rubbed at his chest. "And only when I mentioned the pain his withdrawal was causing his mother did I see even a spark of my Lucien."

Basil leaned forward, placing a hand upon Edward's knee. "Lucien will eventually find himself again and when he does, you need to be there for him. But before you can do that, you need to forgive yourself, Edward, or it will destroy you."

"Destroy me? I couldn't care less about me. In fact, there are days when I hope that I'm taken from this earth, simply to end the misery." Edward ran his hands over his face. "I've already destroyed my son, now I pray every day that my wife doesn't suffer the same fate all because of my lies."

Basil reached over, placing a comforting hand upon Edward's shoulder. "She deserves the truth."

"Does she?" Edward thrust to his feet, shaking off Basil's hand. "Why didn't you tell me that when Lucien was a babe? How can I tell her that the child she's loved, raised, and built dreams around isn't hers? If she had to know eventually, it would have been more merciful to tell her years ago that her own child had died."

"But you didn't make that choice," Basil said reasonably. "So, it makes no sense to lament something that has already been done. No, Edward, you need to look forward."

"How do I look into a future that is bleak and hopeless?"

"By first looking into the past." Basil laid a Bible upon the table. "Look for your answers in the Book, my friend. You shall find them in there."

Edward's fingers trembled as he stroked the cover. "I don't know if even God can help me find a way out of this mess I've created."

"I know He can." Basil clasped his hands together. "Do you remember when I found out that Lilly had been unfaithful?"

"Of course," Edward replied immediately.

"When I learned of her betrayal I felt myself becoming consumed with hatred, unable to move beyond my pain." Basil shook with emotion. "I wanted to destroy everyone who had caused my pain, to hurt the man who had taken—" He broke off abruptly, taking a deep breath and regaining his composure. "I'm sorry, Edward; I still can't speak of it without getting overwhelmed."

"It's all right, my friend." Edward patted Basil on the arm.

Finally, Basil released a shaky breath. "What I'm trying to tell you, Edward, is I've searched for a way to put my pain behind me and I think I've found it."

Skeptically, Edward eyed his friend because it certainly didn't seem as if Basil had put anything at all behind him. Still, Edward knew it wouldn't help either one of them if he pointed that out.

"You must search in your soul to find your way to inner peace," Basil finished calmly.

Forcing a smile onto his face, Edward wondered if, after all the pain he'd not only caused but endured as well, he still had a soul worth searching.

# 8

*R*osaleen Fleming had returned.

Lucien struggled to regain his composure at her unexpected appearance. After all this time, she'd finally come home. His gaze remained fixed upon her as she spoke with two other ladies whose names escaped him. Hell, rational thought escaped him at the moment. All he could remember was how Rose had felt in his arms, the desire she'd created within him, all those years ago.

But that was another lifetime.

The thought sobered him. Lord, he wished he'd never agreed to attend this affair. Breathing deeply, Luc couldn't keep his gaze from Rose, who seemed to have acquired an air of confidence since she'd been away.

Deep within him, in a part he'd thought long dead from his excesses, there was a spark of happiness that Rosaleen had found the acceptance she'd once craved as he watched the matrons welcome her into their fold.

"St. Cyr! Is that you, old man?"

Luc turned to face his old friend, yet another face from his past. "How have you been, Ridgely?"

"Me?" Peter tossed back his head to laugh. "I'm not the one who's stopped coming around. The real question is how are you doing?"

Lucien spread his arms. "I am as you see."

"Is that good or bad?" Peter asked with a wry smile.

"I suppose that depends on one's perspective."

"Lord, St. Cyr, you've become bloody cryptic!" Peter frowned slightly. "First I don't see you for literally years, then I finally run into you again and you talk in riddles. What the devil's happened to you?"

"The Devil is indeed what happened to me," Luc replied, unable to resist the play on words.

Peter's frown deepened. "I don't know what you're talking—" Breaking off his response, Peter directed his gaze across the room. "But I don't believe this is the time to have this discussion."

Luc lifted an eyebrow.

"The lovely Miss Fleming is coming our way," Peter clarified. A side of his mouth tipped upward as he murmured, "And somehow I don't believe I'm the one she wants to see."

As soon as Ridgely moved along to the nearest group of ladies, Lucien turned to watch in horrified delight as Rosaleen hurried toward him, her hands outstretched and a smile of warm welcome softening her beautiful features.

"Oh, Luc," she breathed, clasping both of his hands between hers. "I was so hoping that you would be here tonight."

She rendered him speechless.

Rose leaned closer. "You alone know how difficult it was for me to come to a ball given by Lady Foley . . . and in my honor no less. How the mighty have fallen," she finished with a laugh.

Luc responded without conscious thought. "No, Rose, they haven't fallen at all; they've merely opened their eyes to appreciate your beauty."

Her gasp contained pure joy. "Oh, Luc," she murmured, squeezing his hands tightly. "How I've missed you."

Missed him? Hell, she didn't even know him anymore. Lucien pulled his hands free. "I heard you took Europe by storm."

"Actually, my entrance into Continental society is a very amusing story, and surely you remember how I love amusing stories," Rose replied brightly.

A chuckle, rusty from lack of use, rumbled from Luc. The way she gazed at him made him long for the man he once was, for things that would forever be beyond his grasp. Still, he was unable to resist a touch—one touch to remind him of when he'd once hoped for more.

Slowly, he raised his hand, stroking the tip of his finger down the softness of Rosaleen's fine cheek. Her smile faded away at the touch and her eyes darkened. The velvet of her flesh teased his senses, creating longings within him best left for another man, an unsoiled man.

"It doesn't appear that those three years in Europe changed the Fleming chit at all!"

Stiffening at the insult, Luc dropped his hand to his side and turned to face Lady Howard.

"And you, sir, didn't you learn your lesson?" Lady Howard asked loudly. "After you met her, your reputation slid downward at an alarming rate."

"No, madam, the fault rests with me," Luc pointed out softly, his tone menacing. "I believe the same holds true of you."

Lady Howard gasped, pressing her hands to her chest. "Why, I never—"

"How *dare* you come to my home!" Lady Foley charged toward them, fury blazing from her.

Lady Howard lifted her nose. "Have you forgotten the invitation you sent to me?"

"That invitation was sent to your *husband*, madam." Crossing her arms, Lady Foley glared at Lady Howard. "I specifically did not address the invitation to include you, Marianne."

"Well—well—" Lady Howard sputtered, frantically looking around the room for support and finding none. Closing her mouth with a snap, she spun on her heel and marched from the room.

Triumph settled into Lady Foley's expression as she waved her arm. "With such a lack of manners, it is easy to see why Lady Howard isn't welcome in polite homes anymore." A tittering of laughter followed Lady Foley's pronouncement. "Please continue about your pleasure."

Lady Foley stepped closer to Rose and Luc. "Miss Fleming, my lord, allow me to apologize for that vulgar attack you suffered in my home."

"That is unnecessary, my lady, though I do appreciate your sentiment," Rose murmured graciously. "You handled the situation with marvelous aplomb."

Lady Foley's hand fluttered to her cheek. "Well, thank you, Miss Fleming." She nodded firmly. "It appears your time in Europe was well spent, indeed."

After Lady Foley walked away, Rose turned toward Luc, a smile on her face once more. "Well, that certainly was unpleasant," she said lightly.

Her attempt to alleviate the tension between them failed. Lady Howard's interruption served to remind Luc of who he'd become . . . and how he now threatened Rose's new-found acceptance.

Stepping back, Luc affected an expression of weariness. The adopted stance of a man utterly bored with his surroundings came easily to Luc.

"Luc?" Rose asked, obviously confused by his sudden withdrawal.

Glancing down at her, Luc dismissed her with a single look. "It has been . . . a pleasure seeing you again," he purposely drawled in an insulting manner. "Still, I must be off now. These affairs are as amusing as death."

"Did I do something to offend you?" Rose asked, confusion coloring her question.

He wouldn't allow himself to be swayed by the glint of pain that flickered in her eyes. "Boredom offends me," he retorted.

Rose drew herself up. "I apologize that you found my company so trying, my lord."

"Don't concern yourself," he offered, flicking

a hand in dismissal. "I'm easily bored these days."

Her beautiful features froze as she drew back her shoulders. "Than I shall make you suffer no more, my lord." She tipped her head down, regal as a queen, before gliding away from him.

Pushing away the spark of pain inside of him, Lucien watched her walk away from him, knowing he should be happy that he'd succeeded in rebuffing her company. It was easy to convince his head that he'd done the right thing, but it was harder to feel it in his heart.

With a growl of disgust, Lucien strode out of the Foleys' townhouse, determined to lose himself, and this new painful memory, in the nearest gaming Hell.

"How dare you!" Marianne Howard screamed at the footmen as they forcibly escorted her through the doorway. "Do you know who I am?"

"An uninvited guest, madam," the butler returned smartly before shutting the door in her face.

In her face!

Marianne stormed toward her carriage, fury pulsing through her. She was no longer welcome in society . . . and it had all started because of the Fleming whores. A strangled exclamation of frustration ripped from her throat.

She was Marianne Howard, Duchess of Greenley!

No one treated her this way. No one.

*      *      *

The cool night air did little to ease the blush burning upon Rose's cheeks. A combination of anger, frustration, and sadness swirled within her as she sat in the quiet corner of the garden.

She'd thought herself invulnerable to insult, yet Luc had managed to pierce her heart without effort. In Europe she'd gloried in the acceptance of her peers and had searched for that one man, that special person, who could touch her heart. Yet, as many suitors as she'd entertained, not one of them had sparked more than the desire for friendship. The dreams she'd found so easy to weave around Luc had remained silent, unstirred . . . until now. One glance at Luc and all of her old dreams and hopes had flooded through her.

Why was Luc the only one who affected her like this? When she'd seen him across the room tonight, the years had melted away, leaving in their place an eager anticipation to reunite with him.

Apparently, only she had experienced that desire.

At first, she'd thought Lucien was glad to see her as well. He'd smiled at her, then he'd touched her cheek, melting her inside with the gentle stroke. His glorious blue eyes had darkened with affection, making her heart race beneath his gaze. He'd seemed different somehow from when she'd seen him last, more dangerous. His features had hardened over the years, making him look lean . . . and very appealing.

When he'd run his fingertip down her face, she'd imagined his sculpted lips closing the distance between them. How often she'd dreamed of Lucien sweeping her into his arms, pulling her closer and . . .

"Excuse me, Miss Fleming. Am I interrupting?"

A gasp of surprise sprang from Rose as she twisted around. Recovering quickly, Rose smiled in welcome. "Of course not, my lady. I was merely taking in a bit of air."

The marchioness waved her hand toward the bench. "Might I join you?"

"Please," Rose offered without hesitation.

Sitting down, Katherine sighed lightly. "Ah, this feels wonderful. I vow my feet always begin to ache at these affairs." Turning with a smile, she murmured, "We haven't been formally introduced. I'm Katherine St. Cyr, Lucien's mother."

"Yes, I know. I saw you with your son a few years ago at a country party . . . before I left for my Grand Tour," Rose clarified.

"Indeed," Lady St. Cyr murmured, a pleased smile playing upon her lips. "From his actions this evening, it would appear that my son remembered you as well."

Flushing with embarrassment, Rose wished that the earth would open up and swallow her whole. "I'm sorry, my lady, about that horrid scene with Lady Howard."

"I wasn't speaking of that nasty woman," Katherine replied quickly. "It was afterward when Lucien seemed . . . bothered by you."

"I believe the correct word would be bored." Hearing the bitter tone in her voice, Rose tried to smooth her response. "While it's true I was unsettled by his behavior, I meant no offense toward Luc, I mean, Lord St. Cyr."

"I'm certain none was taken," Lady St. Cyr murmured, before twisting to face Rose. "Of course, I was quite impressed with how you handled yourself. I am all too aware of how upsetting Lucien can be at times. My son has changed greatly over the past three years." She clasped her hands together. "Lucien has withdrawn from society until he is a virtual hermit, only venturing out to indulge in gaming Hells and other sorts of debauchery that go along with them."

"Luc?" Rose couldn't believe what she was hearing.

"Oh, yes," Lady St. Cyr said, her voice breaking. "I've tried to reach him, to understand why he's changed so, but I never get any answers."

Rose felt Lady St. Cyr's pain in the impassioned cry and was powerless to resist it. "Is there anything I can do to help?"

Slowly, the marchioness lifted her head. "Perhaps you might speak with him; try to find out what has caused him to shut himself off from everyone and everything."

It seemed an impossible task, but Rose could no more kill the hope in Lady St. Cyr's eyes than she could abandon Luc to his fate.

He'd given her his friendship when she'd needed it most.

The time had come to return the favor.

"Very well, my lady. I will see what I can do."

# 9

"What are you doing here?"

Rose turned to face Luc, uncertain where to begin her explanation. What *was* she doing here? Helping a friend, Rose realized as she squared her shoulders. "My, what a warm welcome, Luc," Rose said, determined not to let him see her nervousness. "You certainly know how to make a lady feel at ease."

Luc's cool expression didn't warm at all. "I asked you a question."

Calling upon all of her hard-won composure, Rose laughed lightly. "And phrased it so politely," she retorted.

"I'm not in the mood for games," Luc rasped, his jaw tightening.

"No, I can see that," Rose murmured, wondering how to reach him. "In fact, it is plain to see that you've been feeling poorly."

He scowled at her. "What the devil are you talking about?"

Striding over to the closed curtains, Rose yanked them open, sending dust clouding upward. Her hope that the sunlight now spilling into the study would improve its appearance died with one glance around the room. If anything, the golden rays merely emphasized the room's filthy state. Crusted plates and discarded glasses were piled haphazardly on end tables, layers of dust shaded the tops of chairs, and the ashes in the fireplace spilled out onto the carpet.

Squelching her dismay, Rose nodded at Luc. "Yes, it is obvious that you are quite ill because only a truly sick man would live in such squalor."

"I have no wish to discuss how I live with you," Luc said in a low voice, before turning on his heel to leave the room.

"Luc! Wait!" Rose called, rushing toward him. Abandoning her previous tactics, she grasped his arm, bringing him to a stop. "Please, Luc, talk to me. Tell me why you live like this." She gazed up into his face. "What has happened to you?"

Shuddering beneath her touch, Luc ignored her question, saying instead, "Please leave now, Rose. You shouldn't be here."

"Why not? I still consider myself your friend."

He clutched her shoulders. "Then in the name of that friendship, you must leave. Imagine what would happen if someone saw you enter my home, unchaperoned. The fine reputation you worked so hard to build would be destroyed in an instant."

Bittersweet emotions filled her heart. "Once you didn't care what others thought."

"I still don't care what they think about me, but I won't take risks with you . . . especially since I know how much their gossip hurt you."

"It doesn't matter—"

"It does to me!" Luc tightened his grasp upon her shoulders, pulling her in closer. "I don't want to hurt you, Rose, but if you stay around me, you *will* get hurt."

"You would never harm me," Rose said softly.

"Don't be too sure of that," Luc rasped, his gaze intensifying. "You don't even know me anymore."

"I don't see how you could have changed so much that—"

With one tug, Luc brought her flush against him and his mouth came down upon hers. Her heart tripped against her ribs as Luc's lips took possession of hers, tasting, licking, nipping. This was no innocent touch; instead, it was the hungry caress of a man kissing a woman—his woman.

Not a murmur escaped Rose as Luc pressed her tighter against him. Reeling from the sensations he created within her, she leaned into him and wound her arms around his neck, bringing him closer still. Here, in Luc's embrace, she found what had been missing in all her suitors' kisses. Never before had she felt this pulsing need to touch, to stroke, to taste.

Only Luc made her feel this way.

And as suddenly as it had begun, the embrace ended.

Luc tore himself away from her with a groan.

Taking a step backward, he thrust both of his hands through his hair. "Dammit," he said, his voice low and raw. "At least now you understand why you can't come here anymore."

But Rose didn't understand at all. No, she was still reeling from the passion of his touch. "Because you'll kiss me?" she asked hesitantly.

"Yes, that and more!" Luc ground out.

After the warmth of his embrace, the coldness in his voice chilled her. She didn't know what to say or do.

At her continued silence, Luc laughed, a bitter sound that scraped from his throat. "For all of your 'Grand Tour,' you're still a complete innocent, aren't you?"

Wanting to squirm under the ugly look in Luc's eyes, Rose forced herself to remain strong. "Hardly," she retorted, praying her voice didn't waver.

Luc twisted his lips in disbelief. "Of course you are," he challenged, taking a step closer. "You have no inkling of what I'd like to do to you at this moment—how I'd like to pull you back into my arms and savor the rest of your delectable sweetness or how I yearn to lay you against the couch to see if all of your flesh is as soft as your lips."

Fighting the urge to back up from Luc, Rose placed her hands on her hips. "You are merely trying to frighten me, Luc."

"Yes, but you've yet to realize that you *should* be frightened of me, Rose. I no longer belong in your world and you certainly don't fit into mine." Luc's expression hardened. "Unless you'd like to replace

Miranda—as my mistress," he finished with a dry laugh.

A gasp broke from her at the horrible insult. Holding back her tears of pain and shock, Rose glared at Luc one last time, allowing her hurt to show in her eyes, then she fled his home, leaving behind the tattered remains of their friendship.

The moment the door shut behind Rosaleen, Lucien sank into a chair, hating himself for bringing pain into her eyes. He realized he'd had no choice. At least by hurting her now, he'd protected her reputation. And Rose would never know how hard it had been for him to send her away.

Hell, he was still restless and hungry for another taste of the sweet Rosaleen. Disgusted with himself, Luc poured a strong dose of brandy and downed it in one gulp. The burning along his throat did nothing to ease the burning in his loins.

Damn her! Even now he could smell the lingering scent of her perfume, tantalizing him, reminding him of all he'd sent away. A harsh groan broke from Luc. Tonight he would have to visit his newest mistress, the alluring Miranda Worth, to see if he could ease the burning inside of him with her luscious charms.

But even as Lucien planned to visit Miranda, he knew deep inside of him that only one woman could quench his thirst.

Luc wondered which desire would prove greater—his desire to protect Rose or his desire for the woman herself. From the heat still pulsing in his body, he feared the answer was all too obvious.

By the time Rosaleen stepped into her family's townhouse, her composure had returned, but inside she still smarted from Luc's assault—against her body and soul.

Fingers of pain inched through her heart even at the memory, so Rose forced it away. Wandering into her house, the sound of her mother's quiet sobbing captured her attention.

"Mother?" Rose asked as she rushed into the parlor where Elinor stood, crying, wrapped in her father's arms. "What's wrong?"

Her mother hid her face against Reggie's neck.

"What is it?" Rose asked again, pressing a hand to her mother's shoulder.

The grim cast to her father's expression only increased Rose's alarm. "Your mother just received—"

"Reggie, no!"

Her father glanced down at Elinor. "Rosaleen is a member of this family; she has a right to know."

Tears streaked down Elinor's face as she gazed up at her husband. "But she's only just returned after being away for so long and I don't want to burden her."

Stepping forward, Rose insisted, "I want to know, Mother. Whatever it is, I want to help if I can."

Her mother's hand shook as she held out a note.

Curiosity filled Rose as she accepted the proffered missive. The words on the parchment struck terror in her heart.

"Temptress of the flesh,
You shall torment man no more.
Prepare your soul for Judgment Day."

"What is this?" whispered Rose.

"It's a threat against—"

Her mother cut off Reggie's explanation. "Someone wants to kill me . . . just like Lucienda and all the others."

Rose's fingers trembled as she glanced back down at the note. "No, it can't be," she rasped, unable to believe that someone would want her sweet mother dead.

Her father's gaze was bleak. "As the rumors have it, a note exactly like this one was found with all of the victims."

"Why Mother?" The question burst from Rose. "Why now?"

Her father shook his head. "I don't know. It doesn't make any sense."

"Once a whore, always a—"

Reggie pressed his fingertips against Elinor's mouth to halt her words. "You've never been anything but a wonderful, loving woman."

"Thank you," she whispered, before straightening away from Reggie. "What do we do about the note?"

"I've already notified the magistrate, so hopefully he will be here momentarily. After we speak with him, we will know the best way to proceed." He squeezed Elinor's shoulder.

Feeling the need to help in some way, Rose rubbed her mother's back. "Can I get anything for you, Mother?"

"A glass of sherry would steady me," Elinor said with a shaky smile. "A *large* glass."

Lucien looked down at the naked woman beneath him . . . and felt nothing. Perhaps the bottle of brandy he'd drained earlier in the day had dulled his senses. Determined, he slid his hand onto the full curve of her breast, stroking upward, bringing a moan from Miranda's lips.

She arched into his touch, her hands clutching at his shoulders. "Oh, yes, Lucien."

Automatically, he intensified his caress, using his fingers to tease her nipple into a hardened peak.

"Your hands are magic," Miranda moaned, her words low and sultry.

Still, he was unmoved.

Lucien gazed down at his mistress and knew that by all rights, he should have been aroused and yearning for surcease within her beautiful body. Instead, he felt oddly detached and nothing he did seemed to help him overcome the feeling.

But how could he lose himself within another woman when his mind was consumed with Rosaleen? The memory of Rose in his arms accomplished what the naked woman in bed with him could not. Stiff and aching, Lucien twisted onto his side, throwing an arm over his eyes.

He'd been so sure that once he had Miranda in his arms, she would arouse his desire and make him hungry for her womanly charms. Yet, here he lay, unable to rouse even the most remote interest in bedding the luscious Miranda.

"Lucien?"

Miranda's hand curled across his chest, the seductive touch leaving him unaffected. Frustrated, Lucien swung his legs over the edge of the bed to pull on his discarded britches.

"Lucien? What is wrong?"

"Nothing's wrong. I'm just in a foul mood this evening." He rose unsteadily and went to the sideboard where he poured himself a drink.

"Then why don't you come back here and I'll see if I can make you smile," Miranda purred, allowing the blanket to puddle in her lap as she sat up.

Lucien gazed dispassionately at her perfect breasts, unable to do more than simply appreciate them for their beauty. "I'm sorry, Miranda." He took a gulp of his brandy. "I shouldn't have come here tonight."

"Have I done something to upset you?" Miranda lifted the sheet to cover her nakedness.

Cursing himself for his clumsy apology, Luc regretted making Miranda feel self-conscious. Luc set down his snifter of brandy and tried to clear his thoughts, hoping he could soothe her hurt feelings.

"Miranda, it's not you," he began in a soft voice. "I'm simply preoccupied."

She winced, tucking the sheet in tighter. "You're not making me feel better," Miranda said dryly. "It's hardly flattering to a woman, never mind a naked one, to know that she can't even distract a man from his thoughts."

"I can see I'd be better served if I simply stopped speaking."

"You are fumbling quite a bit, which is unusual for you, my charming Lucien." Miranda tipped her head to the side, a pretty smile lighting her face. "I'm afraid I don't understand why you requested my time when you're so obviously uninterested."

Confusion brought a frown to his face. "But I didn't, Miranda, I simply came around to see if you were available."

Her smile faded. "So, you didn't send around a note asking to arrange for the servants to be gone so you could meet me in private?"

"No," Luc replied, shaking his head.

"Oh, dear Lord," Miranda whispered, an expression of terror twisting her features.

"What is it?" Lucien stepped forward, grasping the bedpost. "What is the matter?"

Her eyes were glazed over in fear. "I received a note a month or so ago. At first I was worried, but when nothing happened, I dismissed it, considering it a tasteless prank."

"What did the note say?"

Miranda waved him away, yet despite her efforts to appear unruffled, Luc noticed the tremor in her hand. "Something about my being a temptress of the flesh and that I should prepare for Judgment Day, or something to that effect." She looked up at him. "As I said, a tasteless joke . . . or so I thought. But if I consider the note I received tonight, I don't believe it's a harmless prank anymore."

A chill ran through Luc as he realized exactly what plans had been in store for Miranda. Luckily, he had shown up this evening, undoubtedly saving her in the process.

"Get dressed, Miranda, and pack a few of your things," Lucien directed, reaching for his shirt.

"Why? Where are you taking me?"

Luc tugged on his shirt, leaving it unfastened, as he headed for the door. "Somewhere safe. Don't worry, Miranda. I'll protect you."

Miranda's hand fluttered to her throat. "Surely you don't think that someone is—"

"Trying to kill you?" He ran his hand through his hair. "I don't know, but this entire situation is extremely suspect. We can't discount the truth; a growing number of your friends have been murdered in their own homes."

Miranda paled even further. "God help me," she whispered, pressing her fingers to her mouth.

Pulling open the door, Luc paused with his hand on the knob as bitterness speared through him. "God seems to have forsaken us mere mortals, Miranda, so I wouldn't look to Him for help."

Miranda's horrified scream reverberating through the room was the last sound Luc heard before everything went black.

# 10

White light twinkled before him as Lucien tried to open his eyes. His head throbbed with pain and his neck felt stiff. How long had he been lying here . . . and why was he on the floor?

Suddenly, his last memory assailed him. Panic tightened his chest as Luc frantically blinked, trying to regain his sight. The room lay silent, too silent. On his hands and knees, Luc crawled over to the bed, levering himself into a standing position by grabbing hold of the bedpost.

Though the edges remained fuzzy, his sight had returned by the time Luc got to his feet. Part of him wished to God that it had never returned when he saw what lay before him. Impressions slammed into him all at once, broken phrases of horror.

Miranda. Blood staining the sheets. Eyes still open in terror. Her mouth twisted in a frozen

scream. Stab wounds marking her chest. A note
left on her bloodstained body.

"NO!"

The word ripped from Luc as he stumbled backward, remembering how he'd promised her that
he'd protect her.

Help. He needed to find help.

It was the only thought able to reach his pain-
ridden brain. Luc's stomach rolled as he ran from
the room.

Holding his aching head in his hands, Lucien
wished more than anything that he would awake to
discover this was all simply a bad dream. Finding
Miranda cold and lifeless upon her bed was a memory he knew would haunt him for the rest of his
days.

"So, you didn't see anything or hear anyone?"

Luc's head pounded as he lifted it to gaze at the
magistrate questioning him. "No, Mr. Duncan, I
didn't."

James Duncan squinted down at him. "You expect me to believe that the murderer was close
enough to you that he could knock you out, yet
you didn't hear a sound."

"Yes, I do." Lucien touched the back of his
head. "As I told you, I'd already pieced together
that Miranda—" At her name, another wave of
grief slammed into him. Not only was his life
damned, but it appeared that anyone he touched
was sentenced as well. Miranda's senseless death
was his fault.

"Go on," the magistrate urged.

"As I said, we'd already decided that she was in danger." His hands dropped back into his lap. "I know you found the message left on her body, but did you find the first note that Miranda spoke of?"

Mr. Duncan nodded. "It was tucked into her armoire."

"Is it similar to the others?"

The expression on Mr. Duncan's face closed even further. "I'm afraid I can't discuss that information."

"Why not?" An ugly suspicion arose within Luc. "Do you believe that I murdered Miranda?"

For a long moment, the magistrate remained silent, until he finally said, "While that wound on the back of your head couldn't have been self-inflicted, it doesn't mean that you're not under suspicion." He crossed his arms. "After all, there might be two people committing these murders."

Frustration flashed through Luc. "Don't be ridiculous. I didn't murder anyone, much less my own mistress."

"If you're innocent, you have nothing to fear."

As if he'd fear such a bumbling idiot, Luc thought, anger churning inside of him. With Mr. Duncan in charge of the investigations, Luc suspected Miranda's murder would never be solved.

His emotions raw, Luc wanted to leave. "Am I free to go?"

Mr. Duncan nodded once. "For now."

The reply only strengthened Luc's determination to investigate the murders on his own. It was time for him to stop the downward spiral his life had taken. He couldn't do anything to save his mother from her ultimate discovery that he wasn't her son, nor could he alter the fact that Griffin Kingston was his natural father. The past was set; nothing could bring back Miranda.

But in seeking vengeance in her name, perhaps he could regain a measure of his own honor.

And, in doing so, perhaps he could reclaim a part of himself.

Marianne Howard rounded on her husband the moment he entered their townhouse. "Do you know what time it is?"

Jonathan Howard glanced disinterestedly at her. "I have an inkling." He slid out of his topcoat. "What are you doing up at this hour?"

"Waiting for you," she answered from her perch on the stairs. The scent rising from her husband told of his evening's debauchery. "How dare you come home at this time of night, reeking like a whorehouse?"

"How astute of you, my dear," Jonathan responded smoothly. "I did indeed visit a little place down near the waterfront that caters to exotic pleasures."

Fury and humiliation combined into a powerful hatred, shimmering throughout her entire body. "You disgust me," she sneered. "You and your whoring ways."

Pausing on the stairs, Jonathan glanced down at Marianne. After a long moment, he murmured, "What did I ever do to deserve a lifetime with you?"

If he'd slapped her, it wouldn't have shocked her more. Speechless, Marianne watched as Jonathan turned and walked up the remainder of the stairs, disappearing down the hallway. Hatred hardened in her very core. Those awful Cyprians had taken everything from her. Everything.

First, they'd stolen her husband, and then she'd been robbed of her place in society. Slowly, Marianne made her way back up the steps, fury consuming her in hungry bites. Then she thought of the murders and smiled. The day of reckoning had already come . . . and none too soon.

"Did you hear they found another Cyprian last night?"

Griffin Kingston looked up from his paper. "Pardon?"

"They found another one." The young lord leaned forward on his chair. "This time though, a gentleman was present. They say that he woke in his mistress's bedchamber to find her dead on the bed!"

"Really?" Griffin folded the paper, placing it in his lap. "Who was the unfortunate fellow?"

"The Earl of Berwyn."

Shock ripped through Griffin. His son. Regaining his composure, he adopted the cool pose that came so easily to him. "Poor sot. You say he was found in the same room. He wasn't hurt, was he?"

"Nothing other than a knock on the head," Lord Willerby clarified.

"Interesting." His murmur revealed not an ounce of the turmoil inside of him. "Isn't that a break in the pattern? I thought the ladies were always alone for the evening."

"They always *were* in the past. I don't know what happened this time."

"Perhaps our killer has tired of the game and seeks to add new thrills to his crimes," Griffin speculated.

"If that's the case, then I feel sorry for St. Cyr for being caught unaware." Lord Willerby nodded solemnly. "I know in the future I'll be extremely careful whenever I go to visit my mistress."

"As will I."

Tapping the arm of his chair, Lord Willerby frowned. "It's surprising that the killer didn't kill St. Cyr as well. How could the killer be sure that St. Cyr hadn't seen him?"

"I don't know, but it's a bit of good fortune for St. Cyr."

"He's not in the clear yet," Lord Willerby corrected. "Apparently, St. Cyr is now under suspicion for the murders."

"How preposterous!"

The young lord shrugged. "I would have agreed with you a few years ago, but lately St. Cyr has slipped beyond the pale."

"And what does that have to do with anything? Good God, man, if that is all it takes to be a murderer, then I myself must be one," Griffin asserted. "After all, I'm well known for my indulgences."

"I suppose you're right. It does sound a bit ridiculous," Lord Willerby conceded.

"I'd say so." Griffin felt sick at the realization that he could have lost his son before he'd ever really found him. Nothing had turned out the way he'd thought it would when he'd confronted Lucien with his true parentage. Griffin had been so sure that once Luc had been given time to acclimate himself to the truth he would come around. Griffin had imagined teaching his son all he knew, having a companion with whom to enjoy all the delights the world had to offer.

Instead, he'd received nothing but distance and overt anger every time he'd tried to approach Lucien. Griffin knew he probably wouldn't be much of a father, but he wanted to know his own son.

"Well, if you hear anything further, please let me know," Griffin murmured nonchalantly, not wanting to reveal how eager he was for news of the son he could never publicly claim as his own.

# 11

*R*osaleen clasped her mother's hand. "You wished to speak with us, Father?"

Reggie glanced at the magistrate who sat next to him. "There has been another murder," Reggie said flatly. "Mr. Duncan called to let us know so that we might take more serious precautions."

Feeling the tremor that ran through her mother, Rose squeezed Elinor's hand reassuringly.

"While I know you're afraid, I want you to know that I'm doing everything possible to apprehend the killer," Mr. Duncan explained. "In fact, we now have a suspect."

"Who is it?"

Rose glanced at her mother. "I don't believe Mr. Duncan can reveal that information."

"Indeed, I cannot," Mr. Duncan confirmed. "But I can tell you that the suspect was at the scene of the crime."

"If he was found in the house, then why haven't you charged the man with the murders?" Reggie demanded, placing his arm around his wife.

"Because the evidence isn't clear-cut."

"What could be more clear than finding the man at the scene of the crime?"

Elinor patted Reggie's leg. "Calm down, darling. Yelling at poor Mr. Duncan doesn't help matters."

"No, it does not," the magistrate said quickly. "And, for your information, the reason we can't charge the man was because he claims to have been knocked out by the murderer." Anticipating Reggie's question, Mr. Duncan continued, "And he had a lump on his head to prove it."

"Then why is he still a suspect?" Rose asked, finding it hard to follow Mr. Duncan's logic.

"Because St. Cyr could have had a partner helping him. He could have had the other man knock him on the head—"

"St. Cyr?" Rose gasped, interrupting Mr. Duncan. "Lucien St. Cyr?"

"Blast it all!" Mr. Duncan pounded his fist against his thigh. "I seem to have done it again."

"You can count upon our discretion," Reggie assured the magistrate. "Can't he, Rose?"

"Of course. I wouldn't tell a soul." Rose leaned forward in her chair. "But I fear you are gravely mistaken in your suspicions, Mr. Duncan, for I am acquainted with Lord St. Cyr, and while he may have a few undesirable qualities, I assure you that the capability of murder is not among them."

Mr. Duncan shifted on his chair. "If that is true,

then he has nothing to fear from our investigation."

"Yes, but—"

Holding up his hands, Mr. Duncan rose from the chair. "I'm not at liberty to discuss anything further," he announced. "Good day to you all."

It would appear that she now had no choice but to call upon Luc once again. Dread filled her at the very thought, remembering far too well their last encounter. Yet, the threat hanging over Luc's head outweighed her desire to avoid him. It was painfully obvious that Luc would receive no help from Mr. Duncan in discovering the true murderer, thereby clearing Luc's name.

Mr. Duncan had mentioned Luc far too easily for Rose to assume that the magistrate hadn't made that same mistake with others. And that meant only one thing.

The ton had undoubtedly absorbed this tidbit of news and had already begun to feed upon what remained of Lucien St. Cyr's reputation.

Rose lay in wait.

Her ball gown pooled around her as she leaned forward to peer out of her carriage window. At the ball this evening, she'd discreetly asked about Luc's haunts. The gentlemen she'd questioned had been reluctant to name the places, leading her to conclude that they were less than reputable. Still, she'd persevered . . . which is how she'd ended up at the waterfront, lurking in her carriage.

She would hail Luc the moment he left the tavern. Her decision to seek Luc out tonight had been strengthened by the vicious rumors she'd heard about him that evening. Those at the ball spoke about him as if he were already convicted of the murders. Ignoring the damp night air, Rose shifted closer to the window as two men stumbled out through the sagging front door, allowing it to bang shut.

Rose jumped at the noise, then took a deep, calming breath. While she knew she needed to help Luc, part of her wanted to call a halt to her folly and return home. Only dearly held memories stayed her course. Hearing the door open again, Rose looked up to see Luc exiting the tavern.

Gathering her courage, Rose stepped from the carriage. "Luc," she called out, uncertain of his reaction.

Luc's head snapped upward as he pierced her with his gaze. His features tightened before he glanced around. Immediately, Luc strode forward, directing her back into the carriage. "What the devil are you doing *here?*"

Rose lifted her chin against the onslaught of Luc's fury as he took the seat opposite her. "I tried to call upon you this afternoon but you weren't at home, and since you didn't attend the White-stone's soirée this evening, I decided to seek you out."

"Of all the lackwit ideas—" Luc broke off his grumbling with a shake of his head. Rapping on the ceiling of the carriage, Luc ordered the driver to take them to Rose's home, before returning his attention to her. "Do you realize what would happen to your reputation if you were seen here tonight?"

Rose sighed wearily. "Let's not discuss that again. We have far more important matters to address."

"Such as?" Luc asked, crossing his arms.

"Such as the murder last night," Rose retorted, annoyed at Luc's unyielding attitude.

Luc's eyes darkened, and his face became an unreadable mask. "I will *not* speak of last night."

Compassion flooded her. Leaning forward, Rose placed her hand upon his knee. "But we must, Luc."

"There is no *we*, Rose. This doesn't concern you in the least."

"But it does," she corrected, shifting back in her seat. "My mother received a note this morning."

"*Your mother?*" Luc exclaimed. "Why?"

"Because of her past."

"What bearing does that have on the present?" Lucien rubbed a hand down his face. "Lord, is this madman determined to wipe clean anyone who has ever slipped from grace?"

"It would appear that the sins of the past can haunt the present," Rose concluded.

A bitter laugh ripped from Luc. "How well I've learned that," he murmured.

Before Rose could question his odd remark, Luc said, "And that fool of a magistrate investigating the murders actually believes I might have killed Miranda."

"I know."

Luc pinned her with his fierce gaze. "How could you possibly know that?"

"Mr. Duncan mentioned your name in connection with the murders when he spoke to my family." Rose swallowed before continuing. "But that's not the worst of it, Luc. At the ball this evening, a few people spoke of Mr. Duncan's suspicions."

"Isn't that just perfect?" he ground out. Closing his eyes, Luc leaned his head back against the cushion. "So now everyone believes I'm a murderer."

"Not everyone," Rose asserted, "and certainly not me."

Slowly, Luc opened his eyes to look at her, making Rose wish the carriage were well lit so she could read the thoughts in his gaze. "I tell you to leave me alone, then insult you, yet still you believe, without question, in my innocence."

"As I told Mr. Duncan, you may be many things, Luc, but you're not a murderer."

For a long moment, Luc stared at her. "I envy you the strength of your convictions."

Rose jolted at the quiet statement. "Excuse me?"

"It's been a long time, a very long time, since I've felt such passion, such confidence, in any*thing*, much less any*one*."

"I believe in you," she stated firmly, "and together we can discover the identity of the murderer and clear your name."

"Together?" Luc echoed. "I've already told you that I will handle this matter on my own."

"Yes, but that was before you found out my mother received a note."

"I realize you're concerned, Rose, but I don't

think it's wise for you to become involved with the investigation."

Rose frowned at Luc. "My mother is being threatened and the dunderhead magistrate is convinced you are the murderer, which means he'll be focusing all of his efforts on trying to prove you did it. Nothing about this situation seems wise."

"I realize that and that's the reason I'm investigating the matter myself."

"But I can help." Leaning forward, Rose touched his knee again. "I'm privy to the ton's gossip and can listen for clues."

Luc seemed to consider her argument for a moment, before shaking his head. "I doubt if you'd overhear anything of value from the matrons of polite society."

"How can you be so certain? After all, at the heart of most gossip is a kernel of truth," Rose pointed out earnestly. "For instance, while you didn't kill anyone, the fact remains that you *were* witness to the murder. So, if I do hear something, perhaps it would help us to find the killer." She pressed Luc for an answer. "Doesn't that make sense?"

Before Luc could respond, the carriage pulled to a stop and Luc jumped out. Holding his arms up for Rose, he assisted her out of the hackney, then paid the driver for his services.

"Why did you dismiss him?" Rose asked as the carriage drove off. "How will you get home?"

"It's not too far to walk."

In a flash of understanding, Rose knew why Luc

had sent the carriage away. "You didn't want anyone to notice a strange carriage in front of my home, did you?"

The coming dawn had brightened the sky enough for Rose to see the flush staining Luc's face. "I will not jeopardize your reputation," he replied stiffly.

"Oh, Luc." His concern vexed her, yet warmed her at the same time, creating a confused mix of emotions. "Do you have any idea how frustrating this is for me?" She pressed a hand against his chest. "You have to stop protecting me."

Luc gazed down at Rose and wondered if she could feel his heart racing beneath her fingertips. The farther he tried to push her away, the closer she managed to come. Trying to shield Rose from harm was proving more difficult than he'd ever imagined. He'd hurt her, yet she'd come to help him despite it.

"I've never known anyone like you," Luc whispered, unable to keep himself from touching the smooth skin on her cheek.

"Then let me help you," Rose urged, taking a step closer.

Sliding his fingers down her neck, Luc felt her pulse leap. "I'm sorry for insulting you yesterday," he apologized, purposely not responding to her plea. He had no intention of allowing her to get embroiled in the investigation despite the fact that he agreed with the logic of her argument.

"Apology accepted," Rose whispered, her voice breathy. "I understand now why you wanted to anger me."

His heart began to pound harder when he saw her eyes soften with desire, making it impossible for him to concentrate on her response. Drawn by a force greater than his will, Luc cupped her face with his hands and bent toward her. "I shouldn't do this," Luc groaned as he closed the distance between them.

"And I shouldn't let you," Rose answered, going onto her tiptoes to meet him.

Gently, he molded his lips onto hers, the soft touch an apology unto itself for his forceful kiss yesterday. Her breath fluttered out as Rose melted into him, bringing their bodies together.

Unable to hold back, he deepened the kiss, opening her lips with his, claiming her as his own. A moan echoed in Rose's throat as she twined her arms around his neck. Sliding his hands down her neck, over her shoulders, and along the length of her back, Luc pressed Rose into him, molding her against his body.

Luc angled his head to intensify their kiss, wanting to taste all of her, needing to touch—

"Attaboy, St. Cyr!"

At the shout, Luc broke off their embrace, lifting his head in time to see a carriage slowly passing on the road with four men peering out the window. Groaning at his stupidity, Luc thrust Rose behind his back, praying none of the men had identified his companion.

"Is the chit as tasty as her mother?" yelled Lord Howard. "I still have fond memories of sweet Elinor."

Luc cursed, realizing he'd hoped in vain.

"We'll leave you to your pleasures then." At Lord Evans's quip, all four men laughed, their loud guffaws ringing out over the clatter of the carriage wheels.

Turning back to Rose, Luc grasped her by the arm and propelled her toward the rear of her townhouse. "What was I thinking to kiss you in the middle of the bloody street," he mumbled, furious with himself.

"Luc, we need to talk," Rose protested, trying to dig in her heels.

Luc wasn't having any of it. "Not now," he replied firmly. "Someone else might drive by and see us alone at this time of the morning."

"I believe the damage has already been done," Rose pointed out.

She was right, of course, but he still wasn't going to tempt fate further. Once at Rose's kitchen door, he nearly shoved her through the entrance. "Good night, Rose."

"But, Luc, I want to—"

He shut the door on her protest.

# 12

Looking out his window, Luc watched the sun finally crest the horizon, sending streaks of sunlight onto London. Yet, not even the brightness of the morning sun could penetrate his dark thoughts. How could he have been so careless?

The entire way home from Rose's he'd berated himself for kissing her, right there in the middle of the street. His determination to protect Rose's reputation had melted beneath the warmth of her concern, leaving him powerless to resist his desire for her.

All he could do now was pray that the men who'd witnessed their embrace were discreet. But what if they weren't? Luc thrust his hands through his hair, wishing he had an answer to that question. Well, he'd deal with the problem if it arose.

The more immediate problem facing him was

how best to proceed with his investigation. First he would discover all the similarities between the murders, then he'd decide where to go from that point. Rose's idea about listening to the rumor mill was a sound one, yet he'd never involve her in such a dangerous undertaking. This was murder they were investigating and Luc didn't want it to touch Rose's life any more than it already had. Hell, she was burdened enough by the fact that her mother had received a note. No, there had to be another way to learn the gossip without asking Rose to do it.

Suddenly, the perfect person came to mind . . . if only Luc had enough courage to face him.

The hushed whispers grew to a steady din as Luc made his way through the main salon at White's, a place he hadn't visited in years. Luc remained focused upon the only man who cared enough to help him clear his name—Edward St. Cyr.

Lucien waited silently until Edward noticed him standing next to his chair. "Hello, sir," Luc said quietly.

"Lucien!" The paper Edward held in his hands shook as he folded it onto his lap. "Lucien," he whispered again as if he were having trouble believing his eyes.

"I need your help."

Hope brightened Edward's expression as he eagerly waved Luc into the chair next to him. "Of course, of course," he said immediately. "Anything within my power is yours . . . just as always."

Luc felt the tight knot of doubt inside of him unravel. He'd been right to come to Edward. "I've no doubt you heard about the murder two nights ago."

"Of your mistress?" Edward nodded solemnly. "Yes, I've heard a few rumors." He placed his hand upon Luc's shoulder. "It must have been very difficult for you."

Luc swallowed the lump that had suddenly formed in his throat. "It was," he confirmed. "The magistrate in charge considers me a suspect."

Edward's eyes widened. "What rubbish! I'd heard something like that, but I simply dismissed it as nonsense. What can the man be thinking to believe you capable of such a horrific act?"

Smiling over his father's automatic defense, Luc realized that there were two people who had believed in him without question. "Mr. Duncan doesn't know me at all. How would he know that I'm not a murderer? Once he discovers that I'm not guilty, then he will return to uncovering the real killer."

"What a bloody waste of time," Edward groused.

"Yes, it is, which is why I've decided to investigate the murders on my own . . . and that's where I need your help."

Leaning forward in his chair, Edward asked eagerly, "What can I do?"

"I would like you to listen to what people say about the murders, try to pick up any clues that might lead to the murderer."

"Of course. I'm glad to do it." Edward tapped

his fingers against the arm of his chair. "Exactly
what sort of information are you looking for?"

"I don't know, but anything interesting might
help solve the case."

"Once you've found—" Edward broke off, shaking his head. "No, it's not my affair."

"Please, ask your question." Luc knew he owed
him as much.

Edward cleared his throat. "Very well, I was
simply wondering if you would return to your . . .
former self once your name is cleared."

Luc fought back the tide of resentment that
threatened to swamp him. "There is nothing to return to. I've done a rather thorough job of de-
stroying my reputation."

"That's not true. While your habits have
changed, you've done nothing that would put you
beyond the pale," Edward asserted firmly.

"How can you say that?" Luc asked, incredu-
lous. "My God, you're the one who taught me
that—"

Edward lifted his hand, cutting off Luc's
protest. "I am hardly a paragon of virtue, as you
well know. Do not measure yourself against me."

Luc bit back the urge to defend his father. It was
still hard to turn away from the teachings of his
youth. "Even so, my behavior has—"

"What behavior? Gambling? Visits to houses of
ill-repute?" A short laugh lifted Edward's shoulders. "Good Lord, Lucien, if that's all you believe
it takes to fall from grace, than you're in good
company." He nodded at the other gentlemen in
the room. "Look around you, Lucien, and you'll

find your peers indulge in the very same pleasures."

Lucien gave his father a disbelieving look. "You cannot convince me that you approve of my actions."

"You didn't ask me if I approved or not and I am hardly in the position to offer my opinion," Edward pointed out. "I am merely disavowing your belief that you've slipped from welcome in society because of your indiscretions." He sat back in his chair. "However, if you *were* to ask my opinion, I'd be quick to tell you that your mother and I have always admired your adventurous spirit."

"What?" Luc asked, stunned.

Curving his fingers over the arms of his chair, Edward smiled with a tinge of sadness in his expression. "I should have told you a long time ago, Luc, but I've always envied the joy you found in life. You were never content to just live your life; no, you *reveled* in the essence of life. How could I not admire you for that?"

Stunned, Luc didn't know how to respond as his father's words evoked long-buried emotions. Nodding once, Luc thrust to his feet, driven to escape the confines of the room.

"Won't you stay and join me for a drink?" Edward offered with a touch of desperation in his voice.

Part of Luc longed to accept the invitation, to forgive his father for the lies and the pain, but the wounds were still raw, even after these long years. Slowly, Luc shook his head. "I'm sorry, but I can't stay."

Trying to hide his disappointment, Edward glanced away. "Perhaps another time, then."

"Yes," he agreed quietly. "Another time."

"I'm sorry your wife couldn't join us in town," Katherine said to Basil as she left the confessional. "I always enjoy Lilly's company."

Basil tucked his hand beneath Katherine's elbow. "I prefer she remain in the country," he murmured tersely.

Katherine mentally reprimanded herself for her blunder, remembering too late about what had happened in London four years ago. Edward had told her all about how Lilly had met some man in the nearby park and the innocent visits had turned into a torrid affair, devastating Basil when he'd discovered the truth. For a while, she and Edward had worried that Basil would never recover from the pain, but he'd slowly come around. Still, it was little wonder that he preferred his wife to remain in the country.

"Lilly enjoys the country," Katherine said breezily. "But I'm so happy that you could accompany us to town."

As they left the small chapel that had been built behind the St. Cyr townhouse, Katherine saw Edward hurrying across the rear yard toward them. "Edward? Is everything all right?"

"Yes, yes," he said in a rush. "Better than all right, in fact. I've just come from speaking with Lucien."

Katherine couldn't believe her ears. "You did?"

"Yes, and he even asked for my help."

"The Lord has blessed you," Basil said with a smile.

"Indeed," Katherine agreed, overjoyed. "What did Lucien need? Is there anything *I* can do to help him?"

Quickly, Edward repeated Luc's request to Katherine and Basil. ". . . so you should pay close attention to any gossip concerning the murders."

"It will be a hardship as I detest gossip, but I will do anything if it helps our son. Goodness knows, I hear the latest *on-dit* even when I'm trying to avoid it. Why, just this morning, Lady Foley called upon me for the sole purpose of repeating a rumor she found particularly interesting. Naturally, it involved Lucien." Katherine twisted her lips. "However, her tale was some rubbish about how Lucien and Miss Fleming were seen kissing on the street outside her home at dawn this morning."

With a laugh, Katherine added, "It is the gospel truth . . . according to Lady Foley, who heard it from Lady Haverstram who heard it from Lady Mallon who heard it from Lady Platson," Katherine finished with a smile. "And all this was passed along before noon today!"

Both Edward and Basil chuckled over her news.

"Personally, I believe it is utter nonsense." Receiving doubtful looks from both men, Katherine demanded, "You think it's true?"

Edward grinned at his wife. "It seems the dear Miss Fleming may bring our Lucien back to us, after all."

# 13

With his cravat hanging untied around his neck, Luc hurried downstairs. "Rose?" He'd been stunned when his butler had announced her. "Is something—"

"What is the meaning of this?" Rose demanded, slapping the missive against his chest. "While I know you don't want me helping you investigate the murders, this is an underhanded way to dissuade me. I find it in extremely poor taste."

Lucien steadied her with one hand. "What are you talking about?"

Ignoring him, Rose paced across the foyer. "Last night, I'd been foolish enough to believe you'd kissed me because you . . . well because." A bright flush colored her cheeks. "Now I realize it was an effort to manipulate me, to disorient me with your embrace until I couldn't think straight, much less argue with you."

"Rose, Rose," Luc protested, pulling her to a stop. "I have no idea what you're ranting about."

"This." She waved the paper in front of his face.

"May I see it, please?"

"As if you don't already know what it says," Rose retorted, before slapping the missive in his outstretched hand. "I can't believe you would do something like this!"

The first words leapt off the page at him.

*"Temptress of the flesh . . ."*

His heart froze within his chest as he tried to absorb the shock. "This came to you?"

"Yes," she returned quickly. "It was left at the servant's entrance of our house with my initials on the envelope."

The image of his mistress, bloody and stiff, shifted in his mind, until it was Rosaleen lying upon the bed. Terror raced through him. Slowly, he lifted his gaze to meet her furious one. "I did not send this note, Rose."

She grew very still. "You didn't?"

"No." He glanced down at the parchment. "But I have seen one of these before."

"When your mistress received her note," Rose accurately surmised.

Lucien nodded, his throat tight. "It lay next to her dead body."

Tears sprang forth in Rose's beautiful blue eyes, making Luc wish he could protect her from this pain. "But why me?"

"It makes no sense that . . ." Lucien's words trailed off as a horrible notion struck him. "Dear God," he whispered.

"What is it, Luc?"

"It's me," he breathed, staring blindly down at the note. "I'm the connection."

Rose shook her head. "That's impossible. You didn't even know the other women who were killed."

"No, but I am the reason that *you* received a note."

Luc could see by the light in Rose's eyes that she was going to protest again, so he cut her off before she could utter a word. "What other reason could there be? It seems too much of a coincidence that first my mistress is murdered, then you receive a note two days later . . . after we are seen kissing in the street."

Her brows drew downward. "Perhaps, but it seems highly improbable."

"I know," Luc admitted, "but at the moment it is the only reason I can think of as to why you received the note."

"You might be right," Rose agreed quietly.

Guilt cascaded over Luc. After all, if he was correct in his theory, it was his fault that she'd been singled out by a madman. He reached out to cup Rose's face, turning it up toward his. "I'm so sorry, Rosaleen, for embroiling you in all of this."

"No, please," she murmured, shaking her head. "Don't blame yourself. I'm the one who waited for you outside the tavern."

Turning away from Rose, Luc rubbed his hands

over his face. "I should have resisted kissing you last night, but when you looked up at me—"

Rose placed her hands upon Luc's back. "You shouldn't torment yourself over this, Luc. We can't change the past, so there's no point in belaboring the point."

He drew in a deep breath. "True enough," he murmured, before facing her once more. "We need now to decide what we're going to do about your note."

A tremulous smile wavered on her lips.

Confused at her reaction, Luc touched his fingertips to her cheek. "What's this all about?"

"You said 'we.' "

"Of course I did," he replied swiftly. "Even if I didn't hold myself responsible for your receiving the note, I would never allow you to face this on your own."

Tears gathered in her eyes. "Thank you," she whispered.

"Oh, Rose." Tenderly, Luc tucked a loose strand of hair behind her ear.

"I'm afraid," she admitted brokenly.

Her confession pierced his heart. Without further thought, Luc gathered Rose into his arms, holding her close in comfort, wishing he could protect her from worry. Breaking down, Rose shuddered against him, her tears dampening his shirt.

"I won't let him hurt you, Rose," Luc promised, smoothing his hands along her back. *Pray God that my words are true.*

As her quiet sobs trailed off, Luc continued to

caress her back and shoulders while murmuring reassurances. He wasn't certain how he would keep her safe, but he vowed to himself that he would find a way . . . or die trying.

Finally, Rose sighed deeply. "I'm sorry for—"

"Don't apologize," Luc interrupted, pressing a kiss onto the top of her head. "You've every right to cry."

Resting within the circle of his arms, Rose lifted her head. "What am I going to do?"

He looked at her pointedly.

"What are *we* going to do?" she amended with a shaky smile.

"I believe the most important thing is to ensure that you're never alone." He lifted a brow at her. "Coming to call upon me without a chaperone must end, Rose."

"The only reason I did so today was because I thought you'd sent the note to me."

"Now you know differently." Luc released her, needing distance between them in order to concentrate fully on her safety. "What precautions has your father taken to protect your mother?"

"He's hired four men to guard the house and to escort my mother whenever she steps outside."

"Excellent," Luc said, his brow furrowed in concentration. "We'll need to extend that protection onto you as well. I'm certain your father will—"

"I haven't told my parents about the note yet."

"What?" Luc exclaimed, disbelief in his voice.

"Well, of course I didn't tell them." Rose shook her head at him. "Why would I do that when I believed you had sent me the note?"

Conceding the point, Luc said, "Fine, but that will be the first thing we correct." He turned and called for his butler. As the servant approached, Luc directed, "Storrs, please stay with Miss Fleming while I finish dressing."

"Luc, I don't believe this is necessary," Rose protested quietly. "We're in your house, after all."

He felt his heart expand as he gazed down at her. "I don't want to take any chances with you," he finally replied, before heading up the stairs. "I'll only be a few moments, then I'll escort you home."

Luc hurried toward his bedchamber, a grin coming to his face as Rose's voice drifted up the stairwell. "Now sir, tell me. Is Storrs your first name, or your last?"

Reggie's fist slammed into Luc's face, sending him sprawling against the wall.

"Get up, you bastard, so I can hit you again."

"Reggie, please," Elinor protested, pulling on her husband's arm. "Leave him be."

"*Leave him be?* Did you hear what he did to our little girl?" Reggie exclaimed, pointing a finger toward Luc.

"Of course, I did, darling, but—"

Cutting off Elinor's reply, Reggie shouted, "He kissed her on the bloody street! The fact that carriages were going by didn't stop him. No, by God, St. Cyr plays fast with our baby's reputation and takes liberties where everyone can see!"

Rose had heard quite enough. "Luc escorted me home after I shamelessly followed him to the tavern."

Fingering his jaw as he rose to his feet, Luc said, "Regardless, Rose, your father is justified in his anger."

"As if I need you to tell her that!" Reggie rounded on Luc again. "This is all your fault! Because of you, a madman is threatening my daughter. It wasn't enough that I needed to worry about my wife. No, now my daughter is in danger as well," he finished, his voice cracking on the last word.

Feeling the depth of her father's pain, Rose placed her arms around him. "I understand why you're so upset, but please don't blame this entirely upon Luc."

Before Reggie could respond, their butler knocked on the door, then opened it to announce the magistrate.

"My lord, my lady," Mr. Duncan addressed Rose's parents, pausing only when he caught sight of Luc. "Lord St. Cyr. This *is* unexpected."

Composing himself, Reggie welcomed the magistrate. "Thank you for coming so quickly," he said, stepping forward. "Early this morning, we received another note . . . this one addressed to my daughter."

Mr. Duncan couldn't contain his shock. "Your *daughter*? But that makes no sense."

"She was seen kissing me," Luc explained stiffly.

Scowling, Mr. Duncan replied, "While that might be enough to set tongues wagging, it certainly doesn't warrant her receiving a note."

"No, but perhaps the murderer knew about the time I called upon Luc at his home . . . uncha-

peroned. I suppose that could have been miscon-
strued," Rose said hesitantly. "And then there was
that scene Lady Howard created at the Foleys'
ball."

Lifting his eyebrows, Mr. Duncan looked at her.
"Is that everything?"

"Yes," Rose said, before correcting herself. "No,
wait, I forgot to mention how I waited for Luc
outside Miller's Tavern in a hired carriage last
night."

Clearing his throat, Mr. Duncan asked, "Was
that when you were seen kissing Lord St. Cyr?"

Flushing deeply, Lucien moved to Rose's side.
"There is no need to tell—"

"Of course there is, Luc." Rose knew he was
simply trying to protect her again. "How can Mr.
Duncan proceed with his investigation without all
the information available?"

Luc gave Rose a pointed look, reminding her of
his lack of faith in the magistrate's abilities.

Still, she returned her attention to Mr. Duncan.
"When Luc left the tavern, I called him over to my
carriage. Immediately, he insisted that I return
home, so he escorted me and it was on the street
outside my house that we were caught in an embrace."

Reggie groaned loudly, before glaring at Luc.
"What have you done to provoke my daughter to
act this way?"

"Perhaps you haven't noticed, my lord, but your
daughter tends to follow only her own counsel,"
Luc replied dryly.

Wearing a look of resignation, Reggie leaned

back in his chair. "Yes, I'm well aware of that fact. There are times, this being one of them, that I regret having raised her to be so independent."

Eyeing both men, Rose asked dryly, "Now that the two of you are done commiserating, perhaps we can hear what Mr. Duncan thinks about my receiving a note."

"He probably believes I wrote it," Luc pointed out.

"As a matter of fact, I don't." Nodding to Luc, he said, "You are no longer a suspect in this case, my lord."

Disbelief shadowed Luc's expression. "Since when?"

"Just a few minutes ago."

"Nothing's been said that would disprove your suspicions," Luc retorted, clearly frustrated with the magistrate.

"That's not true, because you're unaware that there was another murder attempt around dawn this morning," Mr. Duncan announced, shocking everyone in the room. "Though the message this woman received was from her protector, she had been wary enough to hide in her armoire until she was certain the caller was indeed the gentleman she'd expected. When a darkly cloaked man entered her bedchamber, she remained hidden until he left and notified us immediately."

"And since I was seen by a number of people at that time, it clears my name," Luc concluded.

"Indeed," agreed Mr. Duncan. "I apologize if my suspicions caused you any discomfort."

From Luc's annoyed expression, Rose knew he was thinking of the torrid rumors that had raced through the ton, yet he remained silent.

"While I find it comforting that the man who destroyed my daughter's reputation is not a murderer, that fact doesn't lessen the threat to my family," Reggie said.

"I understand, my lord, and I believe you have taken excellent precautions to safeguard your wife. As to your daughter, I would recommend that you hire additional guards to protect her as well." Mr. Duncan paused, cautiously eyeing Reggie. "And I would like to make one additional suggestion for her safety."

"Please, tell me," Reggie urged him.

Tugging at his cravat, Mr. Duncan glanced at Luc before addressing Rose's father again. "I believe it would be in your daughter's best interest if she were to become engaged to Lord St. Cyr."

Everyone in the room exploded at the announcement.

"Are you insane?" Reggie demanded, launching out of his chair. "That is the man who got my daughter into this threatening predicament in the first place."

"Which is why I believe he is the one who can get her out of it."

Still reeling from the magistrate's suggestion, Rose struggled to find her voice. "I don't see how an engagement could possibly help matters," she finally managed.

Mr. Duncan raised both hands. "It was only an idea for your consideration, though I believe that if Lord St. Cyr makes everyone know that his attentions toward you are honorable, it might save you from harm."

"I have been married for many years, yet I still received a note," Elinor pointed out.

"Yes, but your . . . past remains unchanged." The magistrate shifted on his feet. "In your daughter's case, Lord St. Cyr is the only man with whom she has been involved. Thus, if they become engaged, perhaps the murderer will think he made a mistake by assuming she was Lord St. Cyr's mistress."

Rose was stunned when she glanced at Luc, because he actually appeared to be considering the magistrate's suggestion. "Luc," she said, tapping on his arm. "Don't you believe Mr. Duncan is mistaken in his theory?"

But once more, Luc remained silent.

Shrugging, Mr. Duncan muttered, "It doesn't make any difference to me if you listen to my advice or not." Bowing to Rose and her mother, the magistrate excused himself and left the room.

"Of all the ridiculous ideas," Reggie sputtered as soon as the door closed behind the magistrate.

It didn't escape Rose's notice that Luc hadn't said a word since Mr. Duncan's suggestion. Looking over at Luc, Rose said, "You've suddenly grown very quiet. Surely you aren't actually thinking . . ." Her words trailed off as Luc gazed down at her with a serious expression.

"I don't believe we should dismiss the idea out of hand," Luc said softly.

Elinor shifted closer to Luc. "Nor do I."

Rose couldn't believe that both her mother and Luc were considering something so . . . so . . . drastic.

"Elinor! What can you be thinking?" Reggie asked, looking as astounded as Rose felt.

"I'm thinking of our daughter, Reggie." Elinor lifted her chin. "What if Mr. Duncan is right and becoming Luc's fiancée will eliminate the threat to Rose?"

"And if he's not? Then what?"

"Then Rose will marry a fine gentleman of title," Elinor concluded calmly.

"A 'fine' gentleman? How can you say that after his treatment of her?"

Elinor frowned at Reggie. "Luc has treated Rose with—"

"Excuse me," Luc interrupted, "but I wondered if you wouldn't give Rose and me a moment of privacy . . . so *we* can discuss the matter."

"Privacy!" Reggie exclaimed, anger twisting his features.

Reaching for her husband's arm, Elinor smiled at Rose and Luc as she tugged Reggie from the room.

As the door closed behind them, Luc rubbed his hand along his jaw. "For a moment there, I thought your father was going to hit me again."

Rose touched Luc's arm. "Does it hurt much?"

Grinning down at her, Luc said, "Even if it did, I wouldn't admit it to you."

"Ah, yes, you have an image to uphold," Rose agreed with a laugh.

"Indeed I do." Luc's grin dimmed as he turned

somber. "Speaking of image, I agree with Duncan that the best way to repair yours is to become engaged."

Her fingers slipped off his sleeve. "Surely you're not serious."

Luc reached for her hands and cradled them between his own. "Of course I am," he replied, his gaze unwavering. "If there is even the slightest chance that becoming engaged to me would keep you safer, then we must do it. Besides, an announcement would also repair your reputation."

His argument saddened her. "Do you hear what you're saying? You want to marry me in order to protect me." She shook her head. "I'm sorry, Luc, but that's not the kind of marriage I want."

"That's not the only reason," he protested.

"Perhaps not, but it is the primary one." Rose squeezed his hands. "If I married you, Luc, you would want to wrap me up and place me on a shelf to keep me safe."

"I would do nothing of the sort," he retorted. "Not only do I understand your nature, I admire it as well."

"Prove it," she challenged. "Allow me to investigate the murders with you."

Luc scowled fiercely at her. "I've already told you that it is far too—"

"—dangerous and you need to keep me safe," she finished. "And that, my dear Lucien, is precisely why I won't even consider marrying you."

For a long moment, Luc remained silent. "All right, I will let you help me on the investigation," he finally said.

Surprised, Rose simply stared at him.

"Did you hear what I said?"

"Yes. Yes, I did," she stuttered, trying to regain her balance.

"Then you will marry me?"

Sighing, Rose shook her head. "While I appreciate your concession, Luc, I still don't believe that we should marry simply because you want to protect me."

"It's more than that," he ground out, tugging her closer. "You make me feel so many things . . . though I'm not entirely certain I *want* to feel any of them. I've tried so hard to push you away because I knew I was the last thing you needed in your life. And I was afraid that if you didn't leave me alone, I would grab hold of you and never let you go." Luc's breath rushed out of him. "I know I'm making a mess of this, but I want you to know that I believe we could have a good marriage."

Rose's heart pounded as she considered his proposal. Imagining marriage to Luc made it hard to think straight. When she'd been in Europe, she'd dreamed about him, building him up in her mind until no other man could measure up to her image of him. Once she'd returned home, Rose had quickly found out that Lucien St. Cyr was far from the fantasy man she'd created in her imagination.

Still, the man that he was inspired powerful emotions within her—from intense desire when he'd kissed her to melting tenderness when he'd held her as she'd cried. Luc might not be the perfect man, but he made her feel so very . . . alive.

Raising her hands to his lips, Luc pressed a kiss upon her fingertips. "Marry me, Rose."

His soft whisper reached her soul and she gave him the only answer possible. "Yes."

# 14

"You're looking lovely this evening, Mother," Luc murmured as he bent down to kiss Katherine on the cheek.

"Lucien!" she gasped, pleasure mirrored in her smile. "I wasn't expecting to see you."

He glanced around the crowded ballroom. "I hadn't planned on coming tonight, but I changed my mind earlier this afternoon."

Katherine rose from her chair. "This is something of a record for you—two balls in less than a week." She smoothed the front of his jacket. "You have no idea how happy this makes me."

"I believe my next bit of news will delight you even more."

"Really? Do tell," Katherine urged with a laugh.

"This evening, my betrothal to Miss Rosaleen Fleming will be announced."

"Oh, Luc," whispered Katherine, tears filling her eyes. "How wonderful."

"Thank you," Luc murmured, smiling at his mother.

Noticing Rose and her parents entering the ballroom, Katherine tucked her hand under Luc's arm. "There is your affianced now. Why don't you take me over so I might welcome her to the family?"

Without hesitation, Luc led his mother over to where Rose stood with her parents. After greeting her mother and father, Luc turned his attention onto Rose. "How are you this evening?" he asked warmly.

"Splendid," she returned, flushing under his intense gaze.

"Please allow me to introduce my mother, Lady Katherine St. Cyr, the Marchioness of Ansley."

"We've already met," Katherine informed Luc as she nodded at Rose's parents. "Elinor, Reginald, delightful to see you again." Her eyes sparkled as she flashed Rose a smile. "And I hear we are soon to be family." Katherine leaned forward to kiss Rose upon the cheek. "I can't express how overjoyed I am to learn of your betrothal to my son."

My son. His mother's words chilled Luc to the core. How could he have forgotten who he was even for an instant? It had been completely unfair of him to propose to Rose without first telling her the truth about him. She had the right to know that she was marrying a bastard, a fraud with no claim to a legitimate title. Fear gripped him at the thought of Rose ending their betrothal. The strength of his emotion stunned him. If he was marrying her for purely practical reasons, why did the concept of losing Rose terrify him so?

Stepping toward her, Luc held out his arm. "Would you care to take a stroll in the gardens with me?"

"It would be my pleasure," Rose answered, tucking her hand into his elbow.

"I don't know if—"

Elinor cut off Reggie's protest with a rap from her fan, then returned to her discussion with Katherine about wedding plans.

Luc led Rose toward the back corner of the garden. "It's lovely out tonight," he murmured, looking up at the stars.

"Have we run out of topics for conversation already?"

He laughed despite his nervousness and glanced down at Rose's upturned face. She was so incredibly beautiful. If only . . .

Luc bit back a sigh as he braced himself for their discussion. He took a deep breath and began. "No, I didn't bring you outside to discuss the weather, Rose. In fact, I had something very important I wanted to tell you, to explain to you."

Her expression remained open, welcoming. "I'm listening," she encouraged him.

He would rather have faced a firing squad than reveal his past to Rosaleen, but he owed her nothing less than the truth. "Over the past few days, I've done quite a bit of thinking and I realized that if I was ever going to overcome my past, I needed to face it."

"It is the only way," she agreed solemnly. "Believe me, I know all too well."

"Yes, I suppose you do." He frowned slightly. "I'd forgotten."

The smile she gave him could have lit the night sky. "That often happens to me too."

His chest felt tight. "But it used to bother you so much."

She shrugged. "I finally realized that I couldn't change who I was, so I needed to learn how to live with it." Her smile tilted into a grin. "And I did, but what I find most amusing about it all is now that I no longer care about the opinion of others, I've somehow gained their approval. It's really quite amusing when you think on it."

"I suppose it is." Luc snapped off a leaf and began to twirl it between his fingers, eager for a distraction, any distraction that would keep him from meeting Rose's eyes. Clearing his throat, he charged ahead with his confession. "I've decided it's well past time that I deal with my past and move on . . . hopefully with you at my side."

Her brows drew downward in a frown. "I'm afraid you're confusing me, Luc. Your background is impeccable. I fail to see what problems you need to address."

"Not everything is as it seems, Rosaleen," he said quietly. He dropped the leaf and turned to face her. "I am a bastard."

She flushed at his statement. "Don't be ridiculous, Luc."

"No, you misunderstand me." He grasped her upper arms. "I am *really* a bastard born."

Shaking her head in confusion, Rose asked, "Your parents were unwed when you were born?"

"No, what I'm telling you is that I am not a St. Cyr by blood."

Seeing Rose's expression, Luc knew his revelation had shocked her. He waited for her to reject him, to tell him that he was beneath her attention, to end their engagement . . . but Rose remained silent.

"Do you understand what I'm saying?" he finally asked, unable to bear the quiet. "Edward and Katherine St. Cyr are not my parents."

"Yes, they are," she corrected firmly.

Frustration rippled through Luc. "I am the son of Griffin Kingston, the Earl of Ross, and a woman named Sarah Thane."

"I understand perfectly, Luc," Rose replied, her voice calm and level. "However, that doesn't make them your *parents*."

Rose's assertion filled him with the hope that perhaps he wouldn't lose her after all.

"I've seen you with your parents, Luc. I know the love you bear for the Marquess and Marchioness. And how did they earn your devotion? By raising you, caring for you, teaching you to be all that you are. They are your *true* parents."

Luc's hold upon her tightened. "But what of the tainted blood that runs through me? You've heard all of the stories about Griffin Kingston. That is my legacy. How do I overcome its pull?" ·

"You already have." Rose smiled up at him.

"When I first met you, I found you to be one of the finest gentlemen that I'd ever known—"

"That was before I'd learned the truth," Luc told her.

"What difference would that make if it was blood that defined who you were? You were a gentleman because you *chose* to act as such."

Releasing her, Luc turned away from her. "I understand what you're saying, Rose, but I don't think you realize how deeply this will affect you. How can I ask you to marry me, take my name, bear my children, when I am a fraud?"

"You *have* asked me and I've already accepted," Rose pointed out.

"Yes, but that was before you knew the truth. It was completely unfair of me to ask you without telling you of my heritage first, but I was so concerned about you, so caught up in the threat toward you, that I . . . forgot."

He flinched when she laid her hands against his back. "I'm not going to change my answer and I'm not going to allow you to take back your proposal," she informed him.

Immediately, he faced her, grabbing hold of her upper arms. "You know I want to marry you, Rose, but I have to be very certain that it is what you want as well. I need to know that you realize our children will have my bastard blood running through their veins."

Gently, Rose reached up and cupped Luc's face between her hands. "And I'm the daughter of a courtesan," she reminded Luc. "Why would I think less of you, of myself, because of something beyond our control? What matters to me is that you are strong, determined, and honorable . . . and *that* is the legacy you will give to our children."

Feeling a rush of joy, Luc folded Rose into his arms. For the first time in years, he felt like the man he used to be, the man he wanted to become again. He'd offered marriage to Rose out of a sense of duty, never imagining that he would find himself within her heart.

Eager to share his news, Edward hurried toward their family chapel. "Basil? Are you here?"

"Of course," the pastor returned, stepping out from the vestibule. "This is an unexpected visit."

"I know it's dreadfully late, but I couldn't wait to share my good news." Edward beamed at his friend. "Katherine just informed me that Lucien is engaged to Miss Fleming."

Basil's expression darkened. "And you think this is a good thing?"

"Yes, naturally," Edward said, confused by Basil's reaction. "It has been years since Luc has made any regular appearances in society and now he's been out twice. Miss Fleming is responsible for that change."

"But she's the daughter of a whore."

"Basil!" Edward exclaimed, offended by the term. "I have always found Elinor Fleming to be a pleasant lady."

"I meant no offense, Edward," Basil said in apology. "Naturally, I am concerned about what will happen to Lucien in the future if he marries her."

"It is my hope that he will have many grand-children for me to spoil."

Shaking his head, Basil sat down in a pew. "But what if she is unfaithful to him? Even the most pious of women are tempted to stray from their marriage vows, so I don't know how a courtesan's daughter could resist." His shoulders slumped forward. "And the pain of betrayal is ungodly."

Edward sat down next to his friend, placing a hand upon Basil's back. "I know Lilly's infidelity hurt you greatly, but that doesn't mean all women stray. Look at Katherine," he said. "She's been faithful to me."

With anger darkening his gaze, Basil twisted on his seat to face Edward. "And you repay her with lies," Basil retorted. "So, don't hold your marriage up as an example for Luc to follow."

Edward's head snapped back as he tried to recover from Basil's unexpected attack. "I . . . I . . ." Edward began before ending his stammering.

Basil dropped his head into his hands. "Dear God in Heaven, please forgive me." Dropping his hands to the side, Basil met Edward's stunned gaze. "I need your forgiveness as well, Edward. My remarks were cruel and unnecessary."

"It's all right," Edward said as he sat back in the pew and realized that his joy over Luc's engagement had dimmed. Edward knew from experience that it was hard to feel happiness beneath the burden of guilt.

Edward looked at his friend. "Let us pray for Luc that he won't face the trials that we've endured."

Without a word, Basil shifted onto his knees, closed his eyes, and began to pray. Edward followed suit.

As he gazed up at the altar, Edward wondered if God would even hear his prayers . . . or if the Lord had simply stopped listening.

# 15

"I cannot believe that you talked me into bringing you here," Luc grumbled, glancing around the
room. "I promised myself I wouldn't do anything
else to jeopardize your reputation, yet here we are
at the home of the most notorious courtesan in all
of England!"

"How kind of you to notice, sir, though I prefer
the term Fashionable Impure."

Luc stood quickly to face Harriette Wilson, the
Prince Regent's infamous mistress. "I beg your
pardon, madam. I spoke out of turn."

"No, dear boy, you spoke the truth." She ran a hand
over the lace edging of her bodice. "A rarity from a
gentleman, true, but always appreciated nonethe-
less."

Bowing over her hand, Luc murmured, "A
beautiful woman can inspire a man to many
things, madam."

Harriette's brows arched upward. "Aren't you the charmer?"

"Only on my good days," Luc replied with a grin.

Her laughter spilling out, Harriette looked down at Rose, who remained seated. "And who did you bring to me? Is this a new mistress whom you'd like me to train?"

Luc shook his head. "No, madam, this is my fiancée."

"Indeed," Harriette murmured, unable to hide her surprise.

Rising gracefully to her feet, Rose held out a hand to the Prince's favorite mistress. "I am Rosaleen Fleming. I believe you know my mother, Elinor Sandley Fleming."

"Elinor's daughter!" Harriette smiled brightly at Rose, giving her a hug. "Let me look at you." Harriette's gaze swept over Rose. "How can it be possible that one of my friends has such a grown daughter?"

"Perhaps it is because you have not aged at all, so it is difficult to imagine."

Harriette laughed in delight. "And quite the wit, just like your dear mama. You were doubly blessed, my dear, to have inherited not only her beauty, but her intelligence as well."

"Thank you," Rose responded politely.

"It is not a compliment, but the truth." Harriette arched a look at Lucien. "You chose well, my lord."

Lucien smiled into Rose's eyes, making her feel flushed and warm all over. "I quite agree, madam."

"Ahhh," Harriette murmured, draping herself over a chair. "How utterly charming that the sweet ingenue has captured the attention of the dashing lord." She smoothed her hand across the velvet back of her chair. "I do love a romance."

Rose didn't know how to respond to Harriette's teasing. She would hardly call her relationship with Luc a romance, yet whenever she was around him, she felt her heart ache with longing—for his smile, his kiss, his laughter.

"So why have you come to see me?"

Harriette's question broke Rose from her thoughts. "We need your help."

"My help?" Harriette asked, pressing her fingers against her bosom.

Nodding, Luc answered, "Yes. I'm trying to uncover Miranda Worth's killer."

"Because she was your mistress."

"Precisely." Lucien's answer was grim.

Harriette's attention shifted onto Rose. "And how do you feel about all of this? Your fiancé brings you to the house of an infamous Cyprian while investigating the murder of his mistress. Doesn't this bother you?"

"Even if it did, I wouldn't allow it to keep me from accompanying Luc," Rose replied honestly. "You see, madam, my mother has received a threat as well." Rose purposely refrained from mentioning that she'd received one too.

"Elinor?" The answer seemed to shock Harriette. "But she has been married for years and years now. Dear God in Heaven, is no one safe?"

"Apparently not," Luc murmured, glancing at

Rose, "which is why I am determined to discover who is committing these crimes before someone else is murdered."

Harriette sobered. "How can I help you?"

"We would like to try to connect the murders somehow," Rose answered, sitting across from Harriette.

"I should think it quite obvious. They are or *were* all mistresses."

"Yes, we know that and the magistrate agrees with that assessment," Rose acknowledged.

Sitting next to Rose, Luc shook his head. "However, there has to be more of a connection between the women than just the fact that they are courtesans. The women who were killed had obviously been chosen for a specific reason and if we discover that reason, we find the murderer."

Harriette spread her hands wide. "I don't know of anything else."

"What of their protectors?" Rose asked. "We know the women all had different . . . *amoureux* when they were killed, but what about in the past? Did they all have the same protector at one time or another?"

"Now that's an interesting question," Harriette murmured, her brows drawing together. "It will require some thought."

"Your help would be greatly appreciated," Lucien added.

Harriette waved away his thanks. "I am more than happy to help you in any way I can. After all, this madman is a threat not only to me, but to all of my friends as well."

"Will you contact me if you find any connection between the women?" Luc asked Harriette.

"Most certainly," she agreed immediately. "I shall make a list of the women and their various lovers, but it will take me a few days to compile the names."

"You have my gratitude, madam," Luc murmured, bending to kiss her hand once more. "I shall anticipate your correspondence."

Harriette rose gracefully from the chair, her every move a thing of beauty. Rose didn't find it difficult to believe that this woman had captured the devotion of their Prince.

"If you have further need of me, please feel free to call." Harriette smiled at Luc, before turning her attention to Rose. "I shall bid you farewell, sweet Rosaleen, for it would be best if you did not come to see me again, though I have enjoyed meeting Elinor's daughter."

Understanding Harriette's reasoning, Rose hugged the older woman. "It has been an honor for me as well," she replied. "I will be certain to let my mother know that you inquired after her."

Blinking rapidly, Harriette sniffed as she pulled back. "Yes, please do that for me." Drawing herself up, she adjusted the shoulders on her gown. "Now off with the two of you. I'm expecting my sweet Prinny this evening and I need to prepare."

"Give 'Prinny' our regards," Luc said with a grin.

"What a devil you are." Harriette's lips twitched as she advised Rose, "You'll have a challenge keeping this one entertained, my dear, but, I wager you'll never suffer a boring life."

Luc bid Harriette farewell and escorted Rose out of the house before the courtesan could dispense more advice.

"What should we do now?"

Luc looked at Rose across the expanse of the carriage. "We will wait until we hear from Harriette."

"In the meantime, I will listen to the gossips." A wicked gleam lit Rose's eyes. "Can you imagine me asking Lady Foley if she knows which gentlemen keep mistresses?"

"A few days ago, she would have given you my name," Luc replied quietly.

Rose's sparkle dimmed at his observation. "I'm sorry, Luc. That was thoughtless of me."

"No, Rose, I am the one who should apologize." Luc would have kicked himself had he been able. "As Harriette pointed out, this entire situation is awkward at best." He leaned forward, placing a hand upon her knee. "I want you to know that when I saw Miranda that night—"

"I do *not* want to hear this!" Rose insisted, shifting her leg out from underneath his touch.

He couldn't blame her. Sitting back, Luc said, "Then allow me to apologize for putting you through this chaos. You deserve . . . better."

Much to Luc's surprise, Rose's annoyance grew instead of diminished at his apology. "Enough already, Luc. What I deserve is exactly what I'm getting—a husband who has promised to care for me," she said firmly. "And while it does disturb me greatly to think of you with your mistress, I am smart enough to know that she had nothing whatsoever to do with us."

Before Luc could offer his agreement, Rose pointed her finger at him. "Consider this fair warning though, Lucien St. Cyr, if you so much as think about engaging another mistress, I will make you more miserable than you can even imagine possible."

With a grin, Luc grabbed hold of her finger and tugged, causing Rose to fall toward him. Wrapping his arms around her, he settled her onto his lap and kissed her soundly.

When Luc lifted his head a few moments later, Rose gasped, "What was that for?"

"For caring enough about me to threaten me with bodily harm," Luc replied with a laugh.

Shaking her head, Rose grinned at him. "Anytime, my lord."

Three days later, Rose sat listening to Lord Atherby prattle on about his latest literary endeavor and prayed she didn't disgrace herself by falling asleep. Hoping she would hear interesting gossip, Rose had come to Lady Haverstram's literary meeting, but all she'd learned was that Lord Atherby had an appalling lack of humor.

Wondering how much longer she would have to listen before she could politely excuse herself, Rose tried to look suitably impressed with the young dandy's plot.

". . . and that is when the brave hero will thrust his blade into the horrible monster . . ."

"If the hero is as deadly dull as Atherby, the brave fellow won't need his sword; he could simply bore the monster to death."

"Luc!" Rose exclaimed, twisting around in her seat to face him. "I didn't expect to see you."

Glancing around, Luc admitted, "Under normal circumstances I wouldn't set foot in Lady Haverstram's salon, but I needed to see you immediately."

"Oh?" Rose murmured, her curiosity aroused. After Luc had escorted her home from Harriette's house, she hadn't spent much time with him at all, except for brief encounters at the various events she'd been attending. Gathering gossip was an exhausting business.

Luc nodded his head toward the hallway. "Perhaps we could slip away unnoticed and—"

"Lord St. Cyr!" Lady Haverstram stood, cutting off poor Atherby's less than stirring conclusion and ending any hope of going unnoticed. "How *wonderful* that you've come to *my* salon," she exclaimed as she moved toward Luc like a Royal Navy vessel under full sail. "After all that has happened to you over this past week, I imagine you'll enjoy our quiet little gathering."

"Yes, I'm certain I will," Luc murmured politely, rising to his feet, "especially after my . . . trying week."

Rose hid her smile behind her hand, knowing from the sound of Luc's voice that he had no idea what Lady Haverstram was talking about.

"Trying?" Lady Haverstram asked with a frown. "Well, I imagine dispelling that horrid rumor that you were suspected of murder—not that *I* believed it for a minute, mind you—was extremely trying," she agreed. "But I'm rather confused as to why you would consider your betrothal a trial."

Luc coughed discreetly to cover his chuckle. "You misunderstood me, my lady. When I said I had experienced a trying week, I wasn't referring to my engagement to Miss Fleming at all."

"Of course not," Lady Haverstram agreed. "I've already offered your fiancée my congratulations and would like to extend them to you as well."

"Thank you," Luc replied, placing a hand upon Rose's shoulder.

"Lucien would never speak of our betrothal in that manner." Unable to resist teasing Luc, Rose whispered to Lady Haverstram, "Not only does he adore me, but he also introduces me to the most fascinating people. Do you remember that lovely lady we met a few days ago?"

Luc squeezed her shoulder. "Of course, but let's not bore Lady Haverstram, darling."

"You could never do that," Lady Haverstram pronounced.

"Indeed, whenever I am around Miss Fleming, I find the experience to be most exhilarating."

"*Exhilarating!* Oh my!" Lady Haverstram exclaimed with a giggle. "What a positively charming way to describe your feelings." She leaned closer to him. "Tell me, my lord, do you enjoy writing poetry, by chance?"

This time, Luc didn't disguise his laugh. "No, my lady. I enjoy poetry far too much to ever butcher the art."

"Yes, well, if you ever change your mind, I'd be delighted to host your first reading."

"You are most generous."

Lady Haverstram smiled at Luc. "How kind of you to say so," she replied, before turning to the now annoyed Lord Atherby. "Pardon the interruption, my lord, please do continue with your reading."

Instead of resuming his seat, Luc bent down to whisper in Rose's ear. "I shall stroll out now and you can follow shortly."

At her nod, Luc released her shoulder and left the room.

Minutes later, Lord Atherby finally concluded his tale and earned a loud round of applause. As Rose discreetly left the room, she wondered if everyone was clapping in appreciation of his story . . . or in relief that he was finally finished.

Still smiling, she wandered down the hall, uncertain of where to find Luc. As she passed an open doorway, Luc's arm snaked out and he tugged her into the Haverstrams' study. Pressing a hand to her chest, Rose released a heartfelt sigh. "This is the first and the last literary salon I am ever going to attend."

"Come now, you enjoyed yourself when you all but told Lady Haverstram of your visit with Prinny's mistress."

"Ah, yes, it's true." Rose fluttered her eyelashes. "I found that moment to be particularly . . . exhilarating."

Their laughter combined, the joyous sound filling Rose with happiness. Gazing at Luc, she realized her dreams had come true. Here was the man she hadn't been able to forget.

Here was the man she loved.

The certainty of that knowledge took her breath away. Staggering beneath that powerful realization, Rose sank into a chair.

Luc smiled down at her. "Are you ready to be serious now?"

"As soon as I received this missive from Harriette, I came to find you." Sitting down next to her, Luc held out the parchment.

Accepting it, Rose turned it over in her hands. "The wax seal hasn't been broken."

A side of Luc's mouth quirked upward. "Of course not. Since we both went to see Harriette, I thought it only fair that we read her letter together."

Luc could have filled the room with flowers and it wouldn't have come close to touching her heart the way his consideration did. Overwhelmed, Rose pressed a soft, gentle kiss against Luc's mouth.

"You may open all of my correspondence if that is my reward," Luc offered when Rose sat back.

She smiled at Luc, but when she looked down at the letter, her happiness faded beneath the weight of the message she held in her hands. "I wonder how many men are listed."

Sobering, Luc retrieved Harriette's letter. "Let's find out."

The wax snapped as Luc unfolded the stiff

parchment. As Rose watched, all the blood drained from Luc's face. "Luc?" she asked, alarmed.

Without a word, he handed her the letter. There were only two names listed.

Jonathan Howard.

Griffin Kingston.

Dropping the note to the floor, Rose wrapped her arms around Luc, wishing she could somehow erase his natural father's name from Harriette's note.

Her arms fell away when Luc thrust to his feet. "Damn him," he ground out.

"I'm sorry, Luc." Rose watched him pace across the room.

"I always knew he was a wastrel, but a murderer?" Luc smacked his hand against the wall.

The sound made Rose jump as she searched for some way to comfort Luc. "You don't know if he is the killer. After all, these are simply two men who had the same mistresses in common," Rose pointed out in what she hoped was a calm voice. "And according to Harriette's note, Jonathan Howard is the only man who also spent time with my mother. So, that alone makes him the stronger suspect."

His pacing slowed. "That's true," he conceded, his steps finally coming to a halt. "And Howard is even linked to you through his wife."

"Exactly." Rose stood and faced Luc. "So what do we do with these names now? I think we should notify Mr. Duncan immediately."

Luc stiffened at her suggestion. "No."

"But, Luc—"

"Like it or not, Griffin Kingston is my blood relation," he said, his voice raw. "I want to speak with him."

Rose felt torn between what she knew was right in the eyes of the law and what she knew was right for Luc. It took less than a minute for her to make a decision.

"When are you going to see him?"

"Now." Luc rubbed the back of his neck. "The task won't grow more pleasant if I put it off."

Rose placed a hand against Luc's heart. "Would you like me to come with you?"

Horror darkened Luc's gaze. "No, God, no." He stepped back from Rose. "I don't want you anywhere near that monster."

Rose wanted to do nothing more than hold Luc in her arms, but she knew that what Luc needed most from her was time and distance. Griffin Kingston was Luc's demon to face.

"All right," Rose agreed gently. "While you're with Lord Kingston, I would like to tell my mother about Lord Howard. She deserves to know."

"Yes, of course," Luc replied in a distracted tone.

Rose longed for the lighthearted banter that had colored their conversation earlier. And as much as she wanted to tell Luc of her love for him, Rose knew it wasn't the time for her declaration.

Instead, she cupped Luc's face between her hands. "Come to me as soon as you've seen Kingston. I'll be waiting for you."

An expression of gratitude flashed across Luc's face before he headed for the door.

As soon as Luc disappeared from sight, Rose sent a heartfelt prayer winging upward. "Take care of him."

"My, my, my," Griffin Kingston murmured as he leaned back in his chair. "To what do I owe this unexpected visit?"

Luc kept his expression neutral, not willing to show even the tiniest sign of emotion in front of this man. "I have some questions for you regarding your mistresses."

"Why? Are you looking for a few hints with the ladies?"

Swallowing his anger, Luc ignored Griffin's crude response. "In connection with the murders," Luc clarified.

Griffin steepled his fingers together. "And what makes you think, even for a moment, that I will answer your questions?"

Luc shrugged lightly. "If you don't answer them for me, I'm sure that the magistrate will be more than happy to ask them."

One side of Griffin's mouth quirked upward. "I always knew you took after me, you arrogant bastard."

Luc shook beneath his exertion of self-control. "I did not come here to trade insults, Kingston."

"That's too damn bad," Griffin returned, his eyes narrowing. "I've contacted you numerous times, yet you never saw fit to respond to any of my letters. But the moment you need some infor-

mation from me, you come without hesitation."
He pushed to his feet. "So, you are going to
have to tolerate my frustration with you, Lucien, because no matter what you'd prefer, I *am*
your father."

"No, sir, you are merely the man who sired me,"
Luc said coldly. "It takes more effort to become a
father." And, for the first time, he believed it. The
maelstrom of emotions surging inside of him
calmed.

Kingston slammed a fist against the mantel.
"Bloody hell, boy, can't you see that I want a relationship with you? I want to get to know
you."

"You've already offered to show me all of the delights in which you indulge . . . and I declined."

"You seem to have done quite well finding them
all by yourself," Kingston retorted.

"True enough, but those days are over." Luc
straightened, feeling stronger than he had in
years. "I've begun to reclaim my life."

A sneer curled the corners of Kingston's mouth.
"You've tasted the forbidden fruit, Lucien. How
long do you honestly believe you'll be able to resist? Don't you think that I've tried to put it behind
me?" He snorted in derision. "I did. More times
than I care to remember, but each time the lure
proved too great." Kingston gave him a level look.
"And you are, after all, my son."

Luc's greatest fear had just been voiced. Still,
he'd be damned to Hell and back again before he'd
allow Kingston to know how much it affected
him. "I will not falter," Luc said finally, praying to

God and anyone else who would listen that it be the truth.

Wearily, Kingston rubbed the back of his neck. "I hope you don't, Lucien. I honestly hope you can overcome the curse that has haunted me my entire life."

Luc wanted to paint Kingston into a dark, forgotten corner of his consciousness, yet he was starting to see what drove Kingston, to understand why his natural father was so . . . lost.

Closing his eyes, Luc tried to block out the shimmering ray of understanding. Finally, he pushed it from his thoughts, focusing instead on his reason for calling upon Kingston. "Are you ready to answer my questions?"

Kingston sank back down into his chair. "Very well then, get on with it," he said, waving his hand at Luc. "At least you'll be speaking to me."

There was another tug at Luc's heart that he chose to ignore. Instead, he asked calmly, "Do you realize that you have been involved with all of the murdered Cyprians?"

Kingston shook his head. "Have I? Lord, boy, I've been with far too many women to remember them all."

Luc flinched away from the answer, all too aware of how many women he'd been with over the past three years. "Still, it is a bit too much of a coincidence that most of the women who were killed or threatened have been your mistresses at one time."

All of the color drained from Kingston's face. "My God," he whispered, shock echoing in the two words. "You think I did it, don't you? You honestly believe that I murdered those women." His fingers trembled as he rubbed them against his temple. "I knew that you disliked me, but I never imagined that you thought me a monster."

Staring down at Kingston, Luc felt a lash of guilt. For so long he'd thought of Kingston as something less than human, a despot with no redeeming qualities. Yet, as he stood here, gazing down at him, Kingston seemed all too human, merely a man beset by more than his share of failings.

"I don't think you're a monster," Luc finally admitted.

Kingston looked up at him, a wary hope flickering in his eyes. "Thank you for that."

Luc nodded once, wishing he'd never come to see this man. It had been a lot easier to despise Kingston when he'd thought the man reveled in his wickedness. Instead, Luc had found a man who fought against the same demons he, himself, battled.

Rose found her mother speaking with the housekeeper about the dinner menu. When Elinor finished, she turned toward Rose with a smile. "Hello, darling," she said brightly.

Linking arms with her mother, Rose directed them into the parlor. "You're looking wonderful today."

"Thank you . . . and how sweet you are to find me *just* to tell me that," Elinor teased.

Laughing, Rose released her mother's arm. "I

suppose it was a bit too obvious that I wanted to talk with you."

"Just a bit," Elinor agreed as she sat across from Rose. "Now, what did you want to see me about?"

"I wanted to talk to you about . . . the murders," Rose finished softly.

Elinor paled. "Why?"

"Because Luc has uncovered some information that might be important," Rose explained. "If you feel it will be too upsetting to you, then I won't continue, but I believe you would want to hear about what we found."

Elinor smiled softly at Rose. "Of course it will upset me, darling, but everything about this vile business disturbs me." Taking a deep breath, she asked, "So, what did your fine gentleman unearth?"

"That all of the Cyprians who were murdered had two protectors in common."

Elinor's eyes widened. "Really? That is too much of a coincidence, don't you agree?"

"Yes."

A gasp broke from Elinor as horror twisted her features. "Then Jonathan Howard—"

"—was one of the men," Rose finished grimly.

A shiver coursed through Elinor. "No, no, it couldn't be Jonathan. He was so kind to me." She looked up at Rose. "We parted without a harsh word between us. Besides, it happened so very long ago."

"Not long enough for Lady Howard to have forgotten," Rose pointed out. "If she can harbor a grudge toward you all this time, perhaps he too is hiding an unspoken resentment."

"I don't believe it," Elinor stated firmly. "Anyway, it doesn't explain why you were threatened."

"Perhaps it does." Rose leaned forward. "We all thought that it was my indiscretion with Luc that caused me to receive the threat. But what if we were wrong? What if it was really because of the way I teased Lord Howard just before I left England?"

Elinor's hand trembled as she pressed her fingers to her chest. "I had forgotten about that."

"If his wife has a say in the matter, I doubt if Lord Howard's forgotten the incident even for a moment. After all, my actions triggered Lady Howard's explosion, which ultimately led to her being ostracized by the ton."

"I just can't believe anything so horrific of Jonathan," Elinor murmured, distress edging her voice. "It can't be him." Reaching out, Elinor grabbed hold of Rose's hand. "You said that Luc had discovered two protectors in common. Who was the other?"

"I don't believe the other person is connected to you at all," Rose said. "His name is Griffin Kingston, Earl of Ross. Do you know him?" For Luc's sake, Rose prayed her mother wouldn't even recognize the name.

"Oh, yes," Elinor murmured, her expression tightening in anger. "He pursued me unmercifully when I first began my relationship with your father."

Rose's heart sank. She'd wanted to be able to eliminate Luc's father from suspicion.

Swatting at the arm of her chair, Elinor shook her head. "In fact, it took your father's intervention before the earl would stop bothering me."

"Father went to see Lord Kingston?"

"Hmmm," Elinor murmured, rising from her chair. "He never told me what was said, but judging from your father's reaction whenever he sees the earl, it wasn't a friendly conversation." Her skirts swirled around the legs of her chair as Elinor moved to the window. "In fact, your father is unable to bear the very sight of the earl. Can't say as I blame him, though. Lord Kingston is not a nice fellow."

Perhaps not, but he was Lucien's natural father. Rose's spirits dropped even further.

"I presume Luc is going to inform Mr. Duncan."

Rose smiled weakly at her mother. "Yes, I believe so," she answered, simply avoiding any mention of *when* Luc would pass along the names to the magistrate.

"You believe so?" Elinor asked, her eyes widening. "Perhaps we should send off a quick note to Mr. Duncan ourselves, just to make certain he has the information."

Rose tried not to act as alarmed as she felt. "No, Mother, I don't think that will be necessary."

"It's far better to be certain."

"But, Mother—"

"Please, Rose. Don't worry over it." Elinor wiped her hands together. "Now, are we finished discussing this nasty business?"

"Yes, for now," Rose replied, determined to keep her mother busy so she wouldn't have time to send a note to Mr. Duncan.

"Thank God." Walking toward Rose, Elinor held out her hand. "Come with me, Rose. Let's enjoy our tea in the garden. It is far too splendid outside to stay in here one moment longer."

Accepting her mother's hand, Rose stood, eager for a respite from her worry over Luc. Pausing in the kitchen, Rose arranged for a servant to set the table in the gazebo while her mother spoke to their butler about bringing out tea and pastries. Once they'd made their arrangements, Rose and her mother headed out into the garden.

Having ensured that her mother didn't write a note to Mr. Duncan, Rose took a deep breath, feeling calmer. Enjoying refreshments with her mother would help pass the time until Luc arrived with news about his meeting with Kingston.

# 16

*"I* hope you will excuse the intrusion, your grace, but I'd appreciate it if you would answer a few questions," James Duncan said, sitting back in his chair. After receiving a missive from Elinor Fleming's worried butler, he'd decided to pay a visit to Lord Howard. Lord Kingston would be next.

"About what?" Lord Howard poured himself a brandy before taking his seat.

It didn't surprise James that Howard didn't offer him a drink. As a magistrate, he was too far below Howard's rank of duke to be of consequence. In his head, James made note of the man's unconscious arrogance.

James detested men like Howard, who thought themselves so far above others. "Regarding the murders," James said in a cold voice.

"Of the mistresses?"

"Yes," James replied with a nod. "It has come to my notice that you were . . . acquainted with all of the victims, your grace."

"Was I?" Lord Howard shrugged lightly. "Perhaps you're correct." A smile played upon his lips. "I do enjoy the ladies."

"I deduced that much." James paused, before pointing out the one major flaw in suspecting Howard of the crimes. "Which is why I can't imagine you harming them."

"I would never do such a thing." A small frown appeared, before being wiped away with dawning understanding. "My God, man! Do you believe I had anything to do with their murders?" His brandy sloshed over the edge of the glass as Lord Howard stood abruptly. "How dare you come into my house and accuse me of such heinous acts!"

James calmly watched Howard rage, wondering how much of it was superb acting and how much true indignation. He'd interviewed far too many suspects to be moved by the dramatic outburst.

"If you will remember, your grace, I didn't accuse you of anything. I merely pointed out that even if I did suspect you, the motive is not apparent."

Lord Howard slammed his glass down on the sideboard. "I refuse to listen to another word," he sputtered.

"I'm sorry you feel—"

"Are you going to charge me?" Lord Howard demanded, glowering at James.

"No," he admitted. "It's too early in—"

"Then you will leave my home at once." Lord

Howard vibrated with anger as he pointed a finger toward the door.

James knew he'd accomplished what he'd come for. He hadn't expected a confession, but instead he hoped that if Howard was the murderer, he would be rattled. Rattled enough to make a mistake. "Thank you for your time," James murmured before heading out the door.

In the foyer, James paused to straighten his jacket when he heard a strident voice echo into the hallway.

"So your whoring ways have finally caught up with you," a female voice accused. James could only deduce that the speaker was Lady Howard.

"Leave me be," Howard ground out. The tone made James lift his brows. It was obvious theirs was not a happy union.

"I hope they find out it was you. I pray every night that someone will come along and take you away."

The feral quality of the words shocked James. He heard hatred in the woman's voice. Pure, untainted hatred.

"As long as I leave my money behind. Isn't that right, my loving wife?" Howard sneered, confirming that the woman was indeed Lady Howard.

"You earn love, Jonathan." The bitterness in Lady Howard's voice was almost painful to hear. "And you've never done anything to endear yourself to me."

Stepping into the foyer, the Howards' butler passed James and quietly shut the door to the parlor where Lord and Lady Howard argued. The ser-

vant's expression grew censorious when he realized James was eavesdropping on the private conversation.

"Can I help you with anything else, sir?" The
butler's voice dripped with ice.

"No, thank you," James replied breezily.

"Then good day to you, sir." The butler reached
around the magistrate and opened the front door.
Smiling at the butler's disdain, James stepped
from the house.

The murders formed a complex pattern, with
the killer at its core. How did they all fit together?
Did it matter that Howard and his wife were at
such odds? James had no answers and he still had
another piece of the puzzle to try to fit into the
frame. Griffin Kingston.

No time like the present, James decided, and he
walked swiftly to Kingston's home, only to pull to
an abrupt halt when he saw an unexpected visitor
leaving the house.

Lucien St. Cyr.

Shock rippled through James. What the devil
was St. Cyr doing here? The answer came
swiftly enough, casting a grim set to James's
features.

St. Cyr was obviously investigating the murders
on his own.

"I must say, Mr. Duncan, that this is an unexpected pleasure." Raising the decanter of brandy,
Griffin asked, "Would you care to join me?"

An odd smile crossed the magistrate's face as he
declined the offer. "Thank you, but no."

Shrugging, Griffin topped off a glass before sitting. "Please, make yourself comfortable," he murmured, doing his best to put the magistrate at ease . . . hoping to ease Mr. Duncan's suspicions in the process. After Luc's questions, it wasn't difficult for Griffin to deduce the reason behind the magistrate's visit.

"I'd like to ask you a few questions," Mr. Duncan said as he took his seat.

"Ask away." Griffin had to focus simply to keep his hands from shaking, because he was still reeling from Luc's visit. His son . . . here in his house. Hoping it would steady him, Griffin took a sip of his brandy.

"Why was Lucien St. Cyr here?"

Brandy sloshed over the rim of his glass as Griffin jerked at the magistrate's question. Setting his snifter down, Griffin wiped at the damp spot on his vest while trying to act as if he hadn't just been broadsided. "I'm sorry," he murmured. "Who did you want to know about?"

"Lucien St. Cyr," Mr. Duncan repeated slowly. "I saw him leaving your house as I arrived."

"Ah, yes, Lord St. Cyr." Griffin paused for a long moment. "The reason for the earl's visit was a matter between gentlemen."

Mr. Duncan lifted an eyebrow. "Would you prefer I question Lord St. Cyr about the nature of his visit?"

Shaking his head, Griffin released a dramatic sigh. "No, that will not be necessary," he said. "Though I ask that you be discreet with the information I am about to impart."

"Of course." Mr. Duncan stiffened. "It is my job."

"And I can tell at a glance that you are a man of honor, which is the only reason I will consent to revealing such a private matter," Griffin said, doing his best to put the magistrate at ease. Glancing around for effect, Griffin shifted to the edge of his seat, leaning toward the magistrate. "Lord St. Cyr had an outstanding gambling debt with me, so he came to settle his voucher."

Disappointment flickered across Mr. Duncan's face. "I was under the impression that it was a serious matter."

Griffin pressed his hands against his chest. "I assure you, Mr. Duncan, both Lord St. Cyr and I *do* consider this a serious issue." He sat back in his chair. "After all, the young lord is newly betrothed. Imagine how upset his fiancée would be to learn that Lord St. Cyr was short of funds," Griffin finished with an inspired twist.

The magistrate nodded, accepting every detail as gospel truth.

"Your point is well taken, my lord. I shall not mention this to the Viscount of Howland or his family," Mr. Duncan conceded.

"On behalf of Lord St. Cyr, I offer you thanks," Griffin murmured, rather proud of his performance.

Bowing his head, Mr. Duncan accepted the gratitude. "Very gracious of you, my lord," he returned. "I want you to understand that normally I would never dream of inquiring over such a personal matter, but since Lord St. Cyr is connected with the murders, I felt it imperative that I uncover the nature of his visit."

"And now you have," Griffin returned lightly.

"Indeed." Mr. Duncan cleared his throat. "Speaking of my investigation—"

"Were we?"

Griffin's interruption flustered Mr. Duncan. "Yes, well—"

"I'm sorry," Griffin apologized, not certain what had tempted him to tease the magistrate. "What did you wish to ask me?"

As Mr. Duncan asked him where he'd been on the nights of the various murders, Griffin tried to remember, but since the women were killed over a span of years, it proved difficult. Still, Mr. Duncan seemed appeased as he concluded the questioning.

Mr. Duncan stood and bowed to Griffin. "I appreciate your cooperation, my lord."

"An innocent man never fears the truth," Griffin declared, retrieving his brandy as he rose from his chair. "Are you certain you won't enjoy a snifter with me before you go?"

This time Mr. Duncan's smile was real. "Well, I really shouldn't—"

"Ha!" Griffin exclaimed, slapping a hand on Mr. Duncan's shoulder. "A man after my own heart."

The first opportunity Rose had to speak with Luc arose when Miss Penelope Winston finished singing her aria. As everyone clapped, Rose leaned over to whisper, "I waited for you most of the afternoon."

Luc glanced at her. "My visit took longer than I'd anticipated and I only had time to dress for the evening before coming to collect you."

While Rose understood, she didn't like it. Ever since Luc had arrived to escort her to the Winstons' musical evening, he'd been distant, and Rose knew seeing Lord Kingston had greatly disturbed Luc. "I need to speak with you," Rose murmured, glancing around. "Perhaps we can find a private corner somewhere."

"Shall you leave first or shall I?"

Glancing at the front of the room, Rose saw Lady Evans taking a seat at the piano. "I believe I should leave first this time."

A wry expression settled upon Luc's face. "I take it you've heard Lady Evans play before."

Laughing, Rose nodded. "It is only fair that you enjoy the performance. After all, I already had the pleasure of Lord Atherby's reading today," Rose said softly, before discreetly leaving the room.

A few servants glanced at Rose as she waited in the foyer, but otherwise her departure went unnoticed. The off-key strains of Lady Evans's sonata resonated from the parlor, making Rose grin at the thought of Luc sitting through the performance.

Lady Evans's voice had just begun to warble in accompaniment when Luc stepped into the foyer. Wincing, he said, "Sitting through that made me long for the days when I was not welcome in polite gatherings such as these."

"You were never unwelcome, Luc. You simply chose not to attend," Rose explained. She could tell from Luc's expression that he didn't believe her. Frustrated at his stubbornness, Rose pressed the issue. "What will it take to convince you that—"

"It doesn't matter, so I see no point in discussing it," Luc said, interrupting Rose's protest. "Is there somewhere we can go for privacy?"

While she wanted to argue, Rose knew that Luc would simply continue to change the subject. Sighing, she pointed down the hallway. "I believe the library is empty."

Tucking his hand beneath Rose's elbow, Luc escorted her into the empty room. The moment the door closed behind them, Rose turned to face Luc. "What happened at your meeting with Lord Kingston?" She laid a hand upon his arm. "Are you all right?"

Luc walked toward the windows, causing Rose's arm to fall to her side. "I'm fine," he replied in a measured voice. "The meeting went as expected." Luc glanced at Rose over his shoulder. "Kingston denies any involvement in the murders . . . and I believe him."

Nodding at Luc, Rose stepped closer. "I'm glad for you, Luc," Rose said gently. "I was concerned that facing your father would prove too difficult."

"It wasn't pleasant," Luc admitted, facing the window once more. "Still, he wasn't quite what I expected."

"Is that good?" Rose asked, uncertain what Luc meant by his statement.

A dry laugh escaped Luc. "I'm not certain at this point." His shoulders slumped forward as he leaned against the molding. "For so long, I've never allowed myself to see the . . . human side of Kingston." Luc lifted his pain-filled gaze to her, making Rose gasp at the rawness she saw in him. "It was far easier to view him only as a wastrel."

"Because now you'll have to deal with him as a man," Rose concluded, closing the distance between them.

As soon as she touched him, Luc shifted out from beneath her fingers and moved a few steps away. His rejection hurt Rose, but she tried to understand that perhaps Luc was in too much pain to accept her comfort right now.

"Enough about me," Luc said, straightening his shoulders. "Did you have a chance to speak with your mother?"

Pressing a hand to her stomach, Rose answered slowly. "Indeed, I did. My mother was very upset when I mentioned Jonathan Howard. She is convinced he wouldn't murder anyone."

"Just because you wish for something doesn't make it happen," Luc said quietly. "Despite your mother's convictions, Howard is the strongest link between the murders, because Kingston has no connection to your mother."

Glancing away, Rose remained silent.

"Isn't that right, Rose?"

Though she dreaded Luc's response, Rose slowly shook her head. "Apparently your father tried to claim my mother as his mistress and when she denied him, he became . . . assertive toward her."

Luc reached out and grabbed hold of a chair. "I see," he said finally.

Instinctively, Rose took a step forward, her hand outstretched, but she allowed it to fall to her side before touching Luc, remembering his earlier rejection. "It might not mean anything," she stated firmly.

"Yes, it does," Luc corrected. "What it means is that we are no further along than we were this morning."

"That's not true." Rose clasped her hands behind her back to keep from reaching for Luc. "This morning you didn't believe in Kingston's innocence." She smiled gently at Luc. "That has got to be worth something."

"Yes." Luc took a deep breath. "Yes, that was worth a great deal . . . and it made me realize something else as well."

Remaining silent, Rose gazed at Luc, waiting for him to continue.

"It is time I faced my past completely. It's time I ended the lies." Pain flickered in his expression before Luc hardened his features. "It is time I told my mother the truth."

# 17

"Lucien, my darling, what a wonderful surprise." Katherine St. Cyr put down her embroidery and rose to hug her son.

Returning his mother's embrace, Luc enfolded her close, wishing that he didn't have to break her heart. "Hello, Mother."

"I wasn't expecting you," she said, running her hands across his shoulders. "But I am utterly thrilled that you decided to drop by for a visit."

"I was hoping you'd be in." Luc pressed a kiss upon her cheek before stepping out of her arms. "I needed to speak with you alone."

"Oh, you do sound serious," Katherine replied, but her smile faded beneath his grim expression. "It is serious, isn't it?"

"Yes, Mother, I'm afraid it is."

Gently, Luc helped his mother onto the settee.

"I need to sit for this? My, it must be *very* serious." Katherine's voice wavered. "Why is it people never have to sit for good news?"

Katherine's attempt at humor fell flat. Seeing his mother struggle to maintain her composure, Luc felt a rush of anger toward his father for making him be the one to tell Katherine.

Knowing his hesitation only made it harder on his mother, Luc sank onto the settee next to her. "I want you to know that I've had a marvelous childhood. No one could have ever been a better mother to me than you."

"Then you are indeed fortunate, for I am the only one you've got."

"No, you're not," Luc corrected quietly.

Katherine paled. "What are you talking about?"

Clasping his mother's hands, Luc gave her the news that would break her heart. "The child you gave birth to twenty-nine years ago died the day it was born."

"Impossible," Katherine rasped, trying to tug her hands away from Luc. "You are my child."

"In your heart, yes. From your body, no." Luc refused to let her go, needing to tell her of his love for her by his touch. "I am Griffin Kingston's bastard child that Father substituted for your stillborn."

"No, no," Katherine protested, her expression panicked. "Your father would never do that. You must be mistaken." Her fingers began to tremble within his clasp. "That's it, Lucien. You are simply mistaken."

"I wish I was, Mother," Luc said softly.

"Why?" Her broken whisper shook Luc to his core. "Why would your father do something like that?"

"He did it out of love." Luc heard the ring of truth in his words and released a bit of the anger he'd held tightly inside of him. Suddenly, Luc understood how tempting it was to create a grand lie in order to save someone you loved from unbearable pain.

Silent tears spilled over her cheeks as Katherine struggled for breath. "But you're my son," she cried, her voice cracking on the last word.

"I will always be your son," Luc stated earnestly, squeezing her fingers. "This changes nothing."

"It changes everything." Her sobs intensified.

Luc released her hands to gather her close, hugging her shaking body against his own, offering her his strength. "I used to believe that it did change everything, Mother, but now I don't think it does." His arms tightened. "Could you have loved me any more if I were your true son? Would you have given me less if you'd known that I was not of your blood?"

"Of course not." Her sobs softened into hiccups. "When they placed you in my arms, I couldn't believe the happiness that filled me. For the first time in my life, I felt complete." Katherine eased back to look at Luc, her gaze running over his features. "I remember thinking what a beautiful boy you were. Then I noticed how large, how healthy, you seemed for a newborn. Yet, I didn't question it." She grew silent for a moment. "No, that's not true. I didn't *want* to question it."

Not knowing how to respond, Luc did the only thing he could; he held his mother and listened to her pain.

"Perhaps deep inside of me, in my heart of hearts, I've always known that you didn't belong to me," she whispered.

"But I do," Luc insisted. "In all the ways that matter, I am your son. Ever since I found out, I—"

"That's why you withdrew from us, isn't it?" Katherine's eyes grew wide. "You discovered the truth and that's why you pulled away from everyone."

"Yes. It was at the Foleys' country party when Griffin Kingston told me he was my true father." Luc waited for the sharp lance of pain he felt whenever he thought of that horrible meeting . . . yet it didn't come. Time had somehow dulled the edges of the memory, leaving it a dark shadow in his past instead of a raw wound infecting his present.

"Three years."

At his mother's whisper, Luc returned his attention to her.

The grief in her eyes gave way to sparks of anger. "For three whole years, you carried this burden . . . and your father allowed it."

"He didn't want to hurt you." Luc shook his head. "Neither did I, so I held my silence as well."

Releasing Luc's hands, Katherine rose from the settee. "You should have told me sooner, Lucien. You should not have carried the weight of this secret."

Luc stood and faced his mother. "I know, but like my father, I couldn't bear to hurt you."

Pain, ugly and raw, shimmered in her eyes for a moment, before Katherine quelled it. Lifting her chin, she asked, "Don't you realize how much you hurt me by pulling away from me, Lucien?"

Guilt lashed at him. "I'm sorry, Mother. I only did what I thought best for everyone."

"I am tired of you and Edward making decisions for me!" Katherine railed.

Luc understood that his mother's anger was directed more at the horrible realization that he wasn't her true son, rather than at him. "I'm sorry," he repeated.

He didn't know what else to say to his mother, how to ease her pain, then he looked into her eyes and suddenly he knew exactly what she needed to hear.

"I love you, Mother."

"You should have told me."

The accusation chilled Edward to the bone. He glanced up from his book to face the icy gaze of his wife. "Told you what?" he asked, knowing that somehow, after all this time, she'd learned the truth about their son.

"How could you have lied to me all these years?" Katherine asked, as if Edward hadn't uttered a word. "You gave me Lucien, and for that I must thank you, but . . . Lord, Edward, you should have told me the truth!"

He shook under the force of his wife's anger. "How could I? The entire time you were expecting, you worried yourself sick, literally sick, about whether or not this babe would live." He rose to his feet, trying to remain steady while his world crumbled beneath him. "You couldn't have borne the truth."

"How do you know? How the devil do you know?"

"I was there, Katherine. I remember how much you wanted a child."

Katherine closed her eyes. "I desperately wanted a child," she agreed, before lifting her lashes once more. "Perhaps I can understand the reasons behind your decision. But that doesn't justify your lying to me all these years." Her hands closed into fists. "How could you have watched me suffer when Lucien withdrew from us, knowing the reason why, but never sharing it?"

Edward's stomach roiled in a sickening wave. "I thought if you knew the truth it would be worse than Lucien's distance."

"So you lied to me again," she stated baldly, her expression frosted over. "Has our entire life together been one lie after another?"

"Of course not!" Edward responded, desperate to convince his wife of that fact.

"Did it ever even cross your mind to tell me the truth?"

"When would it have been a good time to tell you that the son you adored wasn't really your own?" Edward asked, giving her the question that had remained in his heart ever since that fateful day he'd switched the babies.

Ignoring his question, Katherine lifted her chin.

"But the sin I find truly unforgivable is that you allowed our son to carry the burden of your lie."

Edward didn't know how to respond.

"Not only do you leave him to sort through his personal torment, but you permit him to keep the truth from me." Fury burst from her gaze. "If I had only known, I would have tried to ease his anguish. I would have helped my son to deal with the truth."

"Katherine, I—" Edward searched for words to explain himself to Katherine, but he realized he had no defense against the heavy weight of his guilt.

"You took the coward's way out, Edward," she said in frigid tones. "You let our son suffer in order to hide your sin from me." Katherine shook her head. "I thought I knew you, Edward, but it seems I was mistaken. Our marriage has been built upon deceit."

"No!" he shouted, unable to bear the thought of losing his beloved Katherine. "Everything I did was for you."

Stiffening, Katherine replied, "Perhaps it *was* me you thought of when you gave me Lucien, but you held your silence to benefit yourself, Edward."

How could he deny that truth? He hadn't wanted to hurt Katherine, that was undeniable, but he'd also remained silent to protect himself from his wife's fury. "I'm sorry," he said, knowing the words were pathetically inadequate.

"And is that supposed to make it all better?" Bitterness dripped from the question.

Slowly, Edward shook his head.

Katherine took a deep breath. "I have directed the servants to remove my things to the east wing."

"No," Edward rasped, reaching out to steady himself against his chair. "Please don't, Katherine."

She remained unmoved by his protest. "As far as I'm concerned, this sham of a marriage is over, Edward."

And with that, she turned and left the room, leaving him with nothing.

Thanking the Flemings' butler, Luc turned away from the door. According to the servant, Rose and her parents had gone to the Langstons' ball. Filled with a need to see Rose, Luc seriously considered following her there.

But Luc didn't know if he could act the part of a charming gentleman when he felt so torn inside. No, all he wanted was to find Rose and tell her how his mother had reacted to the news that he wasn't really her son.

Perhaps in Rose's arms, he could calm the emotions swirling inside of him. Still, the thought of facing all of those people when he felt so raw overwhelmed him.

Though he wanted Rose, Luc headed home to seek peace within the golden depths of his brandy.

"Of all my unexpected visitors, you, my lady, are the biggest surprise of all," Griffin Kingston murmured as he bent over Katherine's hand.

Studying Kingston, Katherine could see Lucien in this man's face. The realization shook her. "I apologize for the lateness of the hour, but I needed to see you."

"It is fortunate that I was still at home then."

Griffin gestured to a chair. "Would you care to have a seat?"

"No. No, thank you," Katherine amended, far too nervous to sit down. She still couldn't believe that she had called upon Luc's natural father, but once the thought to meet him had taken hold, she'd been unable to resist the idea. "I appreciate your seeing me."

"I'm always happy to indulge a lovely lady," Griffin drawled with a smile.

The expression on Griffin's face stunned her. "My God, you look just like him."

All the color washed from Griffin's face. "You know?"

"Lucien told me this evening."

Shaking, Griffin lowered himself into a chair. "You'll forgive me if I sit in your presence, but it's that or fall on my face."

Understanding perfectly, Katherine sat down as well, facing the man who had sired her beloved son. "I'm sorry if I shocked you," she apologized. "I didn't mean to blurt the truth out like that."

"I'm not one for mincing words myself, but, my goodness, madam, you put me to shame."

Katherine flushed. "I don't know what's come over me. I was in my rooms, thinking about what Lucien told me, and I just had to see you for myself." She looked into Griffin's eyes. "I needed to meet his father."

"Alas, my lady, I'm afraid I can't lay claim to that title." Sadness tinged his smile. "Something Luc has made perfectly clear."

Thinking of all the rumors she'd heard about the Earl of Ross, Katherine found it difficult to attribute them to the man before her. "You are not at all what I expected," she admitted softly.

Laughing, Griffin replied, "I believe I'll take that as a compliment."

"That wasn't very gracious of me, was it?" Katherine said with chagrin. "I'm usually not so . . . tactless."

"Since there is nothing 'normal' about this situation, your bluntness is perfectly understandable."

Expecting a dissolute wastrel, Katherine was pleasantly surprised to find a charming, aging rake instead. "Would you mind if I asked you a question?"

"Under the circumstance, I would imagine you'd have quite a few."

Katherine took a deep breath before asking the one question that had plagued her since Luc first told her the truth. "Do you know how Lucien came to be with us?"

"Yes," Griffin said, then proceeded to tell her the entire sordid tale—beginning with his seduction of Sarah Thane and ending with her letter to him. Rubbing at his temple, Griffin admitted, "I regret my harshness when I told Luc the truth, but I'd just found out about him and I didn't consider Luc's feelings when I confronted your husband." He sighed deeply. "Unfortunately, I've had quite a few years to rue my actions."

Thinking of the pain Griffin's actions caused her son, Katherine offered no words of comfort.

"Ah, the fierce mother protecting her young," Griffin murmured, correctly reading her silence. He paused for a moment before adding, "You've done a fine job raising your son, my lady."

As the knot of tension uncoiled inside of her, Katherine suddenly knew why she'd come to see Griffin Kingston. She'd wanted to see if he would threaten her claim upon Luc.

"Thank you," Katherine whispered, uncertain if she thanked Griffin for his compliment or for relinquishing claim to his son.

"No, Lady St. Cyr, thank *you*."

Lucien poured himself another glass of brandy. Taking a sip, Luc decided that he wasn't drunk enough yet to forget the pain he'd caused his mother. He'd ripped apart her world, leaving her with nothing but heartache. And how had his decision affected his father?

It was far too easy for Luc to imagine his father sitting alone in his townhouse. With one swallow, Luc drained his glass.

Staring down at his now empty snifter, Luc reached for the decanter to pour himself another, but the memory of Kingston's confession stopped him. Suddenly, Luc understood all too well how easy it would be to slip back down the path of desolation.

A knock on the door broke Luc's dark thoughts. "Yes?"

"Miss Fleming, my lord," his butler, Storrs, announced stiffly, his disapproval evident in every vowel.

Before Luc could say a word, Rose hurried into the room. "Good evening, Luc. I hope you don't mind the intrusion," she rushed, out of breath, "but when I heard you'd stopped by, I had to come to see you."

Nodding at Storrs, Luc waited until the man had closed the study door behind him, then turned his attention to Rose. "I don't think this evening is a good time for you to visit."

Ignoring his warning, Rose stepped closer to him. "Did you speak with your mother tonight?"

He nodded with a jerk of his head.

"Oh, Luc," Rose whispered. "I'm sorry I wasn't home when you came around."

"I wanted to see you, to tell you what happened with my mother." He'd wanted to hold her, Luc thought.

"How did she take the news?"

A bitter laugh escaped him. "As well as any woman can take the knowledge that the child she'd claimed as her own isn't really her son."

Without a sound, Rose walked over to Luc and wrapped her arms around him.

*Finally*. It was the only thought pounding through Luc's mind. This was what he'd needed. This was the comfort he'd sought. Somehow, he'd known that only Rose could provide solace from his painful thoughts.

Immediately, he enfolded her against him, holding her tightly. "I broke my mother's heart tonight."

Stroking Luc's shoulders, Rose asked, "Did you tell her you loved her?"

"Yes," he said, tucking his face into Rose's neck.

"Then you didn't break it at all."

Luc tried to lift his head, but Rose held him against her.

"The only way you could ever break your

mother's heart is if you suddenly stopped loving her." Entwining her fingers into Luc's hair, Rose continued, "Perhaps the truth bruised her heart tonight, but as long as you let her know that you're still *her* son, then nothing's been said that love can't fix."

The maelstrom of emotions swirling inside of him calmed at Rose's reassurances. Slowly, he raised his head to look at her. "Tomorrow I'm going to visit my father and face his anger over my decision to tell my mother the truth."

Rose pushed back a lock of hair. "I doubt if your father will be angry at you, Luc. If you had kept this secret, it would have eventually destroyed you." She smiled up at him. "Your father will understand once you explain it to him."

Gazing down at Rose, Luc felt something inside of him, warm and wonderful, burst to life. He'd never known anyone like her. She'd suffered humiliation and ridicule at the hands of vicious gossips, but she hadn't allowed it to defeat her. Instead, Rose had triumphed, capturing the favor of society while still remaining true to herself.

"Why are you looking at me like that?" Rose finally asked, her smile turning self-conscious.

"Because I've never known anyone I admire more than you, Rosaleen Fleming."

"What a lovely thing to say," Rose sighed.

"It's the truth, not a compliment."

"Oh, my," Rose murmured with a laugh. "How am I supposed to keep my head if you continue to turn it with these wonderful comments?"

Pulling her closer, Luc realized he didn't want her to keep her head. Rose felt so . . . *right* in his arms. Fingers of desire spread throughout Luc, making him burn to kiss Rose. When she'd first arrived, he'd wanted to hold her, now he just *wanted* her. "Rose," Luc rasped, skimming his hands along her spine.

Unable to resist one moment longer, Luc lowered his head and captured her waiting lips. Desire curled through him, intense and fiery. Arching into him, Rose tightened her hold on his hair, clutching the strands, her touch warm and urgent.

Slanting his mouth over hers, he deepened the kiss, tasting the sweetness of her passion. This woman belonged to him. That knowledge intensified his yearnings, creating within Luc an elemental urge to bond with Rose, to claim her as his own.

Luc slid his hands downward, sweeping them over Rose's luscious curves, molding her closer to him. Breaking off the kiss, Luc trailed his mouth along the tender line of her neck. He inhaled her intoxicating scent, so uniquely Rose.

"Luc," Rose entreated, tilting her head to the side.

Instinctively, Luc knew what Rose sought and he wanted nothing more than to please her. Tenderly, he recaptured her lips as he slid his hand around her side, along her waist, up her ribcage, until his fingers toyed with the outer curve of her breast. A moan reverberated in Rose's throat as she arched into his hands, seeking his touch.

Breaking off their kiss, Luc pulled back so he could watch Rose's expression as he moved his hand up and over the fullness of her breast. A gasp broke from Rose and her lashes fluttered downward when Luc swirled his thumb around the hardened peak.

Her responsiveness stirred a hunger within Luc that demanded surcease. Swiftly, he undid the fastenings on the back of Rose's dress, causing the garment to fall forward. Cravings, raw and urgent, rushed through Luc as he lowered his mouth, caressing the nape of Rose's neck with his lips. Inching his fingers across the edge of her chemise, Luc followed the path with kisses, softly licking at Rose's flesh.

She leaned back against the arm he kept about her waist, offering him the gift of her body without limitations. Easing down the fabric, Luc freed her breast to his eyes, his fingers, his mouth. Drawn to touch her, he outlined the dark aureole with his fingertip, watching it harden even more.

Groaning, Luc lowered his head once more, claiming the point with his lips, laving it off with his tongue, before drawing it deeply into his mouth. Rose clutched him to her, her entire body arching toward him as she instinctively pressed her womanhood against his aching hardness.

"Luc," she breathed, pulling him closer. "Oh, Luc. I love you so."

Her declaration raced through him, intensifying the desire pulsing within him. Rose loved him.

Twisting upward, he reclaimed her mouth, eager to taste her lips with her avowal of love still fresh upon them.

A pounding sounded in Luc's ears, but at first he thought it was simply his heart.

"My lord!"

Luc drew back from Rose at the shout.

"My lord, the Viscount of Howland is here for his daughter," Storrs called through the closed door.

When Luc gazed down at Rose, flushed and bemused, he wanted to tell her father to go away, but he knew he couldn't. Rose slid one hand down his shoulder and touched her lips, making Luc forget about everything but his overwhelming desire to claim her.

As Luc lowered his head, a loud bang shook the door. "Dammit, St. Cyr. Open this door!"

Only the thought of Rose's father seeing her so disheveled had the power to stay Luc's desires. Pressing one last kiss upon Rose's lips, Luc turned her around and refastened her dress.

When he was finished, he brought her around to face him. "Rose, we need to—"

"Open this bloody door!" Reggie shouted, pounding on the wood again.

Frustration rolled through Luc. There was so much he needed to speak to Rose about. Lord, she'd just declared her love for him. That thought made him freeze, because he had no idea how to respond to her avowal. Could he return the sentiment? Luc didn't know if what he felt for Rose was love. He knew he admired, respected, and cared for her, but was that love or simply friendship?

"St. Cyr!"

This time, with confusion and doubts swirling in his head, Luc welcomed the interruption. Releasing Rose, he hurried to the door. The minute the lock turned, Rose's father pushed the door open, nearly hitting Luc.

"Rose!" Reggie exclaimed, charging forward. "Do you have any idea how worried we were about you? I didn't know where you'd gone." He grasped her shoulders. "What were you thinking to leave the house without an escort? There is a madman who has threatened you and yet you disregarded all of the protection I've arranged and came here alone."

Before Rose could respond, Reggie hugged her close. "You had me worried."

"I'm sorry," she said, returning her father's hug. "I didn't mean to upset you."

Keeping his arm around his daughter, Reggie walked her toward the door. "Let's go home." He nodded to Luc. "Good evening, Lucien."

He bowed his head. "Fleming," he returned, before looking at Rose. "Good night, Rose."

Rose shook her head. "No, I need to speak with you—"

"—tomorrow," Reggie finished for her. "Now say good night to your fiancé."

"But I need to—"

Watching as her father escorted her firmly out the door, Luc smiled at Rose's sputtering . . . and tried to ignore the fact that he felt as if he'd just been given a reprieve.

Sooner or later, Rose would want a response to her admission of love.

The problem was Luc didn't have an answer yet. And when he finally decided upon a response, would it be the right one?

"Are you certain the lady in question was the Marchioness of Ansley?" James Duncan asked for the fourth time.

The man who had been watching the Earl of Ross's home nodded firmly. "I left Briggs to watch the earl's home while I followed the lady." Langly crossed his arms. "She didn't stay long enough for the visit to have been intimate."

Digesting the information, James slapped his man on the back. "Excellent work, Langly."

"Thank you, sir," Langly replied before James dismissed him.

Alone, James tried to fit the newest piece into the mystery. Lady St. Cyr and Lord Kingston? What possible connection could they have? It seemed like the more he learned about the case, the more confused he became.

He knew he'd been smart to assign men to watch both Kingston and Howard. So far, only Kingston and his surprise visitors had proven of interest—first with Lucien St. Cyr, then his mother.

Who next? James wondered as he tried to find how all the pieces came together.

# 18

*"J* feel empty without her already." Edward turned away from the window to face his pastor. "Last night, she left the house and I have no idea where she went."

"Have you tried to speak with her?" Basil asked.

"Of course." Edward began to pace. "But she acts as if she can't hear me."

"Would you like me to speak with her?"

Tempting as the offer was, Edward knew that it would only raise Katherine's ire even more. "Thank you, Basil, but I believe this is a matter between my wife and myself."

"Very well." Basil paused, then lifted his hand. "If I might, Edward, I'd like to make a suggestion."

"I welcome any advice at this point." Edward felt the loss of his wife keenly.

"Take your wife in hand."

Edward blinked. "Excuse me?"

Basil stood and walked over to Edward. "You heard me, my friend. Women are softer, weaker creatures that need a man's firm guidance to help them find their way to Heaven. As her husband, it is your duty to ensure Katherine's soul remains true to God." He looked pointedly at Edward. "And I'm certain that there is no need to remind you that a woman's place is at her husband's side. It is up to you, Edward, to help her return to her proper place."

Somehow Edward didn't see himself making Katherine do much of anything—especially not while she despised him. Not wanting to offend his pastor, Edward said, "Thank you for your advice, Basil, but I don't believe that is the best way to approach Katherine."

"In the Bible, it says—"

"Pardon, my lord," Edward's butler said, interrupting Basil, "but Master Lucien has just arrived and wishes a moment of your time."

"Please, show him in," Edward said, surprised by Luc's unexpected visit. "Would you excuse me, Basil?"

"Certainly," the pastor agreed, "though I would like to continue our discussion later."

"We'll see." Edward didn't commit himself to Basil before he left the room.

"Good morning, Father," Luc greeted as he entered the study.

Edward forced himself to act calm. "I'm happy to see you, Lucien."

Luc's eyebrows lifted as doubt clouded his gaze. "Are you? Even after yesterday?"

"Do you mean after you told your mother the truth?" Wearily, Edward leaned against his desk. "Yes, of course."

"Then you're not angry?"

Feeling like someone was tearing out his heart, Edward shook his head sadly. "How could I be angry at you for doing something I should have done years ago? It is yet another sin to add to the long list against me." He straightened, standing tall. "It was poorly done of me to leave it to you to tell your mother the truth. Both of you deserved better from me."

Edward stood still, almost afraid to breathe, as Luc approached him. "I'm no longer looking to place blame," Luc told his father. "All I'm trying to do is to put the past in its proper place—behind me."

And for the first time in three years, Luc reached out to his father.

The weight of his son's hand upon his shoulder felt so wonderful. Even though Luc broke the contact a moment later, it was enough for now.

"Well, then, I'd best be off," Luc said, filling in the awkward silence.

Clearing his throat, Edward nodded. "I appreciate your stopping by to see me." Suddenly, he remembered the last time Luc had met him. "And I want you to know that I've been keeping my ears open, but have yet to hear anything of interest."

Warmth filled Luc's gaze. "Thank you. I appreciate it," he said, before leaving the room.

Slumping against his desk, Edward felt connected to his son again, though the irony of the situation didn't escape him. The very same act that had cost him his wife had given him back his son.

"I'm afraid that I don't have much time at the moment, Mr. Duncan," Luc explained as he entered the parlor. "I'm due at a very important function in less than half an hour." Luc tucked his handkerchief into his pocket.

"I won't keep you long," Mr. Duncan promised. "And I do appreciate your agreeing to see me on such short notice."

"I'm always willing to do anything I can to assist you in finding the murderer."

"I appreciate that, especially after I suspected you of committing the murder of Miss Worth."

Immediately, an image of Miranda's blood-soaked body flashed in his mind. "I'd rather not resurrect that, if you don't mind," he said with clipped tones.

"I didn't mean to bring up unpleasant memories," Mr. Duncan replied. "I wanted to know if you could tell me how your mother is acquainted with Lord Kingston."

"My mother and Kingston?" Luc asked apprehensively.

"Yes. She was seen entering his house last night."

It took all of Luc's control to maintain his composure. "I'm afraid I can't shed any light onto that connection."

Mr. Duncan tapped his fingers against the top of a chair. "I thought perhaps she'd gone to see him about your gambling debt."

Gambling debt? Luc hadn't the slightest idea what the devil the magistrate was talking about, but he refrained from mentioning that as well. "No, I don't believe it was on that matter."

"Very well then," Mr. Duncan said as he turned to leave. Before the magistrate had taken more than two steps, he stopped and faced Luc again. "You might want to advise your mother not to visit Lord Kingston for a while."

"Is that because he's still a suspect?"

"He's the *lead* suspect," Mr. Duncan clarified. "At the last murder attempt, we found a button with a distinctive pattern." His eyes narrowed. "Today I discovered those buttons were specially made for none other than the Earl of Ross. You can do as you please, but if it were my mother, I'd urge her not to spend time with Kingston."

Luc nodded, uncertain if he could speak without his voice cracking.

"Good evening, my lord," Mr. Duncan said in farewell.

The moment he was alone, Luc sagged into a chair, trying to still the shock screaming through him. For all his fine denials, Kingston wouldn't be able to talk his way out of the evidence. Pushing to his feet, Luc glanced in the mirror hanging on the opposite wall, but instead of seeing himself, he saw a younger version of Kingston. . . .

A younger image of a murderer.

\*　　\*　　\*

"The party is lovely, Mother." Rose popped a canapé into her mouth.

"Thank you, darling," Elinor said with a brilliant smile. "I'm so glad you're happy. This entire affair is in honor of your betrothal, so it's your opinion that counts."

"And Luc's as well."

Laughing, Elinor patted Rose on the cheek. "Once you're married, you'll soon learn that men could care less for this sort of affair. They merely suffer through it for their wives."

Gazing across the room at Luc, Rose thought the word "suffer" described his reaction to this party perfectly. All evening he'd avoided her and she didn't know why. What had happened to make him go from their passionate embrace the last time they were together to his chilly attitude toward her now?

Whatever his reason, Rose deserved an explanation. But as she headed across the room, Lady Foley waylaid her with profuse congratulations, and by the time Rose managed to extricate herself from the conversation, Luc had disappeared.

"Why did you go to see Kingston?" Luc asked his mother without preamble.

Lifting her eyebrows, Katherine glanced around the Flemings' study. "You dragged me away from your lovely party in order to ask me such an obvious question?"

"I'm not in the mood for games, Mother," Luc warned her. The mere thought of his mother alone with Kingston terrified him.

"I don't understand why you're so upset, Lucien," said Katherine. "I went to see Griffin Kingston because I wanted to meet your natural father."

A shiver rippled through Luc at the thought. "I don't want you to go and see him again."

Frowning at Luc, Katherine replied, "I don't know why not. While his reputation is blackened, I found him to be charming."

"He is a suspect in the murders plaguing the mistresses."

Katherine waved her hand in dismissal. "So were you at one point. What does that have to do with anything?"

"This is far different than the suspicions Mr. Duncan had about me."

"How is it different?" Katherine demanded tartly.

Changing tactics, Luc grasped his mother by the shoulders. "That doesn't matter right now. I am asking you . . . for me, please don't visit Kingston again."

By her heavy sigh, Luc knew she wasn't happy with his request, yet she granted it anyway. "Very well."

Relief flooded Luc at his mother's agreement; he could not bear to lose her.

# 19

"Why have you been avoiding me all evening?" Rose faced Luc, her hands on her hips. Her annoyance at him had grown in proportion to the lateness of the hour. Since dawn had just arrived, Rose was furious.

"Don't be ridiculous." Luc tugged one end of his cravat, loosening the knot. "I haven't been avoiding you at all. In case you hadn't noticed, Rose, there were a number of people who wanted to speak with both of us. I'm sorry if it offended you that I couldn't dance attendance upon you," Luc finished in a dry tone.

Rose gaped at Luc. "Now I *know* something is bothering you," she said firmly. "You wouldn't speak to me so rudely if there wasn't a problem."

Ripping the scrap of silk from around his neck, Luc stormed across the now-empty parlor.

"Dammit, Rose, did it ever occur to you that perhaps I didn't want to have a discussion?"

"No," Rose admitted, sitting down. "I thought since we're to be married that we had begun to share our lives with one another."

"Our lives, perhaps, but does that have to include every single bit of time as well?"

"My parents—"

"—are not a typical example of married life," Luc finished for her. "I hate to tell you this, Rose, but most couples do not adore one another."

"Then we won't be 'most' couples." Rose folded her hands on her lap, remaining calm beneath the sarcastic lash of Luc's words.

"How can you be so sure?" Luc demanded, pacing in front of her.

Opening herself up to Luc, Rose said softly, "Because I *already* adore you."

Luc practically shook with anger as he came to a stop before her. "You only *think* you love me, because I've been behaving myself lately. But you don't even know the man I am inside. You've never seen me when I've let myself go, when I've managed to drink myself into a stupor and fall into the arms of three women at once."

"That's not who you are," Rose said with a shake of her head, ignoring the flicker of hurt she felt at his words. "That was simply the way you chose to behave."

"How can you be so sure?" Placing his hands on the arms of Rose's chair, Luc boxed her into the seat. "What if my father is a murderer? Will you still adore me if you learn that madness runs in my blood?"

Rose rested her hands upon his. "I thought you were convinced of Lord Kingston's innocence."

Ripping away from her, Luc rasped, "That was before Mr. Duncan paid me a visit this evening."

Here was the heart of his anger, Rose realized. "What did he say?"

"A button made specifically for Kingston was found at one of the crime scenes." Luc thrust his hands through his hair.

"But that doesn't mean anything," Rose said, confused by the logic. "All that proves is that Lord Kingston was indeed in that poor woman's house and that fact was never in question." She shook her head. "I don't see how anyone can leap from finding a misplaced button to finding hard evidence for murder."

"Yet Mr. Duncan—"

"—is a dunderhead," Rose finished, frustrated at Luc's obstinacy. "You said so yourself."

Slowly, Luc turned to face her and the pain in his gaze made her breath catch. "But what if Duncan is right this time? What if Kingston is the murderer?" Luc scraped his hand across his face. "All I keep thinking is how I followed Kingston's path of wild excesses and it makes me wonder if I don't contain a spark of madness deep inside of me that will flare to life when I'm Kingston's age."

"Luc," Rose began, uncertain how to convince him that his fears were groundless. She knew all too well the destructive force of self-doubt. "I don't believe—"

"Perhaps you don't believe it, Rose, but that doesn't mean it can't happen." Luc's features tightened into a grim mask. "Madness often runs in families, so if Kingston is indeed the killer, then not only will my children inherit bastard blood, they'll be given a legacy of insanity."

Without another word, Luc strode from the room, leaving behind a stunned Rose.

"Remember, I don't want you anywhere near Lord Howard or Kingston."

Rose struggled to maintain hold of her temper. "Luc, you are sadly mistaken if you believe for one moment that I will obey your edicts like a mindless ninny."

"What I expect, Rose, is for you to listen to my sound advice," Luc said in a measured tone.

"Ah, much as you listened to mine last night?" She still couldn't believe that he'd walked out during their argument. "You can't treat me like this, Lucien."

His jaw tightened as he leaned in closer. "If you simply agree to avoid speaking to Howard and Kingston, there wouldn't be a problem."

"Perhaps not for you, but I would still have one," Rose said, her voice low and tight. "I will not be ordered about like a servant."

Luc leveled a stern glare at her. "And *I* will not discuss this further. Now, I am going to follow Howard into the gaming room and I expect you to stand right here," he said, pointing to the floor, "until I return."

"What gives you—" But before Rose could finish her protest, Luc walked off, leaving her to stew once again. Her anger mingled with hurt as she tried to understand why Luc was behaving so abominably. Where had the wonderful man with the sweet kisses gone? That man was undoubtedly hidden beneath Luc's overwhelming fear of tainted blood.

"May I congratulate you on your forthcoming nuptials?"

Rose pulled herself from her thoughts to look up at Griffin Kingston. "Thank you," she murmured, admittedly curious about Luc's natural father.

"Delightful news," Lord Kingston added, surprising her by his politeness. "Young St. Cyr is a fine fellow."

Rose nodded mutely, uncertain of Lord Kingston's reason for approaching her.

"You know," he began conversationally, locking his hands behind his back. "Quite often a young man needs a bit of help from a virtuous lady such as yourself when he's trying to decide upon his future." He looked at Rose steadily. "I am sure that you will do everything in your power to ensure his well-being."

He was concerned about Luc, Rose realized, trying to hide her shock. Inside, she warmed to Lord Kingston. "Of that you can have no doubt."

His shoulders slumped forward as if he'd been relieved of a heavy burden. "Thank you, my dear."

Feeling a surge of empathy for Lord Kingston, Rose placed a hand upon his arm. "I hope you won't think me too presumptuous when I say this, but I believe that sins of the past can be wiped clean if a person is truly repentant."

A haunted look shadowed his gaze. "Do you honestly believe that?"

"I must," she replied simply. "Or I damn myself."

Lifting her hand, Lord Kingston pressed a kiss upon the back of her fingers. "Thank you," he whispered again, clearly moved.

"Release my fiancée at once."

Luc's sharp demand made Rose jump, causing her to pull her hand free. "Luc!" she reprimanded quickly. "Lord Kingston was merely—"

"Excuse us," Luc ground out, grasping Rose's elbow before propelling her outside.

In the garden, Rose tore herself away from Luc. "How dare you!" she shouted at him, not caring if anyone heard her.

"I would dare far more in order to keep you safe," Luc returned without hesitation. "Do you know how I felt when I saw Kingston touching you? Lord, Rose, don't you realize how unclean his hands are?"

She refused to feel any compassion for Luc when she saw him glance down at his own hands. "I don't know why you're suddenly so convinced that Lord Kingston is the murderer. Just two days ago you'd decided that he wasn't."

"That was before I heard about the evidence Mr. Duncan found," Luc said stiffly.

"And that's it? On the word of an incompetent fool, you've changed your mind, abandoned your own conclusions?"

A muscle in Luc's jaw began to tick. "We're speaking of murder, Rose. I can't afford to ignore the evidence and impressions of others."

"Of course not, but that doesn't mean that you can't form your own opinions, regardless of what others think," Rose responded, unable to believe Luc didn't already know that. "Good heavens, Luc, what if Mr. Duncan suddenly found something that belonged to me at the site of one of the murders? Would you then be convinced that I had committed the crime?"

"Don't be ridiculous."

"I'm not," she returned quickly. "After your re-action toward Lord Kingston, I wonder if your faith in me would falter just as easily." The heat of her anger waned, leaving behind deep sadness. "Has your trust in people been so badly shaken that you'll never be able to believe in someone un-equivocally?"

"There is no comparison between you and Kingston."

"That's not true," Rose said with quiet dignity. "We both care for you."

Frowning at Rose's assertion, Luc scoffed, "You couldn't be more wrong, Rose. That man cares for nothing but his own pleasure."

"He wouldn't have taken the time to speak to me if that was so," Rose protested.

A strangled sound of frustration ripped from Luc. "Why are we even discussing this?" he demanded fiercely. "It doesn't matter whether Kingston cares for me or not. I am a grown man now and have no need for him."

"Yes, Luc, that may be true." She gazed up at Luc, wishing she could help him find a way to overcome his bitterness. "But perhaps he has need of you."

"I do not wish to discuss this!" Luc ground out.

Heavy-hearted, Rose sighed. "Is this how it is going to be between us?" she asked softly. "Are you going to push me away every time you're faced with a problem?"

"How can you ask me that?" Scowling at her, Luc shook his head. "I have shared more with you than anyone else. I've told you about my past and included you in my investigation. What more do you want?"

"What I want, Luc, is to share everything with you." Stepping forward, Rose bared her soul to the man she loved. "I want you to let me help you face your past. I want to know that you'll turn to me when you need to be held. I want to be certain that you trust me without reservation." Gently, she placed her hand upon his arm. "I thought we were close to achieving that bond . . . which is why it hurts me so to have you pull away from me."

"I've given you more than I knew I had to give, yet it's still not enough for you, Rose." He stared down at her. "You have no idea how difficult it is for me to look at Kingston and wonder if he is the killer or not. And then those doubts fester within me."

"Even if Lord Kingston proves to be the murderer, that doesn't affect you, Luc. You need to accept your past."

"You aren't even listening to me, Rose." Luc grasped her shoulders. "I *have* accepted that I'm the bastard son of a wastrel. But this is more than facing unpleasantness. Just as I inherited my looks from Kingston, perhaps he also passed along the madness that might reside within him."

"If that is true, then we'll have to overcome it," Rose replied softly. "Together."

"And what if I can't fight it? Just as I succumbed to the lure of jaded pleasures, what if I sink into insanity? I could be a threat to you, Rose."

Coldness gripped at her heart. "What are you saying, Luc?"

Gazing down at her, Luc replied, "The reason I was so furious at you for speaking to Kingston is because it made me realize that the only way to truly protect you . . . is to stay away from you."

"No," Rose whispered. "You would never harm me. I believe in you, Luc."

He remained silent.

"Even if Lord Kingston is a murderer, I have faith in your ability to overcome anything you might face in the future," Rose said, hoping Luc would agree with her.

"But what if I fail?" He shook his head. "I can't take that risk—not with you."

Her fingers slipped from his arm as Rose stepped back. Fighting her tears, Rose knew that all of her dreams, her hopes, lay in tatters. "I thought I knew everything about you, but I now realize I was wrong." Anger blazed forth. "I never knew you were a coward."

Turning on her heel, she left him standing in the garden. Alone.

Try as he might, Griffin couldn't get his conversation with Rose out of his head as he watched Edward St. Cyr sip at a brandy. Because of the hour, only two other gentlemen besides himself and St. Cyr enjoyed the comforts of White's. Dismissing them with a glance, Griffin returned his attention to St. Cyr and allowed Rose's words to shift through his mind once more.

*The sins of the past can be wiped clean if a person is truly repentant.*

Yes, that was how she'd phrased it, Griffin thought with a nod. He'd lived a lifetime of sin, yet one weighed heaviest upon his soul. And while he'd tried to make amends with Luc, until tonight Griffin hadn't even considered that he owed an apology to Edward.

Before he could think twice about it, Griffin stood and walked toward Edward, who sat in front of the fire. Griffin was almost upon him before St. Cyr looked up.

Obviously startled, Edward made to rise, but Griffin waved him back into his chair. "No, please, St. Cyr, just sit and listen to me for a moment."

An expression of wariness passed over Edward's face, before he settled back into his chair.

Taking a deep breath, Griffin plunged forth. "It just occurred to me that I owe you an apology for my actions all those years ago. I was angry, no, furious with you and, while I don't regret confronting you, I should never have done it with Luc in the room."

The stiffness of Edward's spine softened as he shook his head wearily. "Damn you, Kingston," muttered Edward. "How the devil am I supposed to despise you now?"

Grinning broadly, Griffin eased into the other wingback chair. "I know exactly what you mean."

"I suppose this leaves me no choice but to apologize to you as well," Edward said with a heavy sigh.

"To me?" Griffin asked. "Why?"

"Because you were right to accuse me of taking your son away from you."

"Hardly. I didn't even know of his existence until after Sarah died." Griffin didn't want to admit that he couldn't even remember what the woman had looked like. To him, she'd just been another moment of pleasure, enjoyed, then forgotten. "You didn't steal anything from me."

"She might have gone to you if I hadn't offered to accept the babe as my own," Edward said, his voice low and raw. "You see, her father had tossed her out the moment he'd realized she was expecting, so if I hadn't compensated her, she might have sought you out."

"We'll never know for certain," Griffin murmured, not wanting to think of the fear that poor woman faced when she'd been abandoned by her lover, then rejected by her father. "And it doesn't much matter now." Looking at Edward, Griffin

saw a man far better than he could ever hope to
be. "I wanted to tell you that you did a fine job
raising Luc," Griffin said, emotion clogging his
throat. "I would not have done half as well."

Edward shifted in his chair. "I don't know if
that's true."

"Of course it is," Griffin snorted. "Don't be an
ass, St. Cyr."

Edward laughed out loud.

At the sound, Griffin felt a measure of peace
wash over him; perhaps the young Miss Fleming
was correct—it seemed repentance could do won-
ders for the soul.

## 20

_L_uc watched dawn approach, its pink fingers of light spreading across the dark sky. The night had passed and he'd failed to notice. Inside of him the hollowness resounded loudly, tolling the arrival of his empty life. As soon as Rose left the garden, he'd felt as if he'd torn out his heart and tossed it to the ground.

He'd watched her walk out of his life and had done nothing to stop her. At least now, away from him, he could be certain she was safe. He remembered all too clearly when his fear for her had gripped him. Unable to find Howard in the gaming room, Luc had returned to the ballroom only to find Kingston smiling at Rose.

Suddenly, Luc had imagined himself in twenty years looking exactly as Kingston did . . . and then he'd imagined himself looking at Rose with a sheen of madness in his eyes. Perhaps Rose was right; he was a coward, but as long as there was a chance that his sire might be the murderer, Luc vowed to stay away from her. Slowly, Rose had become the center of his world and he would do whatever it took to keep her safe.

Even if it meant living without her.

Luc still stood at the window when a discreet knock on the door disrupted his thoughts. "Yes?" he called, bidding the servant to enter.

"Your pardon, my lord, but you have a caller." The manservant held out a small silver tray with a single card lying upon it. Retrieving the card, Luc had to read it twice before he could believe what it said.

"Kingston," he murmured in astonishment. What the deuce did the man want with him now?

"Shall I admit him?"

Glancing at the servant, Luc hesitated, uncertain of how to respond. Because of Kingston, Luc had urged Rose to leave him, ending all hope he had for a fulfilled life. How much more would the man take from him? Luc thought with a rush of fury. There was nothing he wanted to say to Kingston, Luc decided. But his refusal to see the man froze on the tip of Luc's tongue as Rose's words came back to haunt him.

*Perhaps he needs you.*

And with Rose's soft urging echoing in his thoughts, Luc found it impossible to turn Kingston away. Finally, he nodded. "Show him into the salon."

"Very well, my lord," the servant said before withdrawing.

Luc took a moment to prepare himself. Facing Kingston would be like facing the embodiment of his worst fear. What would he do if he looked into Kingston's eyes and saw a spark of insanity? The answer to his question stopped Luc cold.

He would do whatever it took to protect Rose.

Heading down to the salon, Luc calmed his thoughts. "Kingston," he said by way of welcome when he stepped into the room.

Lord Kingston leaned against the fireplace mantel. "Thank you for seeing me," he said, his fingers drumming against the marble. "I wasn't sure if you would turn me away."

"I very nearly did," Luc replied, trying to ignore Kingston's nervousness, "but something Rose said—" Luc broke off his words, angry with himself for even mentioning Rose's name. She was definitely not someone he wanted to discuss with Kingston.

Chuckling, Kingston nodded. "That lady of yours has a way with words that worms under a man's skin."

"Why have you come?" Luc demanded icily, refusing to speak of Rose again.

Kingston's smile faded. "I . . . I wanted to let you know that I spoke with your father and we reached an understanding of sorts."

"You came to tell me *that*?"

"Blast it, man!" Kingston exploded, slamming his fist against the stone mantel. "I'm simply trying to make polite conversation." Wearily, he rubbed at his eyes. "Sweet Jesu, atoning for my sins is far more difficult than I ever imagined possible."

Growing colder inside, Luc asked, "What sins do you need to atone for?"

"I would need a week to list them all," Kingston said with a bitter laugh.

"And would any of them have to do with your mistresses?"

Kingston jerked away from the wall. "Of course not! We've already spoken about this. I thought you believed me."

Ignoring the pain in Kingston's voice, Luc said, "An etched button that was made for you was found at the last crime scene."

"And so that means I killed that poor woman?" Kingston tipped his head back. "It's not bad enough that my house is being watched by fools who have sent me harassing notes in addition to following me every time I step outside." He met Luc's gaze. "Yet, none of that bothers me as much as the fact that you believe I'm a murderer."

Kingston's protest jarred something inside of Luc. "Harassing notes?" he asked, picking up on the information that made no sense. "I'm certain the men outside your house work for the magistrate, so I can't imagine them sending you any sort of messages, harassing or otherwise."

Raising his hand, Kingston muttered, "Why do I even waste my time trying to explain? It is obvious that you'll never believe anything I say." He straightened away from the mantel, leveling his gaze at Luc. "But I will try one last time to tell you the truth. I did *not* kill those women."

As he had once before, Luc heard the ring of conviction in Kingston's voice. Longing to believe him, Luc looked into Kingston's eyes; could it be true that Kingston was innocent?

"While I've certainly not led an unstained life, I'm not guilty of those atrocities."

Searching Kingston's features, Luc found no trace of deception or guile—and, best of all, not a hint of madness. Relief poured through Luc, cleansing him of his fear.

"I believe you."

Kingston lifted his eyebrows. "Excuse me if I don't hold you to that statement," he replied dryly. "I've heard it before and yet you managed to forget your conviction."

Flushing, Luc nodded. "I apologize for failing to believe in you when Mr. Duncan told me that evidence pointed toward you." With his doubts washed away, he could see clearly that he'd allowed fear to destroy his better judgment.

"Well," Kingston began, surprise lightening his voice, "your apology was certainly unexpected."

"As was yours," Luc replied in a distracted manner. The note Kingston mentioned tugged at Luc. "I'm still confused, though, as to why you would think the men following you would send you a note. Do you remember what it said?"

Kingston shrugged. "Not verbatim. I believe it mentioned something about having to pay for my sins."

Stunned, Luc stared at Kingston. "Why did you think Duncan's men sent it around?"

"Who else?"

"The murderer, perhaps," Luc pointed out. "Didn't it strike you as odd that notes were left with all of the victims, then you receive one as well, and that's when the magistrate finds evidence incriminating you?"

Kingston sank down into a chair. "Good Lord, I'm being set up."

"Exactly." Luc tried to build a connection between the murders and Kingston. "But why? Do you have any enemies?"

"More than I can keep track of," Kingston admitted.

Retrieving a piece of parchment, Luc sat down across from Kingston. "Then we'd best begin our list now."

"Are you going to include both men and women?"

The thought intrigued Luc. "Women? You believe a woman could have committed the murders?"

"Luc, I've seen women do things that shocked even *my* jaded soul," Kingston admitted with a shake of his head.

"Very well, let's include them."

"Now, when I tell you of all the married women I've known . . . in the biblical sense, do you want to list both the lady and her husband?"

Luc shook his head at his father. "Why do I get the impression that I'm going to need more paper?"

\*　　\*　　\*

Rose looked up in surprise when Luc stepped into Lady Holt's rear garden.

"My lord!" fluttered their hostess, rising to her feet. "What a pleasure to have you call upon us."

Luc bowed over Lady Holt's hand. "I appreciate your gracious welcome. The ton has been abuzz all week about this garden party of yours, so I didn't wish to miss it."

Lady Holt actually giggled at Luc's blatant flattery. Rose struggled to keep from rolling her eyes.

"Lady Fleming, Miss Fleming," Luc murmured, bowing toward them. "It is always a delight."

"Hello, Lucien," Elinor said in greeting. "I'm so glad you joined us."

Rose smiled weakly, wishing Luc hadn't come. She wasn't ready to see him yet.

Luc glanced around. "Might I inquire about Lord Fleming?"

"I believe he is playing croquet." Elinor pointed to the far corner of the rear yard.

"Ah," Luc murmured, before casting his gaze onto Rose. "May I impose upon you, Miss Fleming, to grace me with your company while I walk over to see your father?"

Before Rose could respond with a definitive "no," Elinor slid into her pause. "Don't be silly, my lord. Of course Rosaleen would love to walk with you. You are, after all, her fiancé."

Luc's smile broadened. "Indeed I am," he said.

Rising to her feet, Rose tried to sort through her confusion. Luc had let her walk away easily enough last night, so why had he sought her out today?

Accepting Luc's proffered arm, Rose waited
until they were far enough away from her mother
before asking, "Why have you come, Luc?"

"I needed to speak with you, Rose. So much has
happened."

Luc sounded almost . . . jubilant. "Since last
night?" she asked, not understanding how that
could be possible.

"Yes!" he exclaimed with a laugh.

Anger began to simmer within Rose. While her
heart ached because he'd rejected her last night,
Luc acted as if his life had taken a miraculous
turn for the better. "I'm happy for you," she said
tartly, turning on her heel.

"Why are you upset?" he asked, catching her
elbow.

"Oh, I don't know, Luc. Do you think perhaps it
might be that I just now realized that you never
wanted me in your life?"

"*What?*" he exclaimed with a shake of his head.
"What the devil are you talking about?"

"It's perfectly obvious, Luc. What other conclusion can I draw when you're overjoyed with your
life now that I'm no longer a part of it?"

"You're not making any sense."

"Oh, don't play ignorant with me, Lucien St.
Cyr." She propped her hands on her hips. "Last
night you told me that you wanted to protect
me and that the only way to ensure my safety
was to stay away from me." All the pain he'd
caused her came forth, making her burn with
fury. "Do you know I *cried* over you last night,
Luc? I cried for you, for me, for all we could

have had, yet you seem to have had a grand time."

"I was just as miserable," he answered, not caring that they were beginning to attract attention. "I haven't slept at all. After you left, I wanted to shout at the unfairness of it all. Do you think I wanted to pull away from you? Lord, Rose, you've made me want to be better than I am. I'd do anything to keep you at my side. Anything." He lowered his voice to add, "Even meet with Kingston."

Shock pushed through her haze of anger. "You met with him? When?"

"He visited me this morning," he explained. "And *that* is why I was happy, not because of our argument."

"What happened?"

"We talked about the murders and you were right all along, Rose. I should have remembered why I believed him in the first place, but I was too afraid of the consequences if I was wrong. Last night, I kept thinking if he were the murderer, then I had that madness in me . . . and I could hurt you." His expression softened. "I'd never take that kind of a risk with you."

Rose understood how he'd felt, but it changed nothing. "So you've made your peace with him?"

"In a fashion," Luc admitted, before leaning toward her. "Kingston and I uncovered that he's being set up by someone." Seeing her shock, Luc continued, "The killer made the mistake of sending Kingston a note saying that now he'd have to pay for his sins."

"Judgment Day," Rose whispered, stunned at Luc's discovery. "What are you going to do?"

"I've sent a message to Mr. Duncan and asked him to meet with Kingston and me."

"Won't Mr. Duncan wonder why you are working with Lord Kingston?"

Nodding, Luc acknowledged, "In my note, I simply told Duncan that I'd recently discovered that my mother is a dear friend of Kingston's and that she asked me to help him."

"That sounds perfectly reasonable," Rose said.

"Then I told Duncan that after speaking with Kingston at my mother's request, I'd uncovered some information and, as I said, asked for a meeting."

"So, what are you going to do now?"

"Kingston and I have already made a list—a long list—of people who might bear a grudge against Kingston. We'll share that information with Duncan."

"There's only one thing that doesn't make any sense to me, Luc." Pressing a hand to her chest, she asked, "Why did I get a note?"

Luc's brows drew together. "I don't know. The only connection you have to Kingston is through me, but no one knows about that tie." Wearily, he rubbed his eyes. "I pray we're able to find the murderer before he kills again."

"I do as well," Rose murmured.

"Rose, I want to apologize for my behavior last night," Luc said softly. "I allowed my fears to hurt you and for that I am truly sorry."

Her pain shimmered within her, but Rose

forced it back. "I know that you're sorry, Luc. So am I."

"You didn't do anything," Luc said with a frown. "Why are you sorry?"

"Because things have changed between us." She took a deep breath. "You hurt me, Luc, and while I can forgive you for your actions, I can't forget them. The next time you're faced with something painful, will you push me away again? Will you tell me that it's safer for me to stay away from you? And what if we're married, if we have children, then what? Will you pull away from them as well? I don't know if I could bear that."

With every word, Luc's features grew stonier. Feeling her heart break all over again, Rose gazed up at Luc, wishing things were different for him, for them.

"I don't know," Luc finally said, pain twisting his voice.

Blinking back her tears, Rose admitted, "Neither do I."

His entire body tensed. "So what are you saying, Rose? Am I to consider our engagement over?"

Just the thought of that destroyed her. Dear God, she *loved* this man. How could she bear to live without him? But how could she live *with* him, never knowing if one day he'd turn away from her? Doubts assailed her.

Rose wanted nothing more than to be able to step into his arms and have him reassure her. But life wasn't that easy. So, she gave him the only answer she could. "I honestly don't know."

\*     \*     \*

Rose was positive that the afternoon would never end. When she finally managed to get her mother alone, Rose pleaded, "Mother, I wish to leave now."

"But, Rose, the afternoon is young yet," Elinor said, looking at her daughter with concern. "Is everything all right?"

Rose glanced over at Luc, who was standing next to her father, a croquet mallet in hand. "No," she said, looking away. "No, it's not."

"What's wrong, darling?" Elinor asked, stepping closer.

"Mother, please." Stemming the rush of tears, Rose fought for her composure. "Not now. I can't—"

"Good afternoon, ladies."

Both Rose and her mother started at the intrusion, before turning to face Lord Howard.

"Good afternoon, Jonathan," Elinor murmured politely while Rose wiped discreetly at her tears.

"I vow you and your daughter put the flowers to shame."

Stepping in front of Rose, Elinor shielded her from Lord Howard's attention. "Your flattery is still far too obvious, Jonathan. Obviously, you never learned to temper your compliments."

"If I must have a failing, it is good to know it is such an inconsequential one." Lord Howard grinned at them.

"Give me a moment and I'm sure I could come up with more," Elinor teased.

A wistful light shadowed Lord Howard's eyes. "Ah, Elinor, I have missed your wit."

Hearing the longing in Lord Howard's voice, Rose looked up at him and the expression on his face shocked her. If she didn't know better, she would have sworn that Lord Howard was in love with her mother.

Elinor grew flustered beneath Lord Howard's intense gaze. "Yes, well, it was lovely chatting with you—"

"Wait!" He reached out toward Elinor. "I'm sorry. I shouldn't have gotten so personal."

Immediately her mother softened. "It's understandable, Jonathan. After all, we do have . . . history between us."

"Always," he murmured fervently. "And that is why I needed to speak with you today—" He glanced at Rose. "—alone."

Clasping Rose's hand, Elinor shook her head. "Don't worry, Jonathan; Rose knows of my past. You can speak freely in front of her."

Lord Howard hesitated for a moment before asking, "I presume you know of all the murders."

At her mother's affirmative response, Lord Howard continued, "Yes, well, I'm sure you don't know that all those ladies were my, er, rather, that is—"

"Your mistresses?" Rose supplied.

Lord Howard leapt upon it with a grateful nod. "Yes," he murmured, looking intently at Elinor. "Every last one of them had been at one time or another my mistress."

"Oh, Jonathan," Elinor murmured, giving no hint that she already knew that information.

"The reason I tell you this is so you will take

care, Elinor. I couldn't bear to have something happen to you because of me," he finished on a low note.

Rose's breath caught in her throat. Lord Howard was *warning* her mother.

Placing a hand upon Lord Howard's arm, Elinor murmured, "Bless you for your concern, Jonathan. I shall be fine, so there's no need to worry." Elinor smiled in farewell, before tugging Rose along after her.

"Elinor."

At Lord Howard's call, her mother paused, glancing back at him.

"Are you happy?"

His question made Rose warm toward him.

"Yes, Jonathan," Elinor replied, a smile curving upon her lips. "Very happy."

"Good." Lord Howard swallowed as he tugged down upon his vest. "I'm glad for you." One side of his mouth quirked upward. "Though I can't say that I haven't wished Fleming to the Devil many a time for stealing you away."

"Dear Jonathan," Elinor replied, "I pray you can find the happiness you so richly deserve."

Lord Howard blinked rapidly, before nodding once and walking away.

Needing to burn off some of the frustration seething within him, Luc had gone out for a stroll and somehow ended up at his father's home. He found Edward in his study, sitting before the empty hearth, staring at the dead ash that lay within the cold stone.

"Hello, Father."

Edward started, twisting around to face Luc. "Lucien," he said, injecting a jovial note in his voice. "What a nice surprise."

Eyeing his father, Luc poured himself a brandy. "I hope you don't mind if I help myself." He took a sip and sighed as the golden liquid burned down his throat. "It's been a hard day."

"I know exactly how you're feeling," Edward said as he rose and joined Luc in a drink.

Guilt flickered through Luc. "Is Mother still not speaking to you?"

"Not a word." Edward drained his glass.

"I'm sorry," Luc said softly.

"Oh, no you don't, Lucien." Waving a finger at Luc, Edward said, "The problems between your mother and me are of my own making. Don't you dare burden yourself by thinking you're responsible."

"I'll try not to, but it's an old habit," Luc admitted, taking a seat.

"Perhaps, but that doesn't make it a good one."

Luc smiled at his father. "True enough."

An awkward silence fell between them, before Edward cleared his throat. "How is the lovely Miss Fleming?"

As a conversational gambit, his father couldn't have picked a worse topic, Luc thought, swirling his brandy around in the snifter. "I believe she is fine."

"Believe?" Edward asked, picking up on the word.

"Hmmm." Lifting one shoulder, Luc replied, "At the moment, she's not speaking to me."

"Ah, the joys of being in love," Edward sighed.

Luc stilled. "How do you know I'm in love?"

"Son," Edward began with a laugh, "a woman can only make you this miserable if you love her—heart, soul, and body."

Digesting that statement for a moment, Luc looked at his father and admitted, "I wasn't certain if I was capable of love."

"What nonsense," Edward rebuffed with a roll of his eyes. "Of course you are." Tapping Luc on the arm, Edward lifted his glass. "Love is like brandy. You could live without it, but life just wouldn't be as intoxicating."

Clinking his glass to Edward's, Luc made a toast. "Here's to the women we love—may they one day want to speak to us."

"Hear, hear," Edward cheered, before taking a sip.

Looking at his glass, Luc smiled and shot a glance at his father. "You know, it truly is a shame that women aren't *more* like brandy." Luc's smile shifted into a grin. "After all, if you simply hold your brandy the correct way, it warms to the touch."

Edward blinked, before bursting into laughter. "Lord, son, if only it were that easy."

"Indeed," Luc murmured, sipping at his drink. "If only."

"What are you doing?"

Jonathan didn't even bother to glance up at his wife. "What does it look like I'm doing?"

"It looks like you're directing your manservant

to pack your things." Marianne stepped farther into her husband's room.

"Very observant of you," Jonathan remarked dryly as he continued to gather up his cravats, handing them off to his servant.

"You may go now," Marianne directed the servant.

The man paused, glancing at his master. Sighing deeply, Jonathan nodded in agreement. "I will call for you in a few moments, James. After I've dealt with this situation."

"I am your wife, not a situation!"

"And I can't tell you how often I wished that weren't the truth." Lord Howard tossed a pair of boots next to his bed.

"I demand to know what is going on here." She pushed her hands onto her hips, hoping that her eyes were deceiving her.

"If you think on it, I'm sure you'll be able to come up with the answer yourself," her husband answered blandly.

It was the lack of heat in his response that alarmed Marianne the most. "Are you returning to the country?"

"No."

Her throat tightened, but she forced the next question out. "Are you leaving me then?"

Jonathan chuckled grimly. "I suppose you could say that. For myself, I prefer to think of it as ending my term in Hell."

Marianne gasped, pressing a hand on her chest to keep her heart from pounding free. "But . . . but . . . you are my husband."

"And so I shall remain, unfortunately," Jonathan said, pausing to look at her. "But no longer will I tolerate you and all of your nastiness."

She forced herself to remain still despite the verbal blow. "It shall be a relief for me as well," she returned, not wanting to expose her pain.

"Wonderful. Then it appears my decision will suit us both." Jonathan resumed his packing.

"Where will you go?" she asked, unable to hold in the question.

"I'm not sure. Anywhere but here."

Fury stirred within Marianne as a horrible realization struck her. "You're going to your mistress's home."

"Perhaps," Jonathan agreed.

His nonchalance enraged Marianne even more. "Damn you!" she rasped. "You're so used to whores that you couldn't possibly appreciate a decent woman like me."

Jonathan tossed a jacket onto the bed before he turned on her. "Decent? Lord, Marianne, there is very little about you that I find decent. And most of these women you dismiss as 'whores' have more integrity, more *heart*, than you could ever hope to have."

"Since when have you ever cared for their hearts?" Marianne heard herself shriek as if from a distance. "All that matters to you is that they're pretty . . . like the first one who stole you from me, that whore, Elinor Fleming."

Jonathan grabbed hold of her, shaking her beneath his anger. "Don't you call her that," he ground out. "She is the kindest person I've ever known, not to mention the most giving, sweet, and generous spirit. The biggest mistake of my life was allowing her to walk away from me."

Marianne heard a buzzing in her head, making it impossible for her to concentrate on their argument. She couldn't believe what she'd just heard: Jonathan was still in love with that whore. Too shocked to speak, Marianne stood silently as Jonathan strode from the room.

Grabbing hold of a water pitcher, Marianne flung it against the wall, satisfaction pounding through her at the crashing sound. With rage pouring though her, strengthening her, Marianne tore Jonathan's clothes from the case, ripping them before tossing them onto the floor. Moving onward, she tore down the paintings on the wall, smashing them against chairs, and tipped over his mirror, shattering the glass just as he'd shattered her life with his unfaithfulness.

Only when Jonathan's room lay in shambles did the noise in her head subside.

". . . and here is the list of everyone I've ever angered," Kingston told James Duncan as he handed him a fistful of papers.

Lifting his eyebrows, the magistrate fingered through the parchment. "There must be over two hundred names here!"

"Two hundred seventy-eight, to be exact," Kingston corrected. Glancing at Luc, he shrugged.

"I thought of a few more after we reviewed the list."

"I'd say so," Luc said, unable to believe anyone could have made that many enemies. "May I?" he asked Mr. Duncan, holding out his hand for the papers.

Handing them over to Luc, Mr. Duncan leaned forward across the low table. "I have to tell you, my lord, that while I agree that the murderer has fixated upon you, I don't see how we could possibly investigate that many people." Shaking his head, Mr. Duncan murmured, "Two hundred seventy-five names."

"Two hundred seventy-eight," Kingston said, correcting the magistrate again. Tapping the papers in Luc's hands, Kingston pointed out a few marks he'd made by some of the names. "If the person has a star next to his name, it means that he lost money to me and was convinced I'd cheated him. If there is an 'X' beside a name, it means they were married at the time of our affair. And if there is a checkmark next to the 'X,' that means their spouse discovered our involvement."

Rubbing at his temple, Mr. Duncan fell back into his chair. "Thank you for being so . . . thorough," he said in a weary voice.

Luc couldn't believe his eyes. When faced with proof of Kingston's wild ways, Luc realized just how tame he'd been in comparison . . . and that was when he'd indulged his every whim. Apparently, Luc realized, his excesses weren't very, well, excessive.

"My God, Kingston," Luc murmured, unable to get over his amazement. "When did you sleep?"

Mr. Duncan laughed behind his hand while Kingston propped his boot onto the table. "Alone or with someone else?"

"After looking at this list, I think it's quite obvious you were rarely alone." Shuffling the papers, Luc read off a few of the names. "Marissa Thompson. Elizabeth Valle. Samantha Evans." He shook his head. "Do you even remember any of these women?"

Shrugging, Kingston replied, "A few of them."

"Desiree Amour?" Luc asked with a laugh. "Lovely name, wouldn't you say?"

"Now *her* I do remember." Grinning, Kingston nodded at Luc. "A most . . . inventive woman."

"Allison Kent. Madeline Porter. Lilly Whitmore. Sally Drake." Luc whistled lightly as he handed the list back to Mr. Duncan. "It's a wonder you're still alive."

Kingston smoothed a finger over his eyebrow. "I'm not certain I follow you," he replied. "Are you speaking of a threat from a jealous husband?"

"Hell, no," Luc scoffed. "I'm amazed you didn't die of sheer exhaustion years ago."

Laughing, Kingston pressed a hand to his chest. "Ah, yes, but what a delightful way to leave this world."

Mr. Duncan folded up the list, then tucked it into his coat pocket. "Please refrain from your . . . pleasures while we're looking into this matter, my lord." He patted his pocket. "This list is far too long as it is without any names being added."

Kingston nodded. "I shall do my best."

Clearing his throat, Luc looked pointedly at his father.

Sighing in exasperation, Kingston rolled his eyes. "Very well," he muttered. "I shall live the life of a monk until you've found the murderer."

"Thank you, my lord," Mr. Duncan answered as he rose from his chair. "I shall be in contact as soon as I have some information about any of the two hundred and—"

"Seventy-eight," supplied Kingston.

"Yes." Mr. Duncan shook his head. "If I uncover anything suspicious about any of the two hundred and *seventy-eight* people listed, I'll pass along the information."

"Thank you, Mr. Duncan," Luc said to the magistrate before he left with the list.

"What shall we do now?" Kingston asked.

"I'm afraid I must leave you now. I've a long evening ahead of me."

"Are you attending the Marlboros' ball with the lovely Rosaleen?" Rising to his feet, Kingston smoothed his vest. "I was thinking of stopping by that affair myself."

"No," Luc replied with a shake of his head. "My mother planned a formal dinner with Rose and her parents."

Kingston's hands stilled. "Ahh," he said lightly. "A family function."

And with those three words, awkwardness settled into the room.

"Yes, well, I'm the lucky one," Kingston said, waving his hand. "I imagine family functions are quite the dull event."

"Deadly boring."

But Luc could tell from the look in Kingston's eye that he knew Luc's answer for what it was—

A flat-out lie.

"I'm off," Kingston announced, walking toward the door. With his hand on the knob, he paused, glancing over his shoulder. "Thank you for helping me, Luc."

Before Luc had a chance to respond, Kingston left the room. Only the ticking of the clock broke the silence surrounding Luc.

"How could I not help you?" he asked the closed door. "You are, after all, my father."

# 21

Katherine tucked her hand around Luc's arm. "I am delighted that you could make it this evening. After all, I know this private dinner was something Elinor and I decided upon at the last minute, so I'm thrilled that you were free."

Glancing at his mother, Luc escorted her into the dining room. "Even if I hadn't been, I would have rearranged my affairs in order to come . . . as I have no doubt you know."

"Whatever do you mean, Lucien?"

His mother was the picture of wide-eyed innocence, and Luc wasn't falling for it. "Don't play naive with me, Mother. I'm quite certain that you and Elinor had a lovely chat over tea this afternoon. And I'm also fairly certain she mentioned that Rose was rather . . . perturbed with me." He slanted a knowing look at his mother. "Hence, the impromptu dinner party."

Katherine's gaze sparkled as she chuckled under her breath. "You always were a bit too smart for your own good."

Stopping in the hallway, Luc waited for his father to escort Rose into the dining room, then nodded at Reggie and Elinor as they passed by, before following with his mother. They were a few steps behind Rose's parents when Katherine tugged him to a stop. "Do you love her, Lucien?"

Immediately, he looked at Rose as she smiled up at his father. The answer he'd agonized over had lain in his heart for a long time. "Yes," he replied simply, wondering how he could have doubted it for even a moment.

Katherine sighed in relief. "Both Elinor and I were convinced you did." Tilting her head to the side, Katherine murmured, "She loves you as well."

"I know." And he did . . . with an unshakable certainty.

"Then do whatever it takes to win her," Katherine said, her voice tight with conviction. "True love is far too rare a wonder to waste."

Luc took his mother's hand in his. "Isn't it time you listened to your own advice?"

His mother's swiftly indrawn breath told Luc that she'd understood his meaning. Having said all he needed, Luc led his mother to her seat, before he took his own across from Rose.

He glanced up at Rose, catching her gaze, before she quickly looked away. Watching a flush stain Rose's cheeks, Luc smiled to himself. As soon as dinner was finished, he would find a pri-

vate moment with Rose and tell her that he loved
her. No longer would he hide from his emotions.

"Your mother and I were discussing possible
dates for the wedding," Elinor said to Luc.

"Mother!" exclaimed Rose, her eyes wide with
surprise.

"What is it, Rose?" Not giving Rose a moment to
respond, Elinor smiled at Katherine at the opposite end of the table. "I believe we decided the end
of next month would be the perfect time."

"That sounds wonderful," Luc said cheerfully.
"Doesn't it, Rose?"

Her gaze narrowed upon him. "You know perfectly well how I feel, Luc," she rasped, giving her
mother a glare.

Unperturbed, Elinor smiled at Katherine.
"Would you like to help me arrange for the wedding?"

"Mother!" Rose said again. "We've discussed
this matter."

"To allow Katherine to help with the arrangements?" Elinor asked, being deliberately obtuse.
"I don't believe we have spoken about it at all."

"Don't even waste your breath, darling," Rose's
father urged her. "Your mother has been waiting
to plan your wedding for, oh, sixteen years or so."

Laughing, Edward nodded his head toward
Katherine. "My wife as well," he added. "In fact,
I'm positive she's already dreaming of grandchil-
dren."

*"Enough!"*

Everyone at the table started at Rose's outburst.
Taking a deep breath, she explained, "I shouldn't

have shouted, but it seemed the only way to get your attention. While I would have preferred this discussion in a private forum, you leave me no choice." She glanced at everyone at the table. "I'm certain all of you know that Luc and I have had a . . . disagreement of sorts, so you'll understand that I am not up to planning my wedding at the moment."

"I believe our mothers were going to plan it for us," Luc pointed out calmly.

"Luc, please," Rose murmured, leaning forward. "I don't wish to embarrass us any more—"

"Oh, I assure you, Rose, I'm not embarrassed in the least." He smiled at her, well aware that he was rattling her tenuous grasp upon her composure. "After all, everyone present is family."

"Luc," Rose began again, "I'm uncertain if—"

"Excuse me, my lords, my ladies," interrupted the St. Cyr butler, who was visibly upset. "Pardon the intrusion, but one of Mr. Duncan's men says he must speak with Master Lucien immediately."

"Show him in," Luc ordered as he tossed down his napkin and rose to his feet.

"There has been another murder," the man said without preamble.

All three ladies gasped, terror darkening their eyes. "When is it ever going to end?" Rose whispered.

"Who was killed?" Elinor asked softly.

"Erin Hedley," the man said, before glancing at Luc. "Mr. Duncan wanted me to tell you that there has been a new development in the case."

"Go on, man," Edward urged, coming to stand next to Luc.

"According to the maid, Erin's protector had been with her earlier in the day, yet he was suspiciously absent this evening."

Praying the answer wasn't Griffin Kingston, Luc asked, "Who was it?"

"Jonathan Howard," said the magistrate's assistant.

Relief rushed through Luc and he took a moment to center his thoughts. Not for an instant had it crossed his mind that Kingston could have been the killer, but Luc *had* been worried that this new development was part of the set-up against Kingston.

"I don't believe Jonathan Howard capable of murder," Elinor said softly.

"If he's innocent, it will be an easy matter to prove," Reggie announced firmly. Flashing his wife a look of annoyance, Reggie moved to stand alongside Luc and his father.

"If you gentlemen will follow me—"

"Wait!" Luc interrupted Duncan's man. Glancing at the women, Luc turned toward his father. "I don't wish to leave the ladies alone even for a moment, so would you please—"

"I'll stay with them," Edward volunteered, anticipating Luc's request. "As soon as you and Reggie acquire more information, please be certain to let all of us know."

Nodding, Luc thought to the grim task that awaited him. Another woman lay dead and while Luc did indeed feel deep sorrow for her, he couldn't help feeling a spark of relief. At least Rose remained safe.

Love for Rose crashed through him at that thought.

Unable to stop himself, Luc strode around the table, watching Rose's eyes widen in surprise. Inches from her, he pulled Rose into his arms, gazing down into her face. Knowing he'd go through Hell itself for this woman, Luc lowered his head and in front of his parents, her parents, and anyone else who cared to watch, he kissed her.

Deep and powerful, love flowed through him as he claimed her for his own. Knowing his control hovered on the edge, Luc slowly ended their kiss.

Looking down at her, Luc spoke from his heart. "While I'm gone, I want you to plan our wedding. No more delays or hesitation, Rose." He lightly brushed his lips against hers. "We *belong* together. I love you, Rose," he whispered, willing her to believe his vow. Though she gasped, Rose didn't say a word in response.

Releasing her, he walked to the door, pausing on the threshold to glance back at the still speechless Rose, then followed the two other men out of the room.

"This murder is even worse than the last," Mr. Duncan said grimly.

"Worse? How can that be possible?" Luc still carried Miranda's bloody image in his head.

"It is," Mr. Duncan stated simply, his voice darkened.

Luc didn't want any details. "Have you found Howard for questioning yet?"

Nodding, Mr. Duncan said, "We have word that he was in White's. I've already sent three of my men to bring him back here."

"Good, then I'll have a chance to beat the bastard into a pulp," Reggie snarled.

"Lord Howard is only a suspect at this time," Mr. Duncan pointed out. "There is no concrete evidence against him."

"I demand to know the meaning of this!"

Lord Howard's affronted demand echoed throughout the house. Stumbling through the doorway, Lord Howard turned to glare at the two men who had pushed him. "I shall have your jobs for this insolence."

"I rather doubt that, my lord," Mr. Duncan said coldly. "After all, they are merely acting under my direction."

Howard's eyes widened as he took in Luc, Reggie, and Mr. Duncan. "St. Cyr? Fleming? What in the blazes are you two doing here?"

Stepping forward, Reggie said, "We're here to ensure justice is done."

"Justice? What the devil are you talking about?" Shaking his head, Howard glanced at Mr. Duncan for clarification. "What is going on?" he demanded once more.

"Please follow me, my lord," Mr. Duncan said, before moving out of the room.

Howard frowned. "I asked what—"

"It concerns Miss Hedley."

Alarmed, Howard asked, "Erin? Is she all right?" Horror widened his eyes. "Dear God, no! Not her as well!"

Pushing past the magistrate, Howard rushed up the stairs to the bedchambers. "Erin!" he bellowed, fear reverberating in his voice.

Mr. Duncan was on Jonathan's heels, leaving Luc and Reggie in the study. Watching them leave, Luc had no intention of following; he'd seen enough blood to last him a lifetime.

"Nooooo!"

That single pain-filled shout echoed down the corridor to Luc and convinced him of Howard's innocence.

No one was that good of an actor.

## 22

Shifting in his chair, Edward realized it had been close to an hour since Luc and Reggie had left. Katherine, Elinor, and Rose had made a feeble attempt at conversation, but all three had given up their efforts and were now sipping tea. Everyone's nerves were taut, and Edward felt as if his were close to snapping.

Glancing over at his wife, Edward tried not to think of all that needed to be said. Now was not the time, he told himself, but the temptation called to him. After all, this was the first time she'd been in the same room with him in over a week.

Every minute that ticked by was another moment lost to him. He couldn't stand it any longer. "Katherine," he began hesitantly, "may I have a private word with you?"

The flare in her eyes told him that she wasn't

prepared to speak to him yet. Glancing at Elinor
and Rose, Katherine murmured, "I'm afraid this
isn't the time or the place, Edward."

"I'm sure the ladies would excuse us."

"I'm sure they would," Katherine answered before anyone else had a chance. "However, I believe
it best if we all stay together. Safety in numbers, you
know."

Sitting back in his chair, Edward was still trying
to find a way to be alone with his wife when salvation walked through the door . . . in the form of
Basil Whitmore.

"Basil!" Rising to his feet, Edward greeted his
friend warmly. "I wasn't expecting you to join us."

"I hope you don't mind," Pastor Whitmore said
with an apologetic smile. "I heard the commotion
earlier and came from the chapel to see if there
was a problem. Your butler told me the news."

"Tragic, isn't it?" Edward asked, feeling a twinge
of guilt for wanting time alone with Katherine
while his son investigated another murder.

"Indeed, it is." Pastor Whitmore shook his head.
"I shall pray for the lost soul."

Gesturing Basil forward, Katherine introduced
Rose and her mother. "I don't believe you've had
the pleasure of meeting Lucien's fiancée, Miss
Rosaleen Fleming, and her mother, Elinor Fleming, Viscountess of Howland."

"I am delighted," the pastor murmured, bowing
to them.

"Your arrival is quite fortuitous," Edward told
Basil. Smiling broadly, he said, "Lady St. Cyr and
I wished for a private moment together, but we

didn't want to leave our dear Rosaleen and her mother unattended. Would you mind keeping the ladies company for a short while?"

"It would be my pleasure," Basil said broadly.

Satisfied with this turn of events, Edward held out his hand to his wife. "Shall we retire to the library?"

Hesitating, Katherine looked at Edward; he could see she was about to refuse his request yet again.

Desperate, Edward pleaded, "Please, Katherine, just for a few moments."

Looking at Elinor Fleming, who nodded in encouragement, Katherine finally acquiesced. "Very well, Edward." She gestured toward the two ladies. "That is, if it is acceptable to Elinor and Rose."

"Perfectly," Elinor said breezily. Smiling up at the pastor, she gestured toward the seat Edward had recently vacated. "Would you care to join us for some tea?"

"Indeed, I would," Pastor Whitmore accepted gratefully.

The smile Rose gave Edward made it easy for him to understand why his son had fallen so deeply in love with this woman. "Please take your time. My mother and I will be perfectly content with the pastor for company."

Edward gave her a thankful nod and tried to ignore the slight frown on his wife's face as he escorted her down the corridor.

He'd finally regained his son. Now it was time to earn his wife's forgiveness.

* * *

"Either he is a wonderful actor or else he is innocent," Mr. Duncan concluded with a shake of his head. Sitting with his head in his hands, Lord Howard seemed oblivious to Luc, Reggie, and the magistrate.

"I think he's innocent," Luc said, wishing he could believe otherwise. "I doubt if anyone could fake that response."

Reggie sank down onto a chair. "And if Howard is innocent, our murderer is still free."

*To kill again.*

The words remained unspoken, yet Luc knew they lingered in all of their minds.

"I've questioned the servants and begun a list of Miss Hedley's recent lovers." Mr. Duncan looked at Luc. "Apparently she had only recently separated from a long-time protector."

One look at the magistrate and Luc knew the man's identity. "Griffin Kingston."

Nodding, Mr. Duncan retrieved the list he'd received from Kingston earlier in the day. He took a minute to quickly scan the names. Frowning, he glanced up at Luc. "Erin Hedley isn't on the list."

"Of course not," Luc said, reaching for the list. "She was his mistress, not his enemy."

"Ah, yes." Mr. Duncan shrugged. "Between all of the names and the markings on that list, it's easy to forget why it was created in the first place."

Holding back a sigh, Luc shifted his attention to the long list. Quickly, he scanned the names, still amazed at the sheer number of them. As he started to fold the list up again, one of the names caught his eye . . . and made his heart stop for a moment.

"Lilly Whitmore," Luc whispered.

And with that one name, all the pieces of the investigation fell into place—why the murdered women had all been with Kingston at one time, why the evidence had all conveniently pointed toward Kingston, and why Rose had received a threatening note when she had no connection to Kingston.

The only link between Rose and Kingston was Luc, and that certainly wasn't common knowledge. But there was one person outside of the family who knew all of their secrets—

Basil Whitmore.

"I know who killed them."

Everyone in the room turned to look at Luc after his quiet admission.

"It was our pastor, Basil Whitmore."

Mr. Duncan shook his head. "The pastor? Why would you think he's the murderer?"

"Because it all fits," Luc said urgently. "Both Whitmore and his wife are on the list. The pastor has both the motive and the information he would need to set up Kingston."

Frowning, the magistrate said, "That certainly isn't enough to convince me of his guilt."

"Of course not," Luc said, frustrated at the magistrate's methods. "But it is enough to seek out the pastor and question him, isn't it?"

"Yes." Mr. Duncan nodded. "Let's go speak with him now. Do you know where he is?"

"Undoubtedly at our family chapel." As soon as

he'd said the words, fear gripped at him. "Much too close to Rose and Elinor!"

Luc took off at a run.

"I appreciate your speaking with me," Edward began slowly.

Katherine looked at her husband calmly, trying to hide the nerves jumping around inside of her. "Don't presume too much, Edward."

"Presume too much? What do you mean?"

"I allowed myself to be badgered into coming to the library with you, but I never agreed to speak with you," Katherine pointed out in cool tones.

Rubbing his hand along the side of his face, Edward sank down into a chair. "Lord, Katherine, is it too much to expect you to talk to me?" His hands fell into his lap. "God, I miss you, Katherine. I miss talking to you, looking at you, just being in the same room with you."

Unwillingly, Katherine felt herself soften toward her husband. Despite all the pain he caused with his deceit, she couldn't forget how much she loved him.

Edward gazed up at her. "Every morning I pray that you'll forgive me, that you'll understand why I lied to you, yet every night I go to bed with my prayers unanswered." Rising from his chair, Edward stepped toward her. "I don't want to live the remainder of my life alone, Katherine. I need you with me to be . . . whole."

How his words touched her heart. Katherine struggled to hold on to her anger, but it slipped through her fingers, leaving behind only traces of bitterness.

"I've made my peace with Lucien," Edward told her quietly. "I feel as if I have my son back."

"I'm happy for both of you," Katherine said, meaning every word.

Moving closer to her, Edward murmured, "Now all I need to do is make things right with you, my dear Katherine." His hand shook as he reached out and stroked one finger along her cheek. "There isn't anything I wouldn't do for you, my love."

Tears rolled down her face as his words struck a chord in her heart. "I know, Edward; I understand that everything was done out of concern for me. But I can't forget that you *lied* to me, Edward. Not once, but over and over again. It was a lifetime of lies . . . and I don't know if I can ever trust you again."

Closing his eyes, Edward remained silent for a moment until he finally met her gaze. "So where does that leave us, Katherine?"

"I don't know," Katherine whispered, wiping away her tears.

"Then why don't you give me a second chance?" Edward implored, clasping Katherine's upper arms. "Please let me try to rebuild trust between us. I love you, Katherine. Surely that has to count for something."

Hearing the desperation in Edward's voice, Katherine allowed herself to think of the wonderful life they had shared. Their years together had been happy, so filled with love. Perhaps their bond *was* strong enough to rebuild trust.

"Oh, Edward," she whispered, pressing her fingertips to her lips. "I've missed you so."

With hope filling his gaze, Edward clasped her hand. "Can we begin again?"

Looking up at her husband, Katherine gave him the only answer she could. "Yes."

The salon was empty.

Panic clutched at him, but Luc tamped it down. Just because they weren't in the salon didn't mean that Rose and her mother weren't in the house.

He'd just calmly search the house and—

"*Rose!*" Luc bellowed, unable to rein in his anxiety.

A door clicked open down the corridor and Luc strode toward it, only to pull up short when his father and mother stepped into the hall. "Lucien? Why are you shouting for Rose?" Edward asked.

With the need to see Rose, to reassure himself that she was well, pulsating through him, Luc found it difficult to act calmly. "Where *is* she?"

Confusion brought a frown to Edward's face. "Rose? Why, she's in the salon."

"No, she isn't," Luc said pointedly.

Coming up from behind Luc, Reggie added, "Neither is my wife."

Pausing as Mr. Duncan joined the group, Katherine explained, "They must be around somewhere. We just left them a few minutes ago."

"Pastor Whitmore was with them, so I'm certain that—"

Terror slithered into Luc's very core. "No!" he rasped. "Please tell me they weren't with Whitmore."

"But they *were* with him," Edward said, confusion coloring his voice. "Why do you ask?"

*"Because he's the killer!"*

"Impossible," pronounced Edward. "I've know him most of my—"

"I don't have time to explain it all to you, Father." Grasping Edward by the shoulders, Luc implored, "Please just believe me. I need your help finding Rose and her mother."

When Edward nodded, Luc squeezed his shoulders, then released him and turned toward Mr. Duncan. "Duncan, you and my mother search the house. If you don't find Rose and her mother, question the servants to see if they know anything." He pointed to Reggie and his father. "The two of you come with me to search the chapel and the grounds."

Knowing time was of the essence, Luc raced off in search of Rose, praying with every footfall that he would find her unharmed, though she was now at the mercy of a madman.

Her head pounded viciously, but Rose battled against the pain, struggling to remain conscious. Slowly, she opened her eyes, fear tumbling through her as she saw the cold stone fixtures around the small chapel. The sight of her mother struck terror into Rose, nearly bringing her to her knees.

Her beautiful mother lay tied to the altar, unconscious, helpless, vulnerable.

Rose tried to move toward her, but ropes bound her to a cold marble pillar. With fear pumping through her, Rose fought against her bindings, trying to remember what had happened to them.

Her last memory was of Pastor Whitmore ordering new tea for them, before handing them fresh cups. Elinor had drained hers, but the new tea had tasted odd, so she'd sipped it lightly, not wanting to be impolite. After that, everything had gotten fuzzy . . . and she'd awakened in this tiny chapel. Having no concept of how long she'd been unconscious, Rose fought harder to break the bindings holding her prisoner. The flesh at her wrists grew raw, but still Rose attempted to free herself.

Her struggles stilled at the scraping sound to her left. She searched through the shadows filling the chapel, unable to see anything beyond the candlelit altar. "Who is out there?" she demanded, trying to act brave despite the fear quivering through her.

"Your savior."

Relief flooded her at the sight of Pastor Whitmore. "Please," Rose urged frantically. "You need to help my mother and—"

A scream broke from Rose as he stepped fully into the light, his features twisted into a terrifying mask. A long thin blade lay across his upturned palms and he lifted the knife toward the altar, paying homage to God. Slowly, he lowered his hands and bent down to press a kiss onto the blade.

The pastor's gaze shimmered with the light of madness. "Have you prepared yourself for Judgment Day, Temptress of the Flesh?"

# 23

$\mathcal{P}$ain seared through Rose's wrists as she strained against the ropes binding her. "Please, Pastor. There is no need to harm us," Rose pleaded, frantic to get free. With the pastor's sedative still in her, Rose fought against a wave of grogginess. She needed her wits about her now more than ever.

Rose knew she needed to remain calm, to try and reason with him. Biting back hysteria, she realized there would be no reasoning with a madman. With a quick glance, Rose saw that her mother was still unconscious.

Whitmore shook his head. "I can't let you go," he said. "I'm *saving* you."

"Saving me?" Rose asked, wanting to keep the pastor talking. If she had more time, she might be able to slip free.

"Yes. I'm saving you from yourself. When I offer

you to God, your soul will fly to him instead of down to Lucifer." The pastor took another step closer. "Do you understand now? You are damned because of your sins and the only way to save your immortal soul is to offer it to God."

His demented explanation was terrifying. Rose prayed she could continue to distract the pastor with conversation until she figured a way out of the situation. "And what of you? Isn't it against the laws of God to take another's life?"

Disappointment darkened his expression. "It is obvious that you don't know your Bible," Whitmore chided. "The book of Leviticus tells true believers how to cleanse their souls, how to purify their sins."

"God does not sanctify the murder of innocents," Rose returned swiftly.

"*Innocents?* How dare you stand upon the altar of the Lord and lie?" Whitmore raged, his body quaking. "You tempt a man like Lucien with your harlot's ways. Then the moment he weds you, you'll resume your true nature, spreading yourself for anyone who passes." He clutched at the knife. "Ever since Eve, women have been tempting men into sin."

When the pastor began to move toward her mother, Rose shouted, "But Luc told me you're married. Surely you don't believe all women are temptresses? What of your wife?"

*"Don't mention that whore in God's presence!"*

Shocked, Rose looked on, helpless, as the pastor began to pace before the altar.

"She defiled herself by lying down with that

whoremonger, Kingston." Whitmore slammed his
hand into a pew. "Then, she condemned me by
lying down with me afterward. Unclean!"

The pastor's fury filled the air. " 'He must not make
himself unclean,' " he muttered, pacing in front of
the altar. " 'Men of God must not marry women defiled by prostitution or divorced from their hus-
bands, because priests are holy to their God.' "

With one last pull, Rose yanked her bloodstained hand free. The rope fell to the floor, land-
ing with a soft whisper. Rose turned to face the
pastor, hoping he hadn't heard the rope fall. She
started to breathe again when she saw he was too
focused on his ravings to even notice.

Slowly, Rose crept toward her mother, praying
that the pastor wouldn't see that she was free.

"And that is why I must offer you for my sin."
Pastor Whitmore stopped his pacing and turned
to face Rose, who now stood next to her mother's
prone body. "Ah, what a clever temptress you are,
but you'll not get free of me."

"Please let us go," Rose asked, unable to keep
her voice from shaking. "We've done nothing to
you."

"Haven't you been listening to me?" he roared,
pointing the knife at Rose.

"Yes, I have," Rose hastened to say. "But you
were wronged by your wife, not us."

"My soul was damned because of a woman."
Whitmore's eyes glowed fiercely. "Just like Eve
tempted Adam, so you tempt mortal men. By offering you to God, I help to cleanse my soul and
save yours at the same time."

His explanation held no sane reasoning. Still, she tried to reach the man of God who must have once resided in this murderer. "Listen to yourself. How can you hope to save your soul through the murder of others?"

But the pastor was past hearing her. Spreading his arms wide, he continued, "The first time I offered a temptress to the Lord, I thought I'd found my salvation, but the peace was fleeting. That's when I realized that the only way I could reach God was by continuing in my work to cleanse the world of harlots and whoremongers—until He finally forgives me my sin of lying down with an unclean woman."

"Perhaps you've already been absolved of your sin," Rose said, feeling a spark of hope. "Surely you've . . . sacrificed enough in the name of God."

"Then why am I tormented still?" Dropping his arms to his sides, the pastor shook his head. "When God finally forgives me, my soul will be at peace."

"How can He forgive you when you have killed so many people?"

"Not people who count in the Lord's eyes. I've only touched prostitutes, harlots, whores, and their master," Whitmore explained. "I wrote to each one and told them to prepare for their Judgment Day." His lips twisted into an ugly smirk. "But then you already know that, don't you?"

"I am an innocent," Rose declared boldy.

*"Liar!"* he shouted, stepping forward to slap her across the face, sending Rose's head snapping backward.

She stood her ground because she was all that stood between this lunatic and her mother.

"You're just like the rest of them," Whitmore hissed at her, his features contorted. "You cheat and lie and sell your bodies to anyone with coin."

Rose tried to use the pastor's twisted logic against him. "Then why sacrifice us? Aren't we unworthy?"

For a moment the pastor stopped, his brows drawing together in confusion. "Is that why I am still tormented? Is it because my gift to God isn't pure enough?"

His soft whispers gave Rose hope. "Of course," she said, encouraging him to let them go. "My mother and I are undeserving of your attention."

"But I am saving your soul," he muttered, obviously baffled by his disjointed thoughts.

"Perhaps," Rose conceded, wanting to appease him, "but because of our tainted pasts, it doesn't absolve *your* sin."

Whitmore rubbed at his forehead as he took a step back. She'd done it! Rose thought, careful to keep her elation veiled. She'd managed to talk him out of killing—

Suddenly, the pastor's demonic laughter cut into her thoughts. "Dear Lord in Heaven, you are a smart temptress. You almost made me doubt my course."

Her heart froze as she read the deadly promise in the pastor's eyes. "Surely if you doubt, then—"

"*Silence!*" He took a step forward, his hand shaking as he pointed the knife at her. "Will I be forced to cut out your tongue first? I will *not* doubt my purpose. When that idiot magistrate didn't find all the clues I'd left, I didn't give up my faith. No, I increased my efforts until finally the fool noticed all of the evidence against Kingston." The pastor stroked the flat edge of the knife. "And now I realize that the only reason the other women didn't lift my uncleanness is because I killed them in their homes . . . in their dens of damnation."

He spread his arms wide. "Here, in the house of the Lord, I will find my salvation." Looking at Rose, the pastor smiled gently. "Your blood offered here in this holy place will assure my ascension into Heaven."

Rose braced herself for the pastor's attack.

"Bless you, child, for now you shall greet the delights of eternal paradise."

Her chest tightened, but Rose remained steady as Whitmore rushed forward, his knife pointing straight at her heart. Her blood raced as she swerved to the side, trying to draw this madman away from her mother. Lunging away from the knife, Rose tripped and went sprawling onto the ground at the base of the altar.

The minister fell to his knees next to her. Rose crawled backward, scrambling away from the pastor as fast as possible. Tangling in her long skirts, Rose fell onto her side. Her heart pounding, Rose watched the pastor crawl toward her, his knife scraping against the stone floor.

Frantic, she reached around, her hand finding a metal candle post. Pulling at the base of the post, Rose sent the long metal rod crashing onto the floor next to her. Desperate, she grabbed it up, holding it in front of her like a weapon. "Stay away from me!" she shouted, swinging the tall candlestick with all of her might.

The metal struck the pastor's arm, but he stood and kept coming, closer and closer. Rose could read her death in his eyes.

*"Rose!"*

The bellow came just as she raised the candle post again. Whitmore, caught off guard by the sound of Luc's voice, stumbled and fell backward onto the steps of the altar. A crack echoed throughout the church as his head slammed into a marble step. Slowly, blood seeped out from underneath the pastor, staining the white marble with its dark flow.

*"Rose!"* Luc shouted again.

Hearing Luc, Rose pushed onto her knees, unable to stand. "I'm here," she rasped, tears blinding her as she realized that her nightmare was finally over.

Luc dropped next to her and pulled her into his arms, holding her against his heart. Closing her eyes, Rose drew comfort from Luc. "The pastor . . . wanted to kill me and—"

She broke off, her eyes flying open. "Mother," Rose gasped. "She was drugged as well."

Looking at the altar, Rose saw her father already unfastening her mother's bindings. With Luc's help, she got to her feet. "Is Mother going to be all right?"

Her father gathered the now rousing Elinor into his arms. "I hope so," he whispered, brushing back the hair on his wife's forehead. "Come back to me, my love."

"Reggie," Elinor murmured.

Tears spilled onto her father's cheeks as he held Elinor tightly Relieved, Rose looked at Luc's father.

Standing next to the pastor's body, Edward slowly shook his head. "I can see it for myself, yet part of me still can't believe it."

Rose turned away and pressed against Luc, taking comfort in his strength. Praying that the sins of the past would remain silent now, Rose held onto her future, her Luc.

"All of those deaths simply because of an indiscretion." Wearing a disgusted look, Mr. Duncan shook his head. Bowing to Luc, he said, "Thank you for your aid, my lord."

"You're quite welcome." Keeping one arm firmly wrapped around Rose's shoulders, Luc held out his hand.

Mr. Duncan accepted the gesture, before leaving the St. Cyrs' townhouse.

Edward shook his head. "I'd often heard him speak of finding a way to heal after he discovered Lilly's infidelity, but I never guessed—"

Placing a hand on his father's shoulder, Luc offered him comfort. "You couldn't have helped him even if you'd known," he said softly.

"He was your friend," Katherine murmured, moving closer to Edward. Hesitantly, she reached out and clasped his hand with hers. "But Luc's right. Basil was responsible for his own actions."

"If I'd only known, only suspected, then I might have been able to save those—"

"Don't!" Katherine said, cutting off Edward's guilt-ridden murmurings. "Our lives have been filled with enough pain. Don't you lay more upon yourself, Edward St. Cyr."

Edward lifted his wife's hand and pressed a kiss upon her fingertips.

Luc turned toward Rose's parents. "Would you excuse us for a moment? I would like a word with your daughter."

Reggie waved a hand toward Luc. "Most certainly," he began, "but I believe I shall take my wife home. She is still feeling the effects of the ordeal."

"I'm feeling fine," Elinor protested weakly, "or rather I would be if only the room would stop spinning."

After kissing her parents farewell, Rose turned toward Luc. Smiling, he led her from the room and out the front door.

"Luc? Where are we going?" Rose asked as he assisted her into a waiting carriage.

"Our discussion is far too important to risk any interruptions." Luc followed her into the closed conveyance and took her into his arms again. "We need to talk with no one else around."

Without complaint, Rose settled back into Luc's arms, content simply to be held. Once at his house, Luc escorted her into his study.

Locking the door, Luc leaned back against it. Love filled her as she gazed at him. Suddenly nervous, Rose began to babble. "I don't remember if I thanked—"

"I love you."

Her mouth snapped shut. "I believe you've said that once before," she replied, wrapping her arms across her chest.

Pushing away from the door, Luc slowly moved toward her. "I need you to pay close attention to what I'm about to tell you. Can you do that, Rose?"

Mutely, she nodded.

"Very good." Luc's features were drawn into serious lines, his gaze intense. "You were right all along, Rose. I was afraid to let myself feel too much, so I pulled away, hiding behind my bastard blood. But that was only an excuse and I know that now."

Wonder touched her heart at his words. Keeping her gaze upon his beloved face, Rose willed him to continue.

Luc took a deep breath. "It was only after I'd made peace with myself and with my family that I could look at what's inside my heart." One side of his mouth tilted upward. "I still fear the intensity of what I feel, but I can assure you that I'm through hiding from it."

Reaching out to her, Luc brushed back a lock of her hair. "I'm through running as well. If I'm angry, I'll yell; if I'm sad, I'll talk to you about it; and if I'm happy, I'll share it." He cupped her cheek. "I know you don't have to believe me, Rose, but I'm praying you do. I hope that you'll trust me again."

Rose laid her hands over Luc's heart. "I've already told you, Luc. I believe in you." She smiled at him, feeling as if he'd just given her the world. "I love you, my darling Lucien St. Cyr."

Luc's expression melted her. Bursting with happiness, Rose stepped into his arms and lifted her face for his kiss. Slowly, Luc lowered his mouth to hers, tenderly brushing his lips across hers, the touch a vow of love.

"My darling Rosaleen," he murmured, before deepening the kiss.

Angling her head, Rose met his passion with her own, together they completed one another. Luc's hands roamed across her back, downward to press her into him. His hardness complemented her softness and made her yearn for more.

A groan rumbled in Luc's chest as he slid his hand up to cup her breast, molding the sensitized flesh into his palm. Breaking off their kiss, he leaned down to press his lips against her neck.

Clutching Luc's head, Rose leaned back against his arm, urging him closer, wanting more, needing him.

"Oh, Rose," Luc murmured, his breath feathering along the delicate skin on her chest. Slowly, he lifted his head, his breath rasping out of him, desire darkening his gaze. "We'd best stop now . . . before I lose control."

"And would that be so terrible?" Rose asked, holding him tighter.

A flare of promise burned in his gaze. "Oh, how you tempt me, Rose," he whispered, bending to kiss her. After a long moment, he raised his head again. "But we mustn't indulge in our passion until we're wed." He glanced away. "It's important to me that we honor our love before we express it with our bodies."

Tenderness overwhelmed her. How could he have believed for one moment that he was no longer an honorable gentleman? Brushing back a lock of his hair, she murmured, "Then, I suggest we begin our wedding plans."

The grin he gave her had a decidedly lusty tilt to it, making Rose laugh in response. "Splendid idea," Luc declared. "Can we be married next week?"

"Next week?" Rose sputtered with a burst of laughter. "Hardly. I was thinking that if we could hurry through the arrangements, we might be able to get married in a month or two."

"Unthinkable," Luc returned fiercely, pressing his body against hers. "Two weeks at the most."

"Six weeks."

"Three."

"Four!"

"Done!"

Rose blinked at Luc's pronouncement, before regaining her composure. After all, she ached for him; a long engagement wouldn't serve her at all. Nodding, she agreed, "Very well, Lucien. Four weeks."

With a look of chagrin, Luc shook his head. "Why do I feel as if this is going to be the longest four weeks of my life?"

Rose simply laughed.

Narrowing his eyes, Luc vowed, "Just for that, I'll have to make certain that it is the longest four weeks you've ever experienced as well."

The wicked gleam in Luc's eyes made her pause, then he pulled her back into his arms to demonstrate just how wonderful he was at driving a woman insane.

*One month later*

"I can't believe how you tormented me," Rose exclaimed as she walked into their bridal chamber. "I thought this evening would *never* come."

Instead of answering, Luc swept Rose into his arms for a passionate kiss. Both of them were breathing heavily by the time he pulled back. "I drove myself crazy as well," he admitted. "I thought I'd be perfectly capable of kissing you and caressing you while still maintaining control." He kissed her deeply once more. "I'd rather face a firing squad than that torment again," he admitted when he finally broke off their kiss.

Thinking back upon the past month, Rose agreed readily. Every time Luc maneuvered them into a private situation, he would sweep her into his arms and kiss her, often boldly touching her breasts, until she'd ached for more. But finally, now on their wedding night, they could end the torment. Heat coursed through her at the thought.

"We don't need to wait any longer," Luc said as if he could read her thoughts.

Sliding his hands up her arms, Luc began to unfasten her dress, his gaze never breaking from hers. Rose felt anticipation strum through her;

desires long suppressed surged forth, demanding release.

"Tonight, I'm going to make you mine."

Luc's soft vow sent shivers coursing down her spine as Rose shifted to ease her dress off of her shoulders, then past her hips, allowing it to drop to the floor unheeded.

Smiling with pleasure, Luc loosened Rose's undergarments until all that remained was the thin covering of her chemise and her stockings. Still fully dressed, Luc lifted Rose into his arms, carrying her the short distance to the bed, and deposited her upon the downy coverlet.

Passion pounded through her as Luc knelt before her. Gently, he lifted her right leg and removed her slipper. Slowly, he eased her chemise upward until it lay bunched around her upper thighs. With one tug, he freed the ribbon holding up her stocking.

Closing her eyes against the overwhelming sensations, Rose leaned back on her hands, arching her back as Luc slid his hands over her legs, each fingertip caressing its way toward her toes. Finally, he discarded the stocking, before he began to work on the remaining stocking.

Quivering with desire, Rose collapsed, lying back upon the bed with cravings burning through her. She lay open and vulnerable to Luc's gaze . . . and rejoiced in it. When he began to kiss her toes, she sat up once more. "Luc?" she whispered, suddenly uncertain.

The grin he gave her quieted her fears, and she gave up all resistance as he closed his mouth over her little toe. A shiver coursed through her at the deliciously erotic touch. No further protests came from her as Luc slid his mouth over the crest of her foot, onto her ankle, and to the curve of her calf. He paused at her knee, licking at the hollow behind it, before continuing up her thigh.

Awash with passion, Rose rode out the storm of desire, unable to look away as Luc moved ever closer to her most private core. Hot and aching, she yearned for him to touch her, to end the torment coursing through her body.

A scream broke from her when Luc sent his fingers sliding down the moist length of her womanhood. Sensations, intense and brilliant, overtook her and it required all of her concentration to remain upright.

Suddenly, Luc leaned forward and closed his mouth over the sensitized area. Falling back upon the bed, Rose arched up to meet his mouth as he lavished attention onto her moist core. Licking, tasting, kissing, Luc devoured her, and Rose loved every wicked moment of it.

Fierce satisfaction crashed over her as Luc took her to the pinnacle of desire, then plunged her over the edge. Rose lay quivering with the unbelievable feelings within her, unable to say a word as Luc stood and began to strip off his clothes.

Gloriously naked, he stood before her, his chest rasping in and out, his eyes aflame with unfulfilled desire, and his manhood jutting out boldly. Levering herself up onto the bed again, Rose gazed upon him in wonder. Never had she seen anything so beautiful, so magnificent, as the naked glory of Lucien.

Her fingers trembling, Rose reached out to touch him. Slowly, she trailed her hand across his broad chest, scraping her nails along his abdomen, then onto his powerful manhood. Luc's eyes closed and a groan broke from him as Rose closed her fingers about his length.

Hot and hard, the feel of him sparked to life hungers so recently satisfied, surprising Rose with their force. "I want you," she whispered softly.

Luc's entire body jerked within her hand as her breath rushed over the tip of his manhood. Gazing at him in amazement, Rose saw a gleaming drop of moisture on Luc's hardness. Unable to resist her instinctive desire, she bent forward and licked it clean.

"Rose!" Luc growled, his hands diving into her hair, silently urging her forward.

And she accepted the invitation.

Hungry with desire, Rose pressed another kiss upon the tip of Luc's manhood and received a moan in reward. Encouraged, she opened her mouth and drew him inward, licking delicately at the smooth skin at the peak.

Luc swiveled his hips forward and his fingers clenched in her hair. Craving more, Rose deepened the caress, bringing a groan from Luc. Tasting Luc enflamed her and she couldn't get enough of him. Emboldened, Rose began to run her hands along his inner thighs, testing the soft sacs beneath his hardness.

With a harsh groan, Luc stepped back, breaking contact, before pulling Rose to her feet and into his arms. His mouth closed over hers and his hands molded her into him. Desire burned out of control between them as Luc eased her back only to tug off her chemise. Once freed of the garment, Rose stepped close once more, molding flesh against heated flesh.

Luc crushed her mouth beneath his as he lifted her in his arms and lowered her to the bed again. Fierce pleasure raced through her when Luc began to work his way down her body, kissing her breasts, molding them into his hands. After a long moment, he lifted himself upward, levering his body over hers. Eagerly, Rose opened to him, yearning for a fulfillment that she knew only he could give her.

With one swift rush, Luc filled her.

Pain filtered through the desire, causing Rose to try to shift out from beneath him. Calming her with his caresses, Luc soothed her, all the while remaining joined. Soon, hunger began to build once more and Rose swirled her hips upward, the movement making her gasp with pleasure.

"That's it," Luc encouraged her, kissing her neck. "Feel me in you." He lifted his head, the dark fire in his gaze sparking an answering one within her. "We are one body, one heart, one soul." With each word, he gently pressed forward.

Fiery sensations swept through her, making her burn with the need for more, for Luc. "Please," Rose gasped, arching upward. "Please, Luc."

His control snapped and Luc began to move

within her. Wrapping her legs around Luc's waist, Rose met him with equal passion. Sensations flew through her—love, desire, need—until Rose couldn't think of anything but Luc. Pulsating need clawed through her, driving her higher, harder.

Screaming in delight, Rose arched into Luc as primal satisfaction flowed through her. Luc's fingers tightened upon her hips and he drove into her one last time as a shout broke from him. Quivering, he lowered himself onto Rose as she welcomed his weight, holding him against her.

Pressing a kiss against his shoulder, Rose asked, "How could you have denied us this for an entire month? You never told me how wonderful it is to make love."

Luc lifted himself up onto one elbow to smile into her eyes. "It's because I didn't know." Gently, he pressed a kiss to her cheek. "It's the first time I've ever 'made love.'"

Overwhelmed, Rose blinked back tears, unable to express the love that filled her to bursting.

"What's this?" Luc asked, wiping a tear off of her cheek. "I didn't mean to make you cry."

Rose shook her head, drying her eyes. "You touched my heart when you said that, Luc."

"Still, no bride should cry on her wedding night." Suddenly, a corner of Luc's mouth tilted upward. "I've only one question for you, Lady St. Cyr," Luc asked, gifting her with his wicked grin. "When can we try it again?"

Laughter filled her heart . . . and her life. With an answering smile, Rose reached for her husband.

# Epilogue

## One year later

"Here we have a lovely evening at the theater planned and the ladies will make us so late we'll miss the entire first act." Reggie shook his head. "I've been married for longer than I can remember, and I still can't understand how women can take so long to prepare for an evening."

"Neither can I," Luc admitted, grinning at his father-in-law, "but I *do* know that it's not wise to mention the time delay to my wife."

Edward laughed at his son. "Did you have to learn that from experience?"

"Unfortunately," Luc said with a heavy sigh. "I'll never forget how pleased I was with Rose's calm acceptance of my criticism."

"She taught you the error of your ways the next time you tried to head out together, didn't she?" Reggie placed a hand upon Luc's shoulder in commiseration.

"I waited a full *two hours* for her to be ready." Luc rubbed a finger along his eyebrow. "I believe the Opera Company had just taken the stage for their final bows when we arrived."

"Enough already," Griffin exclaimed with a laugh. "The three of you are beginning to sound like a gaggle of old hens."

Luc accepted the comment for what it was—the truth. "If I ever begin to cackle, you have my permission to knock some sense into me."

"And I'll be just the man for the job," Griffin joked, tapping Luc on the arm.

The four men joined in good-natured laughter. Glancing at Kingston, Luc thought back over the past year and how things had changed for both of them. Luc had invited Kingston to his wedding and ever since then, the earl had become a part of their family.

Luc still considered Edward St. Cyr to be his father, but it felt good to accept his heritage . . . all of it. Now, Kingston was treated more like a favored uncle. He'd even begun to act respectable, though Kingston seemed to find great enjoyment in his numerous "backslides," as he liked to call them.

"The four of you seem to be having a delightful time together," Rose commented as she glided into the room. "We could hear your laughter all the way upstairs."

Rising to his feet, Luc smiled at his wife. Her beauty never failed to entrance him, yet it was her inner glow that utterly captivated him. "Hello, love," Luc murmured, moving forward to kiss his wife. "I've missed you."

The smile she gave him was blinding. "I've only been gone a short while, Luc."

"Far too long for me."

"Ah, Lord, you two have been married long enough. When is this open and constant display of affection going to end?" Kingston grumbled, the smile on his face taking the sting out of his words.

"Leave them alone," Elinor chided as she followed Rose into the room. "And come see my granddaughter."

Kingston eagerly moved forward. "The beautiful Mary," he murmured, sweeping the two-month-old baby out of Elinor's arms. "How is my angel today?"

"Just as well as her brother," Katherine replied, entering the room carrying Mary's twin brother, David.

"We've been blessed with healthy children," Luc acknowledged, accepting his son from Katherine. The baby cooed up at Luc, offering him a smile. Looking down at his child, Luc found it easy to believe in a bright future for him, for his entire family.

Holding his son close to his chest, Luc looked around the room. His mother stood within Edward's embrace. At first, their relationship had remained strained, but over time, they had mended their trust. Now, the love between his parents was stronger than ever.

Luc felt utter contentment with his life now. He'd battled through Hell to get to this place in his life, but he'd made it.

Rose came and pressed a kiss onto her son's cheek.

"What about me?" Luc chided.

"Later," she promised with a gleam in her eye.

Luc met her smile with one of his own. "Later," he agreed softly.

The future was bright indeed.

# Return to
# a time of romance...

**SONNET
BOOKS**

*Where today's*

*hottest romance authors*

*bring you vibrant*

*and vivid love stories*

*with a dash of history.*

PUBLISHED BY POCKET BOOKS

# Visit the
# Simon & Schuster Web site:

# www.SimonSays.com

## and sign up for our
## romance e-mail updates!

Keep up on the latest new releases,
author appearances, news,
chats, special offers, and more!
We'll deliver the information right
to your inbox — if it's new,
you'll know about it.

**SIMON & SCHUSTER**
A VIACOM COMPANY
www.SimonSays.com

POCKET BOOKS

SONNET
BOOKS